A THOUSAND DOLLARS A MONTH

DAVE FELLMAN

To my girls and their boys
Lisa, Alix, Ross, Sidney, and Elliot

1

My phone buzzed. A text from Walker: "Coming your way with a bottle."

It was early May, early in the afternoon, about a month into the Covid stay-at-home order in North Carolina. I mostly worked from home, so my workday life hadn't changed all that much. Plus, I'd already done all the work I really needed to do that day. Walker and a bottle would be welcome.

I'VE KNOWN WALKER FOR twenty years. We lived on the same floor as freshmen at North Carolina State University. He came to play football. I came on an ROTC scholarship. I was skinny, bordering on lean. He was huge, six-foot-three and 280 as a freshman. A lot of it was baby fat then. By our junior year it was 300-plus pounds of hard fat. He explained the difference to me once. Baby fat jiggles. Hard fat doesn't.

By the end of our senior year, he was down to 240. He didn't play at all that year. He blew out his knee playing pickup basketball late in the summer, tearing both the main ligaments. I was there. I heard the pop and watched him fall.

He ended up having three surgeries. Football was over. Sports medicine has come a long way, especially with knees, but they still don't always heal completely.

So Walker announced that he was "going in another direction."

"If I don't have to be a fat boy, I'm not gonna be a fat boy," he said. I celebrated a bunch of milestones with him. It took a while to get down under 300, but once he could start exercising his whole body again, things happened faster. Today, he weighs maybe fifteen pounds more than me. I'm not skinny anymore, or lean. I'm a pretty solid six feet and 200 pounds.

Walker teaches Physical Education at a middle school. He's not teaching now, of course. The Wake County Public Schools have been closed since even before the stay-at-home order. The classroom teachers are giving lessons online, but they decided not to do that with the gym teachers. I would have thought a little supervised exercise would be good for the kids, especially now. But like Walker said, it was a decision made above his pay grade. I know something about those kind of decisions.

"BUNCH OF ASSHOLES down by the Oakwood cemetery," he said, when he got to my place. "They're all gunned up, wearing fatigues and those 'I'm a badass' sunglasses."

"What are they doing there?" I asked.

"Just standing around," he said. "Got a couple of signs about reopening, and protecting our Second Amendment rights. What I want to know, when did the virus thing start being about guns?"

I just shrugged. "You didn't, ah, engage with those guys, did you?"

"I just asked the one guy a question."

"Which was?"

"I asked him when the virus thing got all about guns."

I waited for more.

"He was very polite. He gave me a big smile and said something like, 'we stand for all the rights of all Americans.'"

"Sounds harmless enough," I said.

"Course then the other guy said, 'move along nigger.' He didn't say it loud, kind of under his breath, but I heard what I heard."

"So you kicked him in the balls?"

"No, you taught me better than that. Never start a fight with more guys than you've got hands and feet. I just stared at him for a minute. Gave him some Angry Black Man before I moved along." Walker smiled a nasty little smile. "But you know what? I would like to find a way to fuck those guys up."

I SUPPOSE I HAVE TAUGHT Walker some things about fighting. Which is ironic, because I once learned a major lesson about fighting from him. Our sophomore year at NC State. Another pickup basketball game. A couple of guys yapping at each other, then punches thrown. I moved in to break it up, and one guy's buddy decided I was joining the fight, not trying to stop it. He stepped in and popped me one, which turned into a pretty impressive black eye.

"What you have to remember," Walker said, "is that every guy who starts a fight, always has a friend. Or a bunch of them. Situation like that, you need to be first and foremost watching out for the friends."

Something else I learned from that fight. A black eye isn't that big a deal when you're a kid. I had lots of them. But a black eye is a lot harder to explain when you're twenty, and theoretically more mature. Also when you're trying to impress girls with that maturity.

SPEAKING OF GIRLS, it was Staff Sergeant Kirsten Connolly who started me on the path to actually being a tough guy. She joined the ROTC cadre that year as a Military Instructor. The guys used to call her The Big Girl. She was six feet tall, and weighed probably 180 pounds. Not fat, just big. I remember reading once about someone who was described as a big-boned Midwestern girl. Connolly was from Boston, but she was definitely big-boned.

She had one of those "Baa-stin" accents too. First time she saw me with my black eye, she said "Mistah Cahvah, I really hope the utha guy looks a whole lot worse than you do." I told her I couldn't honestly say, he was gone by the time I came to.

She laughed, then asked me, did I think of myself as a violent man? I said no, not by nature. I told her I tended more toward thoughtful. "I'm pretty competitive," I said. "But I'm usually the guy who'll try to calm things down." I told her how I got the black eye.

"You should consider," she said, "that the Army is in the violence business. The reason we exist is to put force on target."

"Are you saying that I should learn to be violent?" I asked.

"I guess I'm saying that if you don't have it naturally, it would be good to acquire some of it. You want to be a Ranger right?"

I'm not sure how she knew that, but it was true. I'd only spoken to her a couple of times before and never about hopes or dreams or goals or any of that. I had applied to Airborne School for the upcoming summer through the Cadet Advanced Individual Training program, so maybe she'd seen that paperwork.

"Got any advice on how to accomplish that, Sergeant Connolly?"

"Have you ever boxed? Any other hand-to-hand combat?"

"No."

"Would you be willing to give it a try?"

"Sure, I guess so."

"Give me your phone number. I'll have a guy call you. Probably sometime next week."

2

Back in my apartment, Walker opened the bottle. Buffalo Trace bourbon. He raised it to his nose and sniffed delicately, then lowered it to his mouth and took a swallow. "Good shit," he said. He held the bottle out to me.

"I'm not sure we're supposed to be drinking out of the same bottle," I said. "Infectious pandemic and all."

"Yeah," he said. "I think they're pretty sure it doesn't spread that way. Besides, we've both had it."

Neither of us had been tested, but we'd both been sick about four weeks earlier. Me first, then Walker. I'd been in Las Vegas at a trade show in the middle of March, and my symptoms started a few days after I got home. We usually worked out together two or three times a week, so it seemed likely that I'd gotten it in Vegas and given it to him.

I never felt miserable, but I was definitely under the weather for four or five days. Walker was probably sicker. He moved in with me to do his quarantine, not wanting to take any chances with his wife Teisha and their little boy. He felt better after about a week, and by that time, the stay at home order was in effect.

So technically, he wasn't supposed to be at my place, but neither of us felt guilty about it. I took two glasses from a cabinet and handed one to Walker. He poured us each a healthy shot and raised his glass.

"To patriotism," he said, "and all of the rights of all of us Americans."

We both drank. "So," I said. "Are we going to act on this desire to teach your new friends a civics lesson?"

"We might get to that, but I have some other news. Maddie called this morning. She says she has a live one."

Maddie is Teisha's best friend. She's a real estate agent. Also a definite Type A personality. In college, she was a three sport athlete, president of her sorority and captain of the debate team. She's still very physical and very driven. Maddie makes good money in real estate, but she wants more. Which is why she steals.

Although technically, that's not quite true. Walker and I steal. Maddie is the scout.

3

"What's she got?" I asked.

"It's a house in Clarksville, Virginia, just across the North Carolina border. Big house on a lake. New people moved in just before the lockdown, but they're moving out temporarily the week after next. Apparently they'd planned all along to replace the air conditioning, and they figure this is a good time to do it."

"Where are they going?" I asked. "It's not like they can travel anywhere."

"They're just staying with family. This is a retired political guy from DC and his wife. They moved to Clarksville to be close to their son and their grandkids. The son's wife turns out to be in one of the fitness classes Maddie's been taking on Zoom, and she overheard part of a conversation before the class. She heard enough to figure out what house they were talking about, and pulled the particulars. I think it looks pretty good."

I SHOULD PROBABLY EXPLAIN that the stealing is kind of a sideline for both of us. I have a day job as a salesman for a company that sells aftermarket parts for all kinds of heavy equipment. My customers are the dealers who sell all that stuff locally or regionally. I talk to the parts managers and service managers, trying to get them to use our parts for repairs as opposed to the "genuine" John Deere or Komatsu or Caterpillar parts.

It's not a hard job, or especially challenging. Before Covid, I usually traveled about one week a month. Other than that, it's phone calls and emails. It rarely takes more than a couple of hours a day to do what I have to do to earn a reasonable living. I made almost $80,000 last year, which is quite a bit more than I made in the Army.

I did eleven years and nine days in The Green Machine, going out as an O3—a Captain. They made it pretty clear that I wasn't going to make Major, so it was time to start the next stage of my life. I was ready anyway. I took most of a year off, trying to wind down from the way you get after four deployments and a total of almost nine years in war zones. Then I got this job, which let me move back to Raleigh

4

The stealing started as a joke. Walker said, "Let's start a gang." We'd seen something on the news about gang violence in the area.

"Wouldn't we have to do separate gangs?" I asked him. "Seems to me it's mostly black gangs, brown gangs and Asian gangs, and they all fight each other."

"Oh, there's white gangs too," he said. "Just you guys call them clubs. Or brotherhoods." He paused. "Anyway, not that kind of gang. I'm thinking money, not violence."

"So you want to be an outlaw?" I asked, with a smile. "Jesse James Walker?"

He started to answer, but held up as Teisha came into the room. This was before they were married, but they'd been together four or five years. Teisha is a paramedic with the Wake County EMS. She had her scrubs on, with a bright orange backpack hanging off one shoulder.

"I'm off to work," she said. "Byron, don't forget to start the dishwasher." Walker nodded. "Andy, don't you get him in no trouble tonight." I nodded too. She walked over and kissed me on the cheek, then gave Walker a big one on the lips.

WE DIDN'T TALK ABOUT stealing again for a couple of months. This time, we were at my place, drinking beer after a run. Walker was on one of his regular rants about teacher pay.

"Even Mississippi pays teachers more than North Carolina," he said.

I usually listen patiently when Walker goes on like this, but on this particular night, I was in a bad mood myself. I had some work things going on and my knee was hurting.

"Are you sure about that?" I asked him. "Seems to me, North Carolina is pretty civilized. We can't be that bad compared to the whole country."

So I googled teacher pay, and it turns out that North Carolina is in the middle of the pack. Now Walker was in a worse mood. He doesn't mind when you think he's wrong, but he gets sulky when you *know* he's wrong.

"It's still not right," he said.

"No argument here," I said. "No question what you do is worth more than what I do. Although, come on B,"—I couldn't resist digging him— "it's not like you teach math or science or something really important. I mean, you're a gym teacher, you're not Dr. Keller."

That seemed to lighten the mood for both of us. Shepard Keller taught the only class Walker and I ever took together at NC State, Introduction to Atmospheric Sciences. Basic meteorology, which I figured would have some value for an Army officer. Walker took it because he was a weather geek.

"Yeah, they didn't pay him enough either," Walker said. "Anyway, I got a proposition for you. Would you be interested in doing something that would make us both some money?"

"Legal?" I asked.

"No."

"Dangerous?"

"I don't think so."

"Potential to be dangerous?"

"Well, yeah, probably a little."

"Tell me more."

5

Walker always had a second job during the school year. During the summers, he worked for the city's day camp program. That year, he was also pouring beer a few nights a week at a pub on Hillsborough Street. The night before, there'd been three young Black men, middle twenties, Walker thought, at the far end of the bar.

"I wasn't *listening*, but I was hearing, you know? They were talking about going into a house, stealing the furniture, and selling it to a guy who runs a second-hand furniture store."

"B," I said, "I don't think Jesse James ever stole tables and chairs."

"I don't have to be Jesse James," he said. "I'm serious about wanting some money. The other thing is, I know the guy who owns the store."

MARVIN TOWNES WAS A very black man with very white hair. He might have been eighty years old, but he still got around pretty well. If he stood up straight, he would have been taller than Walker, but he was kind of stooped over, so he looked shorter than me. We were in his store two days later. It was a Saturday morning. He gave Walker a big smile.

"Byron, it has been a long time. How is your mother?"

Walker had explained that his mother used to work for Marvin. He'd owned a number of businesses over the years, and Olivia, Walker's mother, had worked in three of them. She'd been a clerk in his corner store and office manager for his construction crew. When Marvin took over the furniture store, maybe twenty years ago, Olivia was the first new person he hired. She stayed with him for five or six years, but they had some sort of falling out and she quit.

"She's probably exactly the same as you last saw her," Walker said. "She's mad at me at the moment. Something I did, or didn't do, I'm not a hundred percent sure which."

"That sounds like Olivia. You tell her that I send my best regards."

He turned to me. "I remember you, but I'm sorry to say I can't remember your name."

I told him. "Yes, the Army man. Please, boys, sit." He pointed to a dinette set, and we each took a seat. "Are you here to buy? I'll give you a very good price, whatever you need."

"Actually," Walker said. "We may have some furniture to sell. Just wondering if you'd be interested."

"Always interested," Marvin said. "A used furniture store needs to find used furniture all the time. What do you have?"

"I think I have to ask you another question first," Walker said. "Does it matter how we happen to have it?"

Marvin stared at Walker for a long moment. It was like I wasn't even there. Finally, he stood up and said, "She shouldn't have told you." He turned and walked away.

Walker got up and followed him. "Marvin, wait. *Who* shouldn't have told me *what*?"

Marvin kept walking. Walker followed him across the store and out a side door. I could see Marvin pulling a cigarette pack from his shirt pocket and struggling to light one. I could see Walker's lips moving, his head leaning in close to Marvin's face. I saw Walker take the matches from Marvin's hand, light one in his own cupped hands, and hold it out to the tip of the cigarette. I saw Marvin pull in a full drag, and then let it out slowly. Then they walked out of sight, so I picked up my phone to see if I had any texts or emails.

WALKER CAME AROUND to the front of the store about ten minutes later. He waved for me to come out and I met him by his car. "Let's go," he said. "Let's get some Starbucks. I'll tell you about the skeleton I just found in my closet."

He didn't say anything as he drove. It was only a couple of miles, and I didn't press him. I've always been pretty comfortable with silence. Walker's the one who always needs to be talking. He pulled into the lot, shifted into park, and turned off the engine. But he just sat there with both hands on the steering wheel.

"So, my mother," he said. "Now I know why she quit working for Marvin at the furniture store. It turns out the cops were sniffing around Marvin and threatening her with an accessory charge. It never came to anything, because Marvin knew who to talk to. But you know my mother. When she found out Marvin really was dealing in stolen property, she didn't want any part of it."

"She never said anything to you?"

"Never a word," Walker said. "I told Marvin about the boys I heard talking. That pissed him off too. Anyway, he said he'd talk to us again, but now wasn't a good time. I'm supposed to call him early next week."

Walker opened his door, but turned back toward me. "The last thing he said, 'let's be sure not to say anything to Olivia.'"

WE ORDERED OUR COFFEE and took it outside. The day had started out cool and cloudy, but the sun had come out while we were in Marvin's store.

"A thousand dollars a month," Walker said. "That's all I'm looking for. Without having to work days and nights and weekends to get it. I'm not sure there's any honest way for me to do that, so I'm willing to try dishonest."

I just nodded. We'd started this conversation on the way to Marvin's store. Walker's idea was to steal from people's houses when they weren't home. No guns, just a truck. I'd asked him about the truck.

"Remember Danny Dodge?"

Danny Dodge. Daniel Darwin Dodge, aka 3D. A high school buddy of Walker's who also went to State for a while. He had some talent as a rapper and quit school to chase his dream. Walker had mentioned him from time to time. He never made it as a performer, but he'd managed to scrape out a living doing sound and lights around the local bar and music scene.

"Danny's got a truck," Walker said. "And he's been known to tread on the dark side. I know a bunch of people get their weed from him."

"So he'd be in the gang?"

"Yet to be determined. And not if you didn't want him in. I'm pretty sure we could use his truck, that's as far as I've gotten."

WE TALKED A WHILE LONGER. I told Walker we had an idea but not a plan. "There's a lot more we need to know," I said, "starting with, how much would we have to steal to come up with a thousand dollars a month? Is that a living room, or a whole house?"

"I'll ask Marvin," Walker said. "But wouldn't it have to be two thousand dollars a month?"

I shrugged. "I guess so," I said. I really hadn't thought much about making money from this. I was in good shape financially. I had a mortgage on my condo, but that was my only big expense. I had a company car and they even sent me a dozen logoed polo shirts every six months to wear on my sales calls. Short sleeves in April, long sleeves in October. I was already contributing $1000 a month to my company 401K and I'd been thinking about increasing that. So another thousand dollars a month wasn't going to make a significant impact on my life.

But Walker had gotten me thinking about something that *was* missing. I was three years removed from the Army, barely forty months removed from war. My life was pretty good, but it wasn't very exciting.

WE FINISHED OUR COFFEE, and Walker drove me home. We made plans to work out the next morning. As I was getting out of the car, he asked me if I was in.

"I'm still thinking on it," I said. "But not tonight. Got a lady coming over for dinner tonight. Time to shift focus."

6

The lady was named Meghan. She worked for one of my customers. She was a couple of years older than me, twice-divorced with two kids. We'd hooked up a couple of times when I called on the dealership she worked at, which was in Sanford, about sixty miles south of Raleigh. The first time, we'd started talking while I was waiting for the Parts Manager to see me. When I finished up with him, she was heading out to lunch and she invited me along.

As we finished our lunch, she asked me if I was up for an afternooner. "I don't want to give you the wrong impression," she said. "This isn't something I do every day. But I woke up this morning with kind of an itch. I can't help thinking you were sent here to scratch it."

"By Ferguson Industries?" I asked, with a smile. That's who I work for.

"Or God, or Buddha, or the Lucky Charms Leprechaun," she said. "Doesn't matter to me."

SHE HAD EMAILED ME a week or so before. She was going to be in Raleigh, at a baby shower for one of her cousins. I invited her to dinner afterwards at my place. I'd done some shopping earlier in the afternoon, a big steak, three ears of corn, a couple of heirloom tomatoes and a bottle of wine.

I watched her pull in from my little terrace, which is basically a small rectangular flat space off the third-floor bedroom I use as an office. It's big enough—barely—for a couple of Adirondack chairs, a small table, and my Fuego gas grill. I lit the burner on the grill as Meghan walked from the car to the door, then hustled down to the ground floor to let her in.

She was wearing a bright yellow sundress. She looked good in it, and I told her so. She smiled and leaned in for a kiss. After that, I offered her a glass of wine.

"So listen," she said. "I can't stay too late tonight. I have kid issues. I need to be out of here by nine-fifteen at the very latest."

I nodded. She continued.

"But I have an idea. Want to hear my idea?"

"Sure."

She reached into her purse and pulled out a tightly rolled joint. Then she looked at me with a Cheshire-cat smile. "Let's smoke this, then let's fuck, then let's eat. If we get short on time, I'd rather eat in a hurry than fuck in a hurry. Wouldn't you?"

WE AGREED ON A SLIGHTLY modified plan. I'd cook the steak and the corn while we smoked her joint, then I'd put the food in the refrigerator. We'd eat it cold with sliced tomatoes later on.

The sex was good. So was the food. Afterward, we sat on my terrace and drank more wine. She apologized for being, what she called, anti-romantic. She said two failed marriages will do that to you.

"Speaking of which," she said, "I had a weird experience the other night. I was out with my friend Amy at this Mexican place, and who should be there but both my exes and their current wives. Archie and Catherine, Raymond and Marianne, all sitting together like the best of friends."

She sipped some wine. "It's not like we've never been in the same place before. Birthdays and school things. Modern families, right? But I never thought I'd see them all together, someplace they didn't all have to be. Raymond and Marianne have always been tense around Archie. Because of Artie, he was around a lot when Raymond and I were married. So was Marianne, but that's a different story. Anyway, there they were, and it sure looked like they were enjoying themselves."

"Did they see you?"

"Oh yeah. They finished before us and they all stopped by for a little chat on their way out. Apparently Archie and Raymond are doing some kind of business together. Amy's going to find out the details and fill me in. Still, very weird from my point of view. Now, I need the ladies room. I know the way."

WHEN MEGHAN CAME BACK, I asked her about Marianne. The different story.

"Oh, Marianne," she said, with a sigh. "Raymond worked for her uncle. Marianne worked there too, though she didn't have to. She had family money, plus a big fat settlement from her first husband, including the big house she and Raymond live in now. You should see this place. It's on five or six acres, all surrounded by dogwoods and crepe myrtles. Allan stays there one weekend every month."

She stretched and smiled. "But enough about them. I have another idea. Three weekends from now, Raymond and Marianne are taking Allan to the beach for two weeks and Artie's going to be at basketball camp. Want to come visit me at my house?"

"That sounds like fun," I said.

"Excellent," she said. "OK, time for me to go. Walk me to my car?"

I did. We kissed goodbye and I waved as she drove away. After that, I went inside, poured the last of the wine in my glass, and started roughing out a plan to rob Raymond and Marianne's house.

7

Walker showed up at 7:15 the next morning. He never knocks or rings the doorbell. He just stands at the door, and if I don't open it in thirty seconds or so, he calls on the phone and says, "I'm here." I was asleep when the phone rang.

"You're still in bed," he said. It wasn't a question.

"I still am. It's early."

"I'm here," he said again.

I walked downstairs and opened the door. Without a word, I climbed back up the stairs to get my workout gear on. When I came back downstairs, Walker was sitting at the counter eating a granola bar.

"Want one of these?" he asked.

"I have some."

"I know, this is one of yours. I'm just offering to serve you breakfast. You obviously had a hard night. She's not still here, is she?"

"No, she left pretty early last night, like nine-thirty or so. I stayed up to do some work."

"You did work? After a date? On a Saturday night?" He shook his head. I just shrugged.

IT'S A TEN-MINUTE WALK from my place to the gym. Walker and I worked hard. Ten or fifteen minutes of stretching, then a rotation through all of the leg machines. We finished on the leg press. Walker set it to the max, 450 pounds. "Whose turn to go first?" he asked. This is part of our routine. Whoever goes first does ten reps. Then the other guy does eleven. We alternate until one of us fails. We do the same thing with the bench press, only we do that with a free bar set with 250 pounds. Whoever goes first on the legs goes second on the chest.

Both of us have good legs, but the reps add up. Walker went first and he banged out the first ten. Neither of us really struggled until his turn at sixteen, but he hung in there and made it. Trying for seventeen, I got to fourteen and died. Then it was on to upper body work. He beat me on the bench press too. If we split, which is what usually happens, there's no penalty. If one of us wins both, the loser has to buy breakfast.

NIGHT KITCHEN IS JUST AROUND the corner from the gym. It's a bakery and café. I eat lunch there a lot. For a Sunday breakfast, we each got fresh-squeezed orange juice, dark roast coffee, and a baguette we split between us. I got butter, Walker likes cream cheese. We also got big slices of bacon and mushroom quiche.

"Let me tell you what I was working on last night," I said, after we sat down with our food. "First thing, mission parameters. We're talking about something that's low gain. A thousand dollars a month, times two. That means it also has to be low risk. We're not doing this for any kind of big score. We're looking at multiple small scores."

Walker laughed. "Dude, I thought you were talking about your salesman work. I apologize for ragging you about it."

I showed him my middle finger and continued. "Low risk starts as a function of time and visibility. With visibility, the issues are distance, obstruction and lighting conditions. Ideally, we're talking about houses that are well distant from other houses, shielded by trees or some other strata, and we're talking about working at night. Beyond that, time will always be critical. There's always one thing that has the potential for the most things to go wrong. Here, that's time. The longer the thing lasts, the more likely it gets compromised."

"Jesus, is this what you were like in the Army?"

I thought about how to answer that. It was a simple question, but in my head, not really a simple answer.

"Yeah, it's part of what I was like. My first tour, in Iraq, I was basically your hard-charging, infantry platoon leader. Just tell me what needs to be done, I'll take my guys out and do it. When I made Rangers, there was a lot more emphasis on *how* you were going to get the job done. Plus, the guys I was leading were really night and day. My first infantry platoon was a bunch of kids with a few older hands. My first Ranger platoon was a bunch of old hands with just a couple of kids. They didn't need to be led so much as they needed to be prepared. Give them what they need to do the mission, and they'll do the mission. When I made Captain and got a Company of my own, I was almost completely an administrator. And I was OK with that. I liked the work. I liked the planning and the problem solving. I also liked that, when I got shot at, I was usually inside of an armored vehicle. So anyways, if we're going to do this, we're going to do it carefully and we're going to do it right."

He nodded.

"So we're not going into neighborhoods, housing developments, places like that. We're targeting places that are remote, like down the end of a road, surrounded by trees. Houses with no close-by neighbors. We also need to think about what's in the houses in terms of the furniture. Your idea is that we sell it to Marvin. We need to ask him exactly what he'd want to buy. You're supposed to call him this week, right?"

"Yes, he said early in the week."

"See if you can get a sense of exactly what he wants, and what it's worth. I mean, let's say he pays a hundred dollars for a couch. Is that even viable for us? We'd have to steal twenty couches to get us each a thousand dollars."

Walker frowned. He obviously hadn't done that math and unfortunately, there was more he needed to consider. "We also need to talk about expenses," I said. "Do we owe 3D anything for the truck? At the very least, I expect we'd bring it back full of gas. All of that counts in a low gain proposition."

He frowned some more. I felt a little like I was piling on him now, but I did have some better news.

"OK," I said. "Talk to Marvin. Talk to 3D. And when you talk to Danny, ask him if we can use the truck on July first and second. That's a Sunday and a Monday, three weeks from now."

That brightened him up a little. "Where does that come from?" he asked. "Do you have someplace already in mind?"

"I do," I said. "But this is very preliminary. I'm gonna do some scouting tomorrow. Then we can talk about it some more."

Walker held up his fist, and I bumped it.

8

The next morning, I spent a couple of hours on salesman work and then went off to an 11:00 a.m. yoga class.

I got started with yoga on my third deployment, which took me back to Iraq. My second tour had been in Afghanistan, mostly in the mountains. The third tour was mostly training and supporting Iraqi forces, sometimes in Baghdad, sometimes out in the countryside. We were on our way back to the Green Zone from one of those countryside missions when our small caravan got hit.

I was in the second vehicle. The major in charge of the Iraqi unit was in the first, a Ford pickup truck with a .50 cal mounted on its bed. They took an RPG right between the headlights. It flipped them right over backwards into the Humvee I was in. My driver swerved hard left, and the impact lifted us up onto two wheels—not an easy feat with a Humvee and its extra-wide wheelbase. I was in the front passenger seat. I managed to reach down with my right hand to grab onto the base of the seat, and up with my left hand to brace it against the roof. The driver reversed his turn, which fortunately brought the wheels down, but not before my right shoulder pulled out of its socket.

We bounced to a stop. One of the guys in the back seat popped the hatch and stood up to man the roof-mounted machine gun. My other two Humvees pulled up beside us and did the same. Behind them, the forty or so Iraqi troops jumped out of their trucks and moved for cover along the side to the road. But there was no more incoming fire. We learned later that it was just two insurgents who hit us, a shooter and a spotter with just one RPG. It was a good mission for them. All three people in the lead vehicle were killed, the Iraqi major, his lead NCO and the driver. Other than my dislocated shoulder, there were no other casualties.

My Platoon Sergeant, Mike Stanton, came up on the radio. "You guys OK?" I could see him in the passenger seat of the Humvee to my right. I looked quickly at my driver and the other man in the back seat, who both nodded. "Yeah, we're good. Let's give this a minute, then dismount and look around. I don't think we can do anything for Major Radi." The Iraqi major's truck was upside down and burning behind us.

"LT, I recommend that we pull up another hundred, and spread out another fifty to give cover. Then we let the Iraqis tend to their major and the others."

"Agreed," I said. "Hey Mike, is Doc with you?" Doc Stevens was our medic, a full-fledged Ranger who'd also had Combat Medic training.

"Affirmative."

"Tell him I think I dislocated my shoulder. It's just starting to hurt. Is there anything special I should do?"

A few seconds went by. "He's coming to you. He says meet him in back of your vehicle. Send, ah, who've you got, Bender? Send Bender over here. I'll switch frequencies and get the Iraqis squared away."

I had to reach across with my left hand to open the door. My right arm was sort of stuck in a weird position, hanging down and turned slightly out. Moving made it hurt even more. When I got to the back of the Humvee, Stevens was already there.

"OK LT," he said, "haven't seen one of these for a while. But it ain't nuthin'. Let me just grab it here,"—his right hand on my bicep—"and here,"—his left hand on my wrist—"and then I do *this*,"—he rotated my wrist away from my body and then lifted my arm up toward the sky. I felt a searing pain, then I felt the shoulder ball pop back into its socket. It still felt tender, but most of the pain was gone.

"Don't be throwing no fastballs for a while," Stevens said. "You'll need a few weeks, but this should heal up fine. We'll get you looked at by the real docs when we get back to camp."

WE WERE BACK IN THE GREEN ZONE in about two hours. It took another hour to debrief, then I walked back to our platoon hootch. It was late evening by this time, so I checked my emails, returned a few and hit the rack. I had almost fallen asleep when Stevens knocked on my door.

"How's it feel, LT?"

"No real pain. But pretty stiff."

"From the swelling," he said. "That's pretty normal. Let me get you an ice pack." He'd brought a few with him along with a roll of flexible tape. "You'll be more sore in the morning. Be careful about moving your arm too fast. No lifting weights. Nothing that might stretch the ligaments and tendons. You're best off keeping the arm below the shoulder. I can get you a sling if you want."

"Can you get him a purple one?" That was Mike Stanton, walking into the room. "It'll go with his Heart. Captain asked me for all the details. Says he'll write you up in the morning."

"I'm not sure this is a Purple Heart-worthy injury," I said.

"Oh, no sir. No question about it. Hell, you're a hero. I wasn't there, of course, but Bender told me you were brave as shit. He said you didn't cry or anything. He said you set a fine example for the platoon."

Bender himself was in the doorway. "I didn't say any of that, sir. Sergeant Stanton is an asshole and a compulsive liar."

Everyone was laughing. I spent a lot of time in the weight room with Stanton and Bender. Rangers are pretty informal anyways, at least at the platoon level.

"No lifting for him," Stevens said. "Not for a couple of weeks at least."

"Know what you ought to do, sir?" Bender said. "You should do yoga with the Transpo Babes. He could handle that, Doc, right?" The Transpo Babes were a group of female soldiers from the transportation battalion. We'd see them doing their yoga sometimes when we hit the gym early in the morning.

Doc said, "That would actually be good, LT. But do everything slow. Don't try to impress the girlies."

I WASN'T EVEN TEMPTED to try yoga the next week. My company commander found some make-work for me to do and my platoon never left the Green Zone. By the week after, though, I was craving some exercise. My shoulder was still stiff and tender, which was a weird combination. I walked over to the gym one morning with Stanton and Bender and a couple of the other guys. I stretched with them for ten to fifteen minutes, and when they started their real work, I went to a treadmill and set it to five, which was pretty much its slowest running speed. Even that hurt my shoulder, so I slowed it to a medium-fast walk.

The treadmill faced into the room where the yoga was going on. There were nine people, eight women and one man. One of the women was obviously the leader. She was facing the others and calling out instructions. They all stood on mats and nobody seemed to be having much fun. They weren't smiling, anyway. But as I watched, I realized they were working pretty hard, leaning into their positions and holding them until it must have hurt some.

I did thirty minutes on the treadmill. It wasn't much of a workout. The other guys probably had another half-hour to go. So I walked into the yoga room, hanging in the back, and tried to mimic what they were doing. The first move was standing on the left foot, and lifting the right knee up to the waist. I was fine for the first few seconds, then I lost my balance. I heard the leader say, "No worries, if you fall out, just climb back in." I was pretty sure she was talking to me. Then we did the same thing on the other side, and I did a little better.

She led the class through three more poses. I was glad I was in the back, where no one could see me. Except the leader, but she actually seemed happy to have a newbie in the room. After the class, she came over to me. "I'm Carol Kane," she said. "Staff Sergeant. First time doing yoga, huh?"

"Yeah," I said. "I hurt my shoulder. I can't do much of anything else, so I thought I'd give this a try. I'm Andy Carver. Lieutenant, Rangers."

She said, "We do this every day but Sunday, sir. Happy to have you join us." By this time, another one of the women had walked over, with her mat slung over her shoulder. "This is my platoon leader, Lieutenant Castillo. Ma'am, Lieutenant Carver."

"Andy Carver. Nice to meet you." I held out my hand and Castillo shook it.

"Same here. I've seen you around. In fact, we've convoyed with you. Last month to Ramadi? Probably a couple of more times."

Castillo was tall, with short dark hair. Not beautiful, not ugly, what the guys would call Standard Army Issue.

"Candy," she said to Kane, "are you teaching tomorrow?"

"No ma'am, Barbara from the Med Group."

Castillo looked at me. "You should come back tomorrow. Barbie Doll is a trip." Kane nodded in agreement, then they both smiled and left.

KANE WASN'T THERE the next morning but Castillo was. She set up her mat right beside me and coached me a little during the class. Barbara from the Med Group turned out to be a civilian who worked for some kind of medical equipment company. She was tall and blond. Definitely not what the guys would call Standard Army Issue. While Kane had been matter-of-fact, calling out the positions and then mostly staying quiet, Barbara provided a steady stream of chatter all the way though. But it was a good workout and I made it through the class without hurting myself.

As we rolled up our mats, Castillo said "You did well." Then she asked if I wanted to go to breakfast. Four days and two yoga classes later, we had sex for the first time. According to Walker, she was Namaste #1.

BACK TO MY MONDAY MORNING yoga class in Raleigh. There was a woman named Charlotte I'd had my eyes on, but she wasn't there that day. It was just as well. I had Marianne and Raymond on my mind. The night before, I'd done some research to find their address. I started with Meghan's Facebook page. I knew she'd gone back to her maiden name after both divorces and I sort of remembered that she had both of her sons as Facebook friends. I thought that would give me the sons' last names, and I was right. Artie was Perez, and Allan was Campbell.

Next, I googled "Raymond Campbell address Sanford NC." The listing had Marianne Campbell and Allan Campbell listed as relatives, so I figured I had my man. When I looked up the address on Google Maps, it looked pretty much like Meghan had described it. When I switched to satellite view, I could see that it was *exactly* as she described it, a large lot almost completely surrounded by trees.

After yoga, I took a quick shower and headed off toward Sanford. It's about sixty miles southwest of Raleigh, right along US Route 1. The address was on Center Church road and I quickly found a mailbox that said Campbell at the head of a gravel driveway. I spent the next fifteen minutes checking out the area. There were two churches, a stable, and a couple of other small businesses on that stretch of Center Church Road, but nothing other than houses on the side roads. Most of the houses were small, and many of them had rusted-out vehicles on the property.

By this time, it was close to 2:00 p.m. I figured they were both probably at work so I decided to risk a turn up the driveway. The first hundred feet or so had thick trees on both sides. Then it ran along the side of the large front lawn and led to a large paved pad in front of a three-section garage. I pulled up in front of the first section and turned off the engine. Then I got out of the car, and looked at the front door. I looked at my watch, trying to play the role of someone who was supposed to meet someone here, maybe puzzled that there were no cars, maybe wondering if I had the time right. I pulled out my phone, pretended to punch in a number, and held it up to my face, all this time reconning the area. I saw no people, no other houses. I could hear cars on the road, but I couldn't see any of them. I saw no signs for alarm or security companies. I pretended to talk for maybe forty-five seconds then I shrugged my shoulders, got back in the car and drove away.

So far, I thought, so good.

9

On Wednesday, Walker and I went to Sanford to do a night recon. We left Raleigh a little after seven, with Walker driving. He'd spoken to both Marvin and Danny Dodge and 3D said we could use his truck.

"I told him we were helping someone move," Walker said. "One of Teisha's crew. He said just replace the gas, that's all he wants."

Marvin had also been helpful.

"First, he said he'd pay us thirty percent of whatever he puts on the price tag. Then he said he ends up giving ten percent off the price tag a lot of the time, so he'd really be paying us closer to thirty-five percent of the actual sale price."

That seemed reasonable to me. It was similar to the dealer pricing structure on the parts I sold.

"As far as what he wants," Walker said. "He said the perfect fit for his store is an eight-hundred-dollar couch."

He said that with a little smirk on his face. He was waiting for me to ask the obvious question, so I did.

"I, of course, asked the same question. Marvin said, 'Go out there on Glenwood Avenue, where all the furniture stores are. They got every-thing from Ethan Allen to Rooms To Go out there. Look at what they sell new for fifteen-hundred to two thousand dollars. If it's in good shape, I can get eight hundred dollars for it.'"

"I've been in that Ethan Allen store," I said. "I don't think you can buy a couch there for fifteen hundred dollars."

"Marvin said that too. He said he's more at the Rooms To Go level. But if we do come up with more expensive merchandise, he said, we'd have two options. One is he'd take it on consignment and pay us forty percent of whatever he could get for it, but not till after he sold it. The other, he's got a guy into higher class furniture. He'll buy stuff off of Marvin sometimes, and Marvin will buy stuff that's not quite good enough for this guy."

"Would we be dealing directly with this guy?" I asked.

"Nope. All through Marvin. Which is better for us, right? Security-wise?"

Walker picks up on things pretty quickly.

IT TOOK ABOUT AN HOUR to get to Sanford. We did a couple of passes up and down Center Church Road in the twilight, then a couple more in full dark. Walker asked what we were looking for. I said whatever there is to see. "Just take it in and see if anything jumps out at you."

After that, I had him drop me off near the end of the driveway. My plan was to walk in along the edge of the gravel, then circle the house a few times. I had a pair of binoculars with me and a notebook. Walker would cruise the area for twenty minutes or so. Then I'd make my way to the nearest of the two churches and text him and he'd pick me up there.

IT WAS VERY DARK along the driveway. Then, all of a sudden, there were headlights coming from the house. I stepped quickly into the trees as the car came into view. As it passed, I saw that it was a BMW 5 Series, with a driver and a passenger. I had no way of knowing if it was Raymond and Marianne or visitors leaving, but it didn't really matter either way. After the car pulled out onto Center Church Road, I waited about a minute and then started moving again.

As the house came into view, I saw a downstairs light turn off and an upstairs light turn on, almost simultaneously. Those were guests, I thought, and now Raymond and Marianne are heading off to bed. That turned out to be wrong, because the next light to turn on was in the far corner of the first floor. I walked out onto the front lawn until I had a straight-on look into that room and raised the binoculars. I could see a man, presumably Raymond, sitting at a desk in the center of the room. He was on a computer, probably checking his emails before going to bed. I walked a little further until I had a pretty good look into the foyer. There was an alarm panel on the wall and the little light was blue, which typically means unarmed but ready to arm.

I went back to the tree line and continued my recon around the edge of the lot. There were lights above the garage doors but they didn't reach as far as the trees. In the back, alongside the pool, I found one of those swing set/play tower combinations. The tower would give me a sight-line into the lighted upstairs room, so I climbed the ladder and raised my binocs. Through the window, I saw a woman, presumably Marianne, standing with her back to me in front of a mirror. From my angle, I could only see her from the middle of her back up, but as I watched, she lifted her dress up over her head, then reached behind her to unsnap her bra. She turned about thirty degrees to her left, and then to her right. She raised he hands above her head and did the same thing again. Then she cupped her hands under her breasts and did it a third time. Checking herself out. With my binoculars, I got a pretty good look. Meghan's were better.

I continued my recon, looking in through the ground floor windows. Lots of furniture. Lots of *stuff*. I couldn't really tell the quality of the furniture, but it seemed likely that it would be pretty upscale. Maybe not perfect for Marvin, but if nothing else, this could be a proof-of-concept mission. Everything I saw reinforced the idea that this was doable.

IT TOOK ME ABOUT FIVE MINUTES to get to the church. I texted Walker and he pulled up about four minutes later. He reached over and pushed the door open as I jogged across the lawn.

"So tell me," he said. I could hear the excitement in his voice.

"It's doable," I said. "There's an alarm, so the whole thing depends on whether they turn it on when they leave the house. If we come back here and it's on, we have to abort. OK?"

"I guess so," he said. "Wait, do we know anyone who knows about alarms?"

I laughed. "I know everything we need to know about alarms. If there is one, it's game over. We're not George Clooney and Brad Pitt. We're Fred Flintstone and Barney Rubble. We are as low tech as it gets. An alarm *clock* beats us."

Walker laughed too. "I understand," he said. Then, a moment later, "Are you Pitt or Clooney? I'm not neither of those prissy white men. I'm Don Cheadle."

Walker can go from serious to silly pretty quickly, but so can I. "You're Bernie Mac," I said.

"Fuck you, I'm not Bernie Mac. Cheadle's way cooler. I'm definitely Cheadle." He said the last part in a horrible British accent. I got it. Cheadle's character in the Oceans movies had one too.

"You're missing the point," I said. "We're not any of those guys. We're Fred and Barney. But you can be Fred."

"SO TELL ME ABOUT July first and second," Walker said as we turned onto US-1.

I told him the whole story as we drove north, starting with Meghan seeing her exes and their new wives together. I told him in detail what I'd seen on both recons and how I thought it could work. He asked lots of questions and had a few good suggestions, including how to attack a set of French doors I'd seen in the back of the house.

"Remember that battery-powered Skilsaw I bought when I was

building those shelves in the garage?" he said. "Just two cuts, one above the locks where the two doors come together and one below the locks. Right across both doors, from glass to glass, then one good pop to take out the whole square. I saw it in a movie once."

Walker watches a lot of movies.

"Another thing," he said, "I forgot to mention that Marvin is interested in kitchen shit. Pots and pans, small appliances, things like that. I've got a couple of big duffel bags. We can bring those along. Maybe a few empty boxes too."

"ONE MORE THING," I said. "We start the mission clock when we turn the truck into the driveway. When the clock hits forty-eight minutes, we leave. If we're in the house we carry one last load out. If we're outside the house we leave with what we've got. I figure five minutes from the end of the driveway, cutting the door, getting into the house. From there, we pick up a sofa and carry it to the truck. We make ten trips for things that take both of us to carry. Each trip takes two minutes, on average. We make ten more trips for things that only take one of us to carry. Same two-minute average. That leaves us three more minutes for whatever. We're going to hustle. We're not going to dawdle. And we're going to err on the side of caution."

"Low reward, low risk," he said.

"Exactly."

We drove on a few miles in silence. Then Walker said, "Damn. We're gonna do this!"

I looked at him and smiled. "We be the Thousand Dolla Month Gang. They gonna write hip-hop anthems about us."

Walker held out his fist, and I bumped it.

"TDM," he said. "Righteous!"

10

On June 30, D-Day minus 1, Walker and I lifted in the morning. Then we walked over to Night Kitchen for an early lunch. He was pretty jazzed.

"I've got one big duffel bag packed," he said. "I've got my Skilsaw, and two other big duffels inside. Plus I've got gloves and four pairs of paper booties. The saw's all charged up."

"Just like you," I said, smiling.

"Yeah, just like me. What else?"

"I've got a bag packed too," I said. "I've got a pry bar, and some other basic tools. I've got gloves too. Good thinking on the booties. Where'd you get them?"

"Teisha's go-bag," he said. "Department issue."

"So technically, you stole them from the Wake County EMTs."

Walker laughed. "Yeah, I guess I went bad long before tomorrow night."

I HAD NO REAL PLANS for that afternoon, other than buying some flowers for Meghan. I figured I'd do that on my way out of town. With nothing better to do until then, I settled in for a nap. Next thing I knew, my phone was buzzing. It was a text message from Mike Stanton, my old platoon sergeant.

I hadn't actually talked to him in a few years, but we stayed in touch with the occasional text or email. He was still in the Army, coming up on twenty years. He'd already been in for five when we served together in Iraq. Mike was an incredibly smart guy who enlisted right after 9/11, dropping out of his senior year at Columbia. By the time I met him, he'd already finished his BS in Psychology through correspondence courses and gotten a good start on a master's in organizational psychology the same way. He also earned his Ranger tab, which he considered a far greater accomplishment. He eventually wrote his master's thesis on "Application of Army Ranger Principles to Workplace Management."

The text said: "Got time to talk?"

I texted back: "Can I call you +45?"

He wrote: "I'll be here."

I'D PLANNED TO LEAVE for Meghan's at 4:15. That would leave time for a quick stop at Fresh Market, which I figured would be a good place to buy some flowers on a Saturday afternoon. I bought a dozen yellow roses. They had white, red and orange roses too, and I was tempted by the orange ones, but I was guided by something Teisha said to me once. She told me I was a yellow roses kind of guy.

"What's that mean?" I asked.

"Red roses say I love you," she said. "Yellow roses say I *like* you. Byron give me red because we lovers. You best off with yellow, 'cause you just got fuckbuddies."

"Not that there's anything wrong with that," Walker piped in.

Teisha gave him a lovely smile. "For him, maybe. Not for you. We clear on that, right?"

I DIALED STANTON once I got out onto Route 1. He answered on the first ring.

"Andy Carver. How the hell are you?"

"I'm good Mike. How about you?"

"Outstanding, as always," he said. "Hey, I thought I was going to be at Bragg the end of next week but the trip got canceled. I was going to see if you wanted to get together while I was down there, but now I figured I'd just call you on the phone and catch up."

"I'm actually driving in that direction right now," I said. Ft. Bragg is in Fayetteville NC, about thirty miles southeast of Sanford.

"Going to Bragg?" he asked.

"No, going to visit a friend in Sanford."

"Well I have news," he said. "I got orders. The reason I'm not going to Bragg is I'm going to the Pentagon."

"Seriously?" I said. "What's a Ranger sergeant gonna do there?"

"He's gonna be working for E-9S himself, on the staff of the Sergeant Major of the Motherfucking Army."

"That's great, Mike. Congratulations. What kind of job?"

"On paper, I'll be a Public Relations Liaison. But my real job is finishing my doctorate. Good deal, right? My wife is crazy happy. No more war zones for me. I can probably ride the Pen all the way to a teaching job at West Point."

We talked for a while longer. He told me more about his family, and asked about my life. I filled him in on my job and promised him I was staying in shape. I finally ended the call as I was turning off Route 1 in Sanford

MY PHONE RANG as I pulled up in front of Meghan's house and her garage door started to open. "Just pull in," she said when I answered. "I don't want to shock the neighbors." I assumed she just didn't want a strange car in her driveway overnight, but that wasn't what she meant at all. The door started down as soon as I crossed the threshold. Meghan was standing in the open doorway wearing something made out of mostly mesh. She struck a pose. "See anything you like?"

The roses slowed her down only a little. "Oh Andy, they're beautiful. And so thoughtful. I'll put them in water—but later."

In twenty or so minutes we were back in her kitchen. I picked my pants and shoes off the floor and started putting them back on. She put on a pair of jeans and a t-shirt that had been hung over a chair.

"What do you want to do now?" she asked.

WE HAD A VERY PLEASANT EVENING. Meghan put together a big shrimp cocktail. We turned on the TV, and ended up watching the last hour of a golf tournament. After the golf, we ordered a pizza and scanned through Netflix for a movie. When the movie ended, we went out for a walk. There was lightning in the sky out to the west, obviously coming our way. When we got back to Meghan's house, she asked me to give her ten minutes and then meet her upstairs. "You can do whatever you need to in the downstairs bathroom," she said.

I used the toilet, washed my face and brushed my teeth. After about ten minutes I called up from the bottom of the stairs. "Is it safe to come up?"

She appeared at the top of the stairs in something slinky and red. "You tell me."

11

We both woke up hungry on Sunday. Meghan suggested that we drive down to Pinehurst for breakfast. As we approached Sanford on the way back, Meghan told me to get into the left turn lane. I knew what was there, Center Church Road.

"Remember I told you about Raymond and Marianne's house?" she said. "You've got to see it. Did I tell you it has a basketball hoop in the front hall?"

I took the turn and passed through the built-up area. I caught myself slowing down as we got close to where I knew the driveway to be. Meghan didn't seem to notice.

"Right there," she said, pointing at the driveway. "It's a gravel road. Pull in and drive right up to the house."

"No one's home, right?"

"No, they're at the beach. They took Allan, remember?"

We pulled up in front of the first garage, right where I'd parked before. Meghan bounced out of the car and up onto the front porch. I followed her and looked inside. Sure enough, there was a basketball hoop on the wall, but it wasn't a full-sized regulation setup, just a nerf-ball hoop set at about regulation height. I was more interested in the alarm panel anyway and I could see that it wasn't armed. The amber "ready" light was lit. Good for us!

MEGHAN WENT DOWN THE STEPS and started around to the far side of house. I followed her. She had a little prance in her step. Obviously she was enjoying herself.

"Come around back," she said. "We can look into the kitchen. Wait till you see their pots and pans. They've got one of those hanging things over the island. Raymond wouldn't even make himself breakfast when he was with me, but Allan says he's some kind of gourmet chef now. And a connoisseur of fine wines." She stretched *connoisseur* into four long syllables.

"Look past there," she said, pointing through the kitchen into the room on the other side of the house. "See that glass door? That's where they keep their fancy wine."

"It's a nice house," I said. I walked over to the French doors and looked in, not seeing anything I hadn't noticed on my initial recon. When I turned around, Meghan was standing beside the pool.

"Feel like a swim?" she asked.

I smiled, but shook my head. "That sounds like a really bad idea. We should get out of here."

"Andy, there's nobody home. There's no way anyone can see us. And I really don't care about swimming, I just want to fuck in Marianne's swimming pool." She pulled her sundress over her head, but I reached out and grabbed her before she got it all the way off.

"I appreciate the thought," I said. "But let's not. People with big houses have security cameras, you know? We might already be on video. You don't really want to make a sex tape, do you?"

"Now that you mention it," she laughed, "that kind of turns me on."

"Be that as it may," I said, "we should get out of here. Thanks for showing me the house. But my experience? Nothing good happens in places you're not supposed to be. Trust me on that."

She put on a sulky face. Then she burst out laughing. "OK," she said, "but you owe me one. And I plan to collect as soon as we get home."

I THOUGHT I PERFORMED pretty well, considering it was the third time in barely twenty hours. Meghan seemed happy to just lie around in bed afterward and that was fine with me. We talked a little and listened to music. I nodded off for a while. I woke up when Meghan jumped out of bed and ran down the stairs. I heard her ring tone playing faintly. She'd left her phone in the kitchen. A couple of minutes later she came back upstairs with her phone in her hand.

"I don't want you to feel like I'm kicking you out," she said.

I smiled. "But you need me to leave."

"Oh, Andy. Sometimes things get complicated."

"No problem," I said. "And no explanation necessary." I dressed quickly and checked my backpack to make sure I had all my stuff.

"I feel like I should explain," she said. "But it's kind of a long story."

"No, really," I said. "But I am a little curious. Does this have anything to do with either of your ex-husbands?"

"My *next* husband," she said. "Like I said, it's a long story."

MEGHAN ASKED ME to take the roses. That seemed to make her sad, but it was probably a good idea. I drove off with a smile on my face from the whole situation.

Walker and I had planned to talk at 5:00 p.m. which is when I'd expected to be leaving Meghan's. It was a little before four now so I just headed home. I was most of the way there when Walker called me.

"Yo," I said. "Everything OK?"

"One little problem," he said, "but I solved it."

"What was the problem?"

"Danny Dodge. I went over to his place to pick up the truck and it wasn't there. Him either. I got him on the phone and he was all surprised, like 'Oh shit, that was today?' He's in Goldsboro, working a show tonight."

"So what did you do?"

"I got us a U-Haul. It's, ah, bigger than Danny's truck, but it came with a mover's package, a bunch of blankets and boxes and a hand truck. It was a weekend special, only $48 for 48 hours. I parked it out on Blount Street.

"That sounds fine," I said. "Where are you now?"

"Sitting in the struck," he said. "You?"

"Just getting off the beltline at Wade Avenue. I'll be there soon."

TEN MINUTES LATER, I pulled up alongside the U-Haul. It was *a lot* bigger than Danny Darwin's ten-foot box truck.

"It's a twenty-six-footer," Walker said. "It was the smallest truck they had. The guy told me none of their ten-footers or fifteen-footers had come back in yet from weekend rentals. But bigger is better than smaller, right?"

"I guess. Who's going to drive it?"

"You can if you want to, or I will," he said. "It's not that bad going forward. If we don't have to back up into anything tight we ought to be OK."

We stood silently for a moment then Walker burst out laughing. "Come on, we're big boys. We the TDM Gang."

I laughed too. "Truck Drivin' Men." I said.

12

We left my place at about 7:15. I had Walker check my bag before we went out to the truck and I checked his. As promised, he had his Skilsaw, the paper booties, a bunch of bungee cords, and two more large duffel bags.

"Do you have any packing tape?" he asked. "For the boxes that came with the truck?"

I nodded, and pulled a roll from a kitchen drawer. I also grabbed a roll of paper towels from my pantry and loaded it all into my bag.

WE DIDN'T TALK MUCH as Walker drove us out of Raleigh, but not long after we got onto Route 1, he looked over at me with a big goofy grin. "I'm, ah, pretty stoked," he said. "But it feels different than football used to. Is this what it's like to go into combat?"

"I don't know that I ever went *into* combat," I said. "We weren't like a medieval army marching into battle. It wasn't like a football game where you know it's going to happen. Most of what I did was uncertain. Out on patrol, back from patrol, you might get hit, but most of the time we didn't. No contact, no shooting, no bombs going off. I was nervous, for sure, but I wouldn't describe it as being stoked or excited."

"Well, I'm definitely stoked *and* excited," he said. "Like we're off on an adventure."

I smiled. "So you don't feel like a criminal?"

Walker paused before he answered. Then turned to me and said, "Not yet."

AS WE GOT CLOSE TO SANFORD, I set a series of alarms on my smart watch. "I'm setting a stopwatch program with alarms at fifteen, twenty-five, thirty-five, and forty-five minutes," I said to Walker. "I'll start the clock when we turn in the driveway. When the last alarm goes off we leave, Three minutes to be in the truck and off the property."

"You'll call them out to me?" he asked.

"I will. I'll tell you how long we've been in and how long we have left."

He nodded. "One more thing," he asked. "Are we turning on lights?"

"No reason not to," I said. "I wouldn't be surprised if they've left some lights on. Most people do when they go away for any length of time. But let's try to turn off any lights that *we* turn on."

WE DROVE THE LAST STRETCH on Center Church Road in silence. Walker slowed and signaled a right turn into the driveway. He clipped a couple of branches on the way in, but it didn't seem to cause any damage. He pulled even with the first garage door and turned hard right away from it.

I jumped out of the truck with the pry bar in one hand, my gloves and booties in the other. I walked backwards towards the garage as I waved him back. When he got to about three feet, I held both hands out to stop him. I slipped through between the garage and the back of the truck. Walker was already out of the truck and on his way to the back of the house.

I caught up with him at the corner. A few more strides put us right in front of the French doors. Without a word, we put on the gloves and booties. Walker held the saw above the lock, parallel to the ground, and hit the trigger. The saw was surprisingly quiet until he pressed the blade to the wood, then it made the normal screaming, cutting sound. It took maybe three seconds to cut from glass to glass. He lifted the blade out, set up below the lock, and hit the trigger again. As he pulled the saw out with his right hand, he pulled on the door handle with his left, and the whole lock section came right out.

"Slick as shit, huh?" he said. We were in.

"GARAGE," I SAID, and headed that way. I opened the inner door and found the garage door buttons just to the left. There were three of them, so I mashed them all. The lights came on as all the doors started lifting. I ran to the truck and raised its roll-up door, then pulled out the loading ramp.

I ran back into the house. Walker was standing at one end of a couch in the family room. I went to the other end, we lifted it up, and carried it to the truck. "Did you see the other couch?" Walker asked.

"In the living room. Yes. Let's get that next."

"Did you see the bikes and the jet ski?" There were two motorcycles and a jet ski on a trailer in the farthest section of the garage.

"Yes," I said. "But first things first."

We ran to the living room and grabbed the other couch. We set it down facing the first one, giving us a little padded bed. "What next?" Walked asked.

"Let's check the front room on the other side. They use it as an office." That room had a small couch and a credenza along with a very modern looking desk and a rolling chair. The desk was basically two side rails and a top, no drawers. It had a computer and a lamp and some other things on the top. The credenza had file drawers on each side. We picked up the couch and carried it to the truck.

"Let's go back into that room," I said. "You clear everything off the desk and I'll look in the credenza drawers. If I can empty them easily we'll take that. Otherwise we'll leave it. Either way, we'll take the desk first because it's closer to the door."

The credenza turned out to be easy. I just piled the files and other things in the corner on the floor. Two more trips and we had both the desk and the credenza along one wall of the truck with the credenza upside down on top of the desk and one of the blankets in between them. My watch buzzed as we ran back into the house.

"Ten minutes gone," I said. "Thirty minutes left. Let's look at the dining rooms."

WE RAN BACK INTO THE HOUSE, through the family room, and into the kitchen. The first dining room had a blond-wood table and six matching chairs. The formal one had a black mahogany table and a matching cabinet along with eight upholstered chairs. The cabinet was full of china and glassware.

"I don't see any way we can handle that monster," Walker said. "The table maybe, but not the cabinet. Even if we emptied it all out."

"Let's take the table and lay it upside down in front of the couches. We can step over it to put smaller things on the couches, then we can stack the chairs on it later on."

We carried the table into the garage and set it down. I ran back into the house while Walker set a couple of blankets on the truck floor. I ran to the office and grabbed the desk lamp, set it on the rolling chair, and pushed them both to the garage.

"Very efficient," Walker said with a grin. We carried the table into the truck and set it down on the blankets. "You know, I think that other dining table would fit upside down inside of this one." He pulled another blanket from the pile and laid it down on the underside of the first table, and we went back in for the other one. Sure enough, it fit perfectly. "What next?"

"Let's get all the dining room chairs and bring them to the garage, but not into the truck." We did that, two trips each for the upholstered chairs. My watch buzzed again as we set the last four down in the garage.

"Twenty minutes gone, B. Twenty more to go. You get the other dining room chairs and I'll grab those side chairs in the living room."

Once we had all of those chairs in the garage, I said to Walker, "Take your bags in and load up with kitchen stuff. I'll grab lamps and other small stuff from the living room. Then I'll start on the stereo gear. All that goes up to the front of the truck on the two couches. Then the dining room chairs. Then we go back in for those two recliners in the family room."

I made three trips into the living room. When I came back into the family room, Walker was carrying two of his duffels and dragging the third. "Got all kinds of good shit in here, man," he said. "Pots, pans, knives, one of those big blenders, a toaster. All fancy brands. I think I cleaned out the kitchen pretty good."

I asked him to bring back a couple of boxes for some record albums I'd found. There might have been a hundred of them. While I wanted for him to come back, I looked into the little room behind the glass door. One quick look and then out. I stacked the tuner and turntable on top of twenty to thirty albums and carried that out to the truck, passing Walker on his way in. My watch buzzed again. "That's thirty minutes. Ten more to go."

I stayed in the garage and started carrying dining room chairs into the truck. I left a lane for Walker to get back to the two couches, which he did, first with one box, then another. "That's all the vinyl," he said. "There's a bunch of DVDs, but I don't think anyone wants those. There's a bunch of books, but they're just books. I didn't see anything special."

"Let's go upstairs," I said. "But no big furniture. Two trips max."

WE RAN UP THE STAIRS. Walker went into the room on the left and I went right. Mine was a music room. It had a bunch of stereo gear, but more importantly, three guitars. Two of them were Fender electrics. The other one was a Martin acoustic. They were hanging on pegs on the wall, but I opened up a closet and found their cases. I quickly packed them up and headed for the truck. Walker was just coming down the stairs when I got back.

"Andy," he said. "Look at this." He held out both hands. One held a shiny wooden box, about a foot square and six inches high. The other one held four banded stacks of bills. "I think this is jewelry," he said, lifting the box a little higher. "It's got a little lock on it, and I didn't find a key. This," he said, lifting up the other hand, "is three-plus packs of hundred-dollar bills. There's a safe in the closet. It was sitting wide open. I think we hit the jackpot."

THERE WERE STILL two leather recliners in the family room. Walker set the money and the jewelry box down on the first one. I bent down at the front and Walker went to the back. He had his hands on the top of the back of the chair when I lifted the front off the ground. Next thing I knew, the leg rest part flipped up and hit me in the chin. It stunned me for a second. I dropped my end of the chair.

"Damn, that hurt," I said. Walker laughed.

"Better carry it from the sides," he said. "We'll have to remember that. Be careful with recliner chairs. They're deadly."

WE GOT BOTH RECLINERS into the truck. "Let's get all the rest of these dining room chairs in. It's OK to close off the lane now." We did that then went back into the house to turn off the lights we'd turned on. Walker ran upstairs and I got the ones on the ground floor. When he came back downstairs, I was standing at the glass door. I had looked at my watch. We were coming up on forty-two minutes.

"Look at this," I said, as I pulled the door open. There were at least ten sealed cartons in the small room. I snapped on the light and we could see that most of them had pictures of wine bottles printed on them. A couple had liquor company names and logos on them. I could see one that said Seagram's and another with a picture of a buffalo.

"Holy shit!" Walker said, then "Fuck, we got a hand truck, but it's buried in the front of the truck."

"That's OK, we just run them out there one at a time. Twenty-second trips. No sweat." We each made four quick trips. When we came back for trip number five, there were three cartons on the floor. "Load me up two," Walker said, "then you get the last one."

MY WATCH BUZZED JUST AS I dropped the last carton in the truck.

"How much time left?" Walker asked.

"None," I said. "We're done."

"I think we should take the motorcycles," he said. "Look, we've got plenty of room in the truck."

He was right about that. "But how are we going to get rid of them?"

"How are we going to get rid of that wine? Marvin said he had a guy for just about anything. We're here, they're there for the taking. I say let's grab 'em now and worry about 'em later."

We rolled the bikes up the ramp and Walker secured them to the side of the truck with a couple of bungee cords. Then he reached for the door handle and pulled it down as he stepped out onto the ramp. After he secured the door, he hopped down and I lifted the end of the ramp and pushed it back into its slot. As it cleared the last few inches, I saw that the truck had a trailer hitch. I looked at Walker. He'd seen it too.

"Pull the truck up about ten yards," I said. "Start turning out toward the road. Then come back and help me."

I lifted the front end of the trailer that held the jet ski and started pulling it out of the garage. It was heavy but I got it moving on the garage floor. Then Walker was there. He went to the back and pushed. I maneuvered the coupler over the ball and held them together. Walker came up and set the locking mechanism and fastened the chain. Then he held his fist up and I bumped it.

"I'm going to close the garage doors and come out through the back door," I said.

"Stop in the kitchen," he said. "They got beer in the refrigerator."

Sure enough, there were four bottles of St. Pauli Girl on the top shelf. I grabbed two in each hand and headed out the back door. Walker slid the truck into gear as soon as I hopped into the cab.

"First thing," I said. "You've got fifteen feet of trailer hanging off the back of this thing. You *cannot* forget that. I'm already worrying that we pushed our luck too far."

"I won't forget," he said. "Slow, wide turns. I'll drive like my Grandma."

"Second thing," I said. "Where's the cash and the jewelry box?"

"I put them into one of the duffels, and I jammed that one in between the couches and the side of the truck."

"Good. OK, third thing." I looked over at him and smiled. "Want a beer, Mr. Cheadle?"

13

Walker drove carefully, just under the speed limit. Neither of us said much until we were northbound on Route 1.

"OK, what did we learn," I asked him.

"This is what you call your mission debrief, huh?"

"That's right. And it's important. So what did we learn?"

He was quiet for a moment. Obviously thinking, getting his thoughts in order. Walker does that when he knows you want a serious answer.

"We were lucky with the truck," he said. "Danny's truck would have been too small. It would have limited us pretty seriously."

"I agree," I said. "What else did we learn?"

He nodded, and ticked off three things with his fingers. "One, if we get a hand truck, don't bury it in the big truck. Two, blankets are important. And three, beware of recliner chairs."

I laughed. "Yeah, that still smarts a little. All right, two more things I think we learned. One, the best thing about that house was its setting. We were invisible. That gave us time, and that made the whole thing work."

Walker nodded his head.

"The second thing is the value of intelligence. We knew the house was empty, and we knew something about what was in it. Some of that was recon, but most of it was Meghan. This mission really started with her."

"Would she help us again?" Walker asked.

"She doesn't know she helped us in the first place," I said. "And we don't want her to. Anyway, I think this was a one-off situation."

Walker nodded again.

"But now I'm thinking," I said, "who *do* we know who's involved with people and houses, and houses that might not have people in them?"

Walker smiled. "Hot damn. Maddie!"

WE PARKED THE TRUCK on Blount Street, disconnecting the trailer and pulling it up on the sidewalk side. On the way home, we'd decided to hold a few items back from Marvin. We unloaded the liquor and wine, the three guitars, the record albums, the cash and the jewelry box. Walker fought his way to the front of the truck and came back with the hand truck. We got everything into my condo in three trips. I brought the hand truck back out and locked the truck with a spare bike lock.

When I got back inside, Walker had one of the banded stacks of bills in his hand.

"Take a look," he said, tossing the bills to me. *Harrah's Cherokee Casino Resort* was printed on the band. "I guess Raymond's a gambler."

"Or Marianne."

He smiled and handed me the jewelry box. It had a round keyhole with a little notch at the bottom. Very old-fashioned looking. I took a long, thin, straight-head screwdriver out of my junk drawer and wiggled it around a little. The lock snapped open and I lifted up the cover. There was a tray full of rings and bracelets. I lifted that out and found another tray, this one with half a dozen necklaces and a couple of watches. Underneath that was a compartment full of silk-looking scarves.

"Got any thoughts on what we do with this stuff?" I asked Walker.

"I do, as a matter of fact," he said. "I think this might be how we bring Maddie into the picture. She knows about shit like this. I remember her telling Teisha about good jewelry and bad jewelry. I don't know how she knows, but she knows.'

"Does this mean we're telling Teisha what we're doing?"

He hesitated for just a second. "She already knows. She wanted to come tonight. I probably should have mentioned that."

I wasn't surprised. We'd never really talked about Teisha knowing, let alone her being involved, but I knew Walker didn't like to keep secrets from her. Better to tell her up front than to have her wondering where the extra money was coming from.

"The booties were her idea, weren't they," I said.

He just smiled, sheepishly.

"OK, why don't you reach out to Maddie. Invite her to dinner or something. In the meantime, we'll take the rest of the stuff to Marvin."

I drove Walker home, then took a shower, brushed my teeth, and got into bed. I lay back with my eyes closed and my mind started reconstructing the mission. I said to myself, *no! Not now! Sleep now!* Amazingly, it worked. That's the last thing I remember until my alarm went off at 6:00 a.m.

14

Walker was at my door at 6:30. We reconnected the trailer and Walker drove carefully through downtown. As we approached the store, Walker pointed at a Cadillac sedan coming from the other direction. "That's Marvin," he said. "Looks like Keila's with him."

We let them turn in first. Marvin pulled in alongside the building and he and Keila got out. She headed for the front door and Marvin waved us forward. Walker stopped the truck as we got even with Marvin and lowered the window.

"You boys headed to the lake after this?" Marvin asked. "I was expecting you to bring me some furniture."

"Oh, we got some of that," Walker said. "But this was there too, so we took it. Wait till you see what else."

"Keila's gonna open up the garage. This truck will fit. Back it right in."

"We need to unhook the trailer," Walker said.

"Why?"

"Because I'm not a very good truck driver."

"You boys get out," Marvin said. "I'll do it."

It took Marvin longer to haul himself into the truck than it did for him to back it smartly into the garage, trailer and all.

He climbed down and said, "All right, now unhook the trailer. Just move it to the side so you can pull the ramp out." We did that, then I worked the lock and rolled up the door.

The first thing Marvin saw was the motorcycles. "What in the name of the Holy Baby Jesus," he said. "What part of 'Marvin's Used Furniture' did you not understand?"

I still hadn't said a word, and saw no need to. Walker said, "You told me you had a guy for just about anything. Besides, just about everything else *is* furniture, or else other household stuff that you told us you could sell."

Marvin walked up the ramp. Keila followed him. "What you think?" he asked her. She walked deeper into the truck, looking over the dining room chairs, then the leather recliners. She worked her way back to the two sofas and all of the stuff we had piled on them. She zipped open all three duffel bags.

"This is all good, Grandpa. It might be too good for some of our customers, but if we price it right, I think it'll sell."

Marvin nodded. "Here's what I think we should do," he said. "I'll ask you boys to unload the truck, set everything upright back in this corner. You take the truck away and Keila will make a couple of lists. One list of the obvious things, that we know we can sell, and we know what we can sell them for. Those are the things I'll pay you cash for right away, three dimes on the dollar. Next list is things not so perfect for us, too good for us really. Like Keila said, we can sell it at a certain amount and I'll pay you thirty percent on that amount. I'm telling you now, though, I'm paying you less than the worth. Someplace else, you understand? Some other store that caters to another clientele."

Walker and I both nodded. "More white people," Keila said. "No offense, Mr. Andy."

"You stop that now," Marvin said. Keila winked at me. "Third list is the things that might interest a friend of mine. He pays thirty, same as me, but you got to split the thirty with me. I give you twenty, I keep ten, but all that takes a bit of time. You understand?"

Walker and I nodded again.

"Byron," Marvin said, "I still wish you hadn't got into this, but you seem to have a knack for it. Someday I want you tell me all about how you did it. But not today. Come see me tomorrow and we can talk about what's what."

We nodded again. Marvin held out his hand, first to Walker, then to me. Keila winked again and they both went into the showroom while Walker and I started unloading the truck. It didn't take long. We were back at my condo a little before 8:00 a.m.

I TOLD WALKER I'D TAKE the truck back later in the morning so he could go right off to work. "Before you go," I said. "Let's split the cash. No reason to wait on that, right?"

We'd stashed the banded stacks in my freezer overnight. Walker said that's the way they did it in the movies. I handed him a full stack and set one on the counter for myself. Then I handed him the other full stack and held onto the partial one. "You split that one, I'll split this one," I said.

Walker counted out two piles of fifty. I ended up with two piles of seventeen. $33,400 in total. $16,700 each. We were both grinning like fools.

15

The rest of my day was uneventful. I made my sales calls and took a couple of small orders. I spoke with my boss for about twenty minutes. He read off my sales figures for June and we talked about the outlook for July. I was apparently in the running for "Big Dog." That's what they call the top salesman every year.

I spent part of the afternoon doing research on the internet, trying to figure out what the wine and liquor we'd taken might be worth. None of the wine was spectacular, mostly between $15-$20 a bottle. We had a case of Seagram's vodka that went about the same. The star of that show was a case of Buffalo Trace Bourbon at $40 a bottle. I was pretty sure Walker would want to keep that.

I looked up the guitars too. The Fender electrics were called Stratocasters. There were hundreds of them listed on eBay and Craigslist, anywhere from a few hundred to a couple of thousand dollars. I figured these two were somewhere in the middle of that range. The Martin was a DSS-17 and it looked to be in perfect condition. Martin's website said it listed for $1999.

Walker texted me at about 4:00 p.m. "Marvin says 7 p.m. at his store. Can U make it?" I texted back, "Yes."

"KEILA SHOULD BE HERE SOON," Marvin said. "She has all the lists. She printed up spreadsheets on her computer at home." He pointed us toward the table we'd sat at the first time and went off to talk to a customer. Keila walked in a few minutes later.

"Hey Byron. Hey Mr. Andy. Hey, I got something I'd like to ask you about, after?"

"Sure thing," I said.

She set some papers on the table. "Let me go tell Grandpa I'm here."

AS SHE WALKED AWAY, an older but still athletic-looking man with a full head of curly gray hair opened the front door and walked in. He looked over at us, looked away, and then right back at me.

"Andy?"

"Denis," I said as I rose to my feet. "It's been a long time."

"It has been far too long. Come," he said, holding both hands up and waving me toward him. I took a step forward and he shifted into a boxing crouch. "Come," he said again, a large smile growing on his face. Then he came out of the crouch and took two fast strides forward, opening his arms wide. I took a smaller step into his bearhug. It was at least ten seconds before he let me go.

"You look good, Andy. Are you home on leave?" Denis was born and raised in Sydney, Nova Scotia. He's probably been in the US for forty years, but he still speaks with a French accent.

"I've been out a while. I'm living here, full-time civilian."

"But you have not come by the gym?"

"As I remember, you told me I wasn't welcome there anymore."

He was quiet for a moment. "Yes. You are right. But did I not also tell you that you would always be welcome in my home?"

16

Denis Chaisson was the guy who called me after my 'violent man' conversation with Sergeant Connelly. She'd told me it would probably be next week, but my phone rang the next day. "My name is Denis Chaisson,"—with his accent, it sounded like Denice Shayson—"I was asked to call you. By Kirsten Connelly. She tells me that you are interested in learning to fight."

"I guess that's right," I said.

"No," he said. "This is not something you guess at. It is something to be serious about. Are you serious about this?"

"Mr. Chaisson, I'm training to be an Army officer. I'm serious about that. But Sergeant Connelly asked me a question and she wasn't completely satisfied with my answer. That's what led to her asking you to call me."

"What was the question?"

"She asked me if I thought of myself as a violent man."

"And your answer?"

"That I didn't."

"But you are training to be part of the most violent endeavor of mankind."

"That's basically what she said."

"I understand. Come to my gym. At the very least, I can provide you with a head start toward the hand-to-hand combat training the Army will put you through. Beyond that, who knows?"

I AGREED TO MEET HIM at his gym after my classes the next day. It was on the second floor of a building on Rock Quarry Road, just off of Martin Luther King Boulevard. The ground floor had two small businesses, a tattoo parlor and a hair salon. When I drove up, there were half a dozen guys sitting on lawn chairs outside the tattoo place, drinking beer and malt liquor out of cans. All Black guys, most of them inked up. They looked at me with interest as I got out of my car, and I definitely felt out of my element. Not just because they were Black. I spent plenty of time around Black people at school, starting with Walker. But these guys weren't college students and I wasn't on campus. This was Southeast Raleigh. The poor side of town. The gang side of town. So I was a little wary.

"You here for tats?" one of them asked me. "I could do some pretty work on that bright white skin."

"For real," another said. "James a artiste."

Everybody laughed, including me. "I'm here for the gym. It's upstairs, right?"

The second talker pointed toward the corner of the building. "Stairs around there. Denis up there,"—pronouncing it Denice—"couple a other dudes. Floatin' like butterflies. Stingin' like bees. Hah!"

Everyone laughed again. I said thanks and headed for the stairs. The gym was an open space, maybe sixty feet by thirty feet with dingy gray walls. Most of it was empty. There was a raised octagonal fighting cage at one end and a square mat about the same size on the floor at the other end. In between there were a couple of hanging bags, a couple of free-standing bags, and a rack filled with sandbags and weight balls. Denis was watching a Hispanic kid, maybe fifteen or sixteen, working on one of the hanging bags. Two older Hispanic guys were doing sit-ups in the middle of the mat.

"You are Andy?" Denis asked.

I nodded. "Come," he said, holding up both hands and waving me toward him, the first of many times I would see that gesture.

"How much do you weigh?" he asked.

"About one-seventy-five."

"How much did you weigh last year?"

"Maybe one-sixty-five."

"Good, you are moving in the right direction. With your frame, you can easily carry two hundred pounds and more. Do you lift weights?"

"Twice a week. My roommate is a football player. I lift with them."

"Do you run?" he asked.

"At least five times a week," I said. "We do three to five miles at morning PT. I try to go long on Saturday or Sunday. Ten or twelve miles.

"And how did you get that black eye?"

"Sergeant Connelly didn't tell you?"

"She told me what you told her. Is there more to the story?"

"Not really. I was trying to break up a fight. In a pickup basketball game."

"And one of the fighters hit you?"

"No, it was actually his friend. I guess he thought I was going to double up on his boy."

"Do you know the Bible, Andy?" Denis asked.

"Not really. I know the basic story, I guess."

"In the book of Matthew, it says 'blessed are the peacemakers.' But whether you are a peacemaker or a warmaker, it is important to know who is who and what is what in a fight. Otherwise, you are likely to be blessed with one of those," pointing to my eye. "That is not what Matthew had in mind, eh?"

I started to say, "I guess not," but caught myself. Instead I said, "They definitely teach us the importance of situational awareness."

"Exactly. As I say, who is who and what is what. Now tell me, what did Kirsten Connelly tell you about me?"

"Nothing, really. She just said someone would be calling me."

"Then let me tell you what I think you should know about me. When I was fourteen, I was the toughest boy on Cape Breton. Do you know where that is?"

"Canada, right?"

"Yes. Cape Breton Island is the eastern end of Nova Scotia. The city of Sydney is there, and many smaller towns. Maybe a hundred thousand people there in all. My father was perhaps the toughest *man* on Cape Breton. He was very tough on me, so much so that I left home at sixteen. I went to Halifax, at the other end of Nova Scotia. And I quickly found out that I was not the toughest boy there. But I found my way from fighting and losing on the streets to fighting and winning in the ring. First boxing, then judo and Muay Thai. Then all of it together. Did you ever hear of the Tough Guy Contest?"

I shook my head no.

"In 1980, in Pennsylvania, near Pittsburgh, was the first contest. The rules were, anything goes. I was twenty. I lied about my age to be twenty-one. I fought a boy about my age and won. In the next bout, I fought a man twice my age and won. Then I fought the man who eventually won the contest and he beat me easily. I earned one-hundred-twenty dollars. A few months later, I fought in another contest and lost to the same man, again, after beating two others. This time I earned two hundred dollars because more people paid to watch. Also, this time he did not beat me so easily. We became friends, he and I. I went to work for the same company as he, loading trucks. Good, physical work. We trained together, sparring, but never fighting again. I twice worked his corner in contests that he won. He once did the same for me. But then two things happened. My friend was arrested, accused of stealing from the company we worked for. That was first. Second, the rules of the contest changed. We fought in weight classes in 1980. I was a middleweight. I weighed just a few pounds more than you do now. The classes were to be eliminated in 1981, which could put a middleweight in the ring with a heavyweight. I was tough, but I was not stupid. On the street, if you have to, you might fight at that disadvantage. In the ring, if you do not have to, only a fool would take the risk. My friend said, 'someone is going to die.' And he was right. A boy who weighed in at one-hundred-sixty-nine pounds went into the ring with a skilled fighter who weighed more than two-hundred-fifty pounds. The people cheered as he was beaten unconscious. Then they jeered as he was carried out. I was not there, but I could see it my mind, you know? I still can. That was the end of my desire to be a professional tough guy."

"So now you train fighters?"

"I train a few. There is still boxing, and the mixed martial arts are better regulated." He pointed toward the two older Hispanics. "These two fight in regional MMA events across the Southeast. They win some, they lose some. They will never be on television but they work hard. They take pleasure in the competition. But mostly I teach self-defense." He pointed toward the teenager. "Like this young man. He has been bullied most of his life. Maybe the next bully will get an eye like yours, eh?"

The kid must have heard that. He threw a crisp punch-punch-kick combination at the hanging bag.

"We also have fitness classes here," Denis continued. "Your Sergeant Connelly teaches kickboxing for fitness. She also assists me with the self-defense classes for the women."

"I wouldn't want to take her on," I said.

"She is formidable. But she is also a very good example of what she calls *Chaisson's Way*. In my life, I have fought because I wanted to. Now, I will only fight if I have to. And I stay out of situations where I might have to. It is the first thing we teach in self-defense. Risk avoidance. You always win the fight that you avoid."

I thought about that for a moment. "I'm not sure that applies to me completely. If I'm ordered into battle, I have to go."

"And if that is the case, you will be better off for your training. But that is not what I am talking about. In your basketball game, how did the fight start?"

"Two guys yapping at each other. Then, I guess, one guy pushed the other guy and they threw down. I didn't see the first punch."

"But one of the combatants threw it. Was it in any way self-defense?"

"Not really," I said. "Probably more about not losing face. In fact, I remember one of them yelling at the other one. "You ain't gonna punk me," or something like that."

Denis turned to the teenager. "Manuel, what will you do if a bully calls you names tomorrow?"

The boy answered, "I will turn to face him, and stand my ground."

"What if he touches you?"

"I will fight him."

"What if he does not touch you. What if he just uses words."

"I will face him and stand my ground. If he doesn't, ah, escalate, I will go on about my business."

"What if there are two of them?"

"I will go on about my business. And wait for a better opportunity."

"And...?"

With a smile. "I will continue to train and learn until I can handle them both at once."

Denis smiled too, and held out his fist for a bump. "Now Manuel, will you ever go out looking for a fight?"

"No, Denis."

"Why?"

"Because that's not what we do."

"And...?"

"Because then I'd have to go in the ring with you. For real. And you'd kick my ass and never let me come back here."

He turned back to me. "I was a violent boy and a violent man. But I have grown in my life. Kirsten says I have the capacity for violence, but not the need for it. I think that capacity is what she seeks for you. So, if you wish, I will teach you what I know. I ask only that you respect my way."

OVER THE NEXT TWO YEARS I learned a great deal from Denis. He had very little formal education but he was unquestionably smart. And very inquisitive. He'd ask me about what I was reading in my classes and sometimes he'd read the same material and we'd talk about it. Usually, he got it better than I did. He was probably worth at least half a point to my GPA. I progressed pretty quickly in my fighting skills and toward the end, I was assisting him with the self-defense classes. I know it's a cliché, but he was almost like a second father to me.

But then I fucked it up. In March of my Senior year, I got in a fight in a bar on Hillsborough Street. I'd had too many beers on top of a very bad day. I'd done poorly on a Military Justice oral exam and gotten chewed out by my professor for my obvious lack of preparation. On top of that, my date was in a pissy mood herself.

We were yapping back and forth and a guy at the next table asked us to cool it. Then he got up and stood up over our table and *told* us to cool it. I told him to back off. He said make me. I said let's go outside and started to stand. He pushed me back down into the booth. I came out swinging. He was a good-sized guy. I hit him twice in the gut. He bent over but he didn't go down. I was lining up an uppercut when my date grabbed by arm. It was just enough to bring me back to sanity. I lowered my hands and stepped back. The guy straightened up, said "Fuck you" and walked away.

The whole thing had happened very quickly. I doubt that most of the people in the place even noticed. But one person who did was in Sergeant Connelly's kick-boxing classes and she apparently told the story there. It got back to Denis. The next time he saw me, he asked me if it was true.

I didn't try to evade or explain. I just said yes, and that I had no excuse. He didn't say a word, he just turned and walked away. I followed him into his little office.

"I know you're disappointed in me," I started to say, but he just held his hand up.

"You graduate in, what, two months?"

"Yes. May fifteenth."

"And then you enter the Army?"

"Two weeks later. June first."

"I am tempted to say, we will continue as we have until then. It is not very long. But I cannot let this go, even as much as I care for you."

"You know I feel the same way," I started to say, but again, he held up his hand.

"You will always be welcome in my home, Andy, but you are no longer welcome here. Go."

There wasn't anything else to say. I remember Walker asking me a week or so later if I'd quit the fighting gym.

"Yeah," I said. "With finals and my last ROTC quals coming up I'm not going to have time for everything. That seemed like the most logical thing to drop." I also kept my distance from Sergeant Connelly.

17

Back in Marvin's store, I was feeling guilty. I probably should have reached out to Denis at some point. He had left that door open, but I guess I wasn't over the original guilt. I decided to keep it light for now and asked him if he remembered Walker. They'd met a few times, but it was a long time ago.

"I am sorry, but I don't," Denis said, turning toward Walker. But then I saw some recognition in his eyes. "Or maybe I do," he said. "You were a football player?"

Walker said yes.

"But you were bigger, no?

Walker laughed. "About a hundred pounds bigger."

By this time, Marvin had joined us. "Byron," he said, "was big from the time he was a baby. You look at him now, you wouldn't believe he weighed three hundred pounds in high school."

"I didn't," Walker said. "That's just an ugly rumor. I never weighed more than two-hundred-fifty in high school. I got to three hundred in the weight room at NC State."

"If you say so," Marvin said. "I only know what your mother told me."

Marvin turned to Denis and held out his hand. "I'm Marvin Townes, the owner of this fine establishment. What brings you here this evening? Tell me what you need and I'll show you what we've got."

DENIS SEEMED AMUSED by Marvin's greeting. Or maybe he was still amused by Walker. He looked at me and asked, "Will you be here for a few minutes?" I nodded yes and he went off toward the back of the store with Marvin. I sat back down with Walker. In maybe two minutes, Marvin came back alone. He pointed toward the back of the store. "Denis would like to talk to you. I'll keep Byron company."

I exchanged looks with Walker then we both looked at Marvin. "It's like they say," Marvin said. "It's a very small world."

I got up and walked back to where Denis was now sitting on a sofa. He patted the seat next to him.

"This is a day of surprises," he said. "First, that you are even here. Second, that you are the associate Marvin has told me about. I came here to take a look at that person. I am always careful about every link in the chain."

"You're not the only one who's surprised," I said. "You're obviously the friend Marvin told us about. The man who buys things he can't sell."

"Marvin and I, we have done business together for quite a few years. We have both benefited and we have never caused problems for each other. But, yes, I am a buyer and seller of things with questionable provenance. That is a good phrase, eh, for stolen property?"

He smiled at the dumbfounded look on my face. "I probably told you that my father was a fisherman." He had. "I probably did not mention that he was also a smuggler. I left his house at sixteen. I probably told you that too, and why. I went as far away as I could imagine, which was only the other end of Nova Scotia. But I made my way in those days with what I could steal. First it was food and other things I could immediately use. Then it was things that I could not use, but could sell to others. Before long, I realized that the people I sold these things too were doing much better than I was. You could say, I suppose, that I aspired to be one of those people."

"Were you doing this back when I was coming to the gym?" I asked.

"Oh, yes, Andy. At best, the gym was a break-even proposition. But it was a labor of love, made possible by my other business. I own the building, you know. I did not back then, but I do now, along with a home and some other real estate. I am not rich by any means, but we have a comfortable life."

"We?" Denis had lived by himself when I trained with him.

"Kirsten is with me. She left the Army a few years ago. She had posted back to active duty after her tour at the university but we stayed in touch. She will be happy to hear that you are back, I think, but maybe not so happy to find what you are doing. And now I must ask you. Why?"

"Well," I said, "I could tell you that it was all Walker's idea. He's a teacher. He scrapes by with a couple of part-time jobs. Then one night, at one of those jobs in fact, he happened to hear Marvin's previous, ah, associates talking. He's known Marvin for a long time. His mom worked for him. So he talked to Marvin. Basically he said, 'how can I get in on this?' And Marvin gave him some ideas, which Walker brought to me."

"And why did you decide to get involved?"

"Besides Walker being my best friend?"

Denis just looked at me, waiting for more.

"OK, it was two things. One is that I'm kind of bored. I spent most of my time in the Army in war zones. Now I sell tractor parts. It's not that I miss getting shot at, but there was definitely something missing in my life. The other thing is, an opportunity sort of dropped in my lap. A woman I know told me about a situation that meshed with what Walker was talking about. I did a careful recon and I thought it was doable, so we did it."

"My father would speak of *droit* and *courbe*," Denis said. "Straight and bent. He would say that *le fric droit* and *le fric courbe*—straight money and bent money—spent the same, but still bent money was better. He would also say that all men have *vol dans nos coeurs*—larceny in our hearts. That is true of me. Apparently it is true of you." He lifted his hands and clapped them sharply in front of his face. "So, we shall be together again. Now we go back to Marvin and your friend and talk business."

MARVIN SEEMED SULLEN when we got back to the table. Walker and Keila were having an animated conversation about something or other. Maybe Marvin was just tired. He pointed to the two empty chairs at the table and asked us to sit, which I did, but Denis remained standing.

"I should be going," Denis said. "I know you have business to discuss. But I do want to say that I think we can all do business together. I will call you tomorrow, Marvin, with my offer. You will be open, yes, on the Fourth of July?"

Marvin nodded.

"Then let me just say one more thing. Byron, as I told Andy, I did not come here to meet you. I only wanted a look at you. Under normal circumstances, I would have been in and out, taken my look, and we would never have met. This complicates things, for both Marvin and I. I do not want Marvin to feel threatened by my friendship with Andy. So, let us all be clear. I am in business with Marvin. You boys are in business with Marvin. Marvin establishes price with me, and split with you. Two separate arrangements. Are we agreed?"

I nodded, and I noticed that Marvin was looking less sullen. Not smiling, but obviously relieved.

He stood up slowly from the table. "Show them the list," he said to Keila. "Let me walk you out," he said to Denis. I watched as they walked to the door. As they shook hands outside, Marvin leaned in close and said something to Denis. I couldn't see Denis's face but Marvin's lit up in a smile. He nodded his head a couple of times, then Denis walked off, and Marvin came back into the store.

KEILA'S LIST WAS LONGER than I thought it would be. She listed every item individually, including all the things Walker had taken from the kitchen. But it all added up to a nice figure: $9225. That made our share $2767.50 and it didn't include the motorcycles or the jet ski, which Denis was going to offer on.

"I have around a thousand dollars on me right now," Marvin said. "I hope you won't mind waiting until tomorrow for the rest. I expect I'll hear from Denis's pretty early. Why don't you come back, ten o'clock, eleven o'clock, around there."

We said that would be fine. Marvin reached into his pocket and pulled out a wad of bills. He counted out $800 in hundreds, and $200 more in twenties and tens. "You want an envelope? Something to put this in?" he asked.

"No need," Walker said. "My pockets been empty a long time. I got plenty of room."

"STILL WANT TO ASK YOU SOMETHING," Keila said to me. "Private?"

Walker smiled and said, "I'll be by the car."

"My friend Julie?" Keila said, after he was gone. "You seen her with me at yoga?"

"I've seen you there with two girls," I said.

"Julie with dark hair. Her people from Vietnam."

I nodded.

"She thinks you're hot."

I laughed. "She said that?"

"No, fool. *I'm* saying that. So maybe talk to her a little bit next time you see us?"

I promised I would.

18

The next day was the Fourth of July. I slept in a little. When I came downstairs just before 10:00 a.m., I found Walker at my door.

"Change of plan," he said. "Denis called Marvin, said he's waiting on a guy and he won't be ready to talk until probably late tomorrow. Marvin called me and said we could still come by and pick up the rest of the money. Maddie's gonna be here between one and two o'clock and Teisha sent me out to buy a few things for dinner. You want to come with me? First Marvin, then Fresh Market?"

I said sure, and we got into his car and drove off. When we got to Marvin's store, it was busier than I'd ever seen it. We stood just inside the doorway for a minute before Keila noticed us and held up one finger. After another minute or so she came over.

"Crazy here today," she said. "Fourth of July sale. Already sold one of your sofas and the two recliner chairs. Be a while before Grandpa gets free, though. Any chance you can come back later?"

"No problem," Walker said.

I said, "Why don't we just see him tomorrow?"

"That'd probably be best." Keila said. "I'll tell him you'll call him in the morning." She hurried back to her customers.

Walker and I drove on to Fresh Market. "What do we need?" I asked.

"Pretty much everything. Burgers, chips, salad stuff, watermelon, something for dessert. Beer for you and me, tonic and limes for the girls. I told Teisha about the vodka. She's says it gonna be vodka-and-tonic day for her and Maddie."

We did our shopping and loaded the bags into the car.

"Want to come over now," Walker asked. It was still only around 11:00 a.m.

"No, just drop me at home. I'll come over around two o'clock."

"You'll bring a couple of bottles of the vodka?"

"Yep, and the jewelry box."

WHEN I GOT TO WALKER'S PLACE, Maddie was already there. "What you been up to Andy Carver?" she asked.

"I joined a gang," I said as I handed Walker the two bottles of vodka.

"No shit? You a Crip or a Blood?"

"I'm a TDM. Me and Byron. We're the whole gang."

"What's TDM stand for?"

"Thousand Dolla a Month."

She turned to Teisha. "What's this boy talking about?"

"Byron's Don Cheadle and Andy's George Clooney."

"What are *you* talking about?"

"Let them tell you," Teisha said.

Walker had opened one of the bottles by this time and mixed two generous drinks. He put one in front of Teisha and the other in front of Maddie. "It all starts with," he said, "I don't have enough money."

"You and me both," Maddie said.

"And Andy does have enough money, but he's sympathetic to my situation."

"So what you going to do, start some kind of company?"

"No. Like he said, we started a gang."

"And this gang is going to get you more money?"

"It already has. Me and Andy robbed a house last weekend. We stole a bunch of money, a bunch of furniture, and a bunch of other stuff. We stole that vodka you're drinking. Hell, we stole two motorcycles and a jet ski!"

Maddie looked at Teisha. "Is this for real?"

"Very real. And they want you to join the gang."

Maddie stood up. "All right, but first, I'm gonna go to the bathroom. And if I come back and you're just laughing at me, I'm gonna fuck somebody up."

"I have to get something from the car," I said. "I promise I won't be laughing at you. We think you can help us, and we think you're gonna want in."

WHEN I CAME BACK with the jewelry box, Walker and Teisha were sitting at the kitchen table. Maddie was standing by the refrigerator with her arms crossed.

"Maddie, you know something about jewelry, right? Take a look. Tell us if any of this stuff is any good."

I handed her the box. She turned it around to look at it from different angles. "The box is really nice. This thing alone is probably worth a few hundred dollars." She set the box down on the table and opened the lid, then lifted both trays out and set them on the table too.

"Where did you get this stuff?"

Walker answered. "Like I said, we robbed a house."

"A rich person's house?"

I answered that one. "We had reason to believe they were pretty well off."

"You did a home invasion?"

I looked at Walker. He nodded at me to go on. "We went into a house we knew was empty. The people were at the beach."

"And how did you know all this?"

"Let's not get ahead of ourselves," Walker said. "Tell us what you think about the jewelry."

"No. I want to know this first. You got tipped off by someone in my business, didn't you?"

"We got tipped off by someone in *my* business," I said.

"Really? Don't you sell lawnmowers or something?" I just nodded. "Well, if you're going to do it again, I can help you, for sure. Realtors definitely see who got the good stuff."

She started separating the rings and bracelets and things from the first tray into three piles. When she finished, she pointed at the first pile. "This here is crap, costume jewelry. Some of it's pretty but it's not valuable."

She pointed to the second pile, which was the largest of the three. "This here is what you get at the mall. Kay or Zales or a department store jewelry counter. There's real gold and silver and diamonds here and a couple of these bracelets are nice, but it's not, you know, rich people jewelry."

Then she pointed to the third pile, which was a ring, three bracelets and a brooch pin. "And this isn't really rich people jewelry either. Not rich, rich anyway. But it came from Bailey's or someplace like that." Bailey's is probably the most upscale jewelry store in Raleigh.

"And then *these*," she said, lifting out two pearl necklaces from the second tray and looking them over carefully. "These are beautiful. This *is* rich people jewelry."

She handed one of the pearl necklaces to Teisha and fixed the other one around her own neck. "Look at us. *Look at us!*" They both started to giggle. "What are you going to do with these?" she asked Walker. "I'll tell you what you *should* do. You should give them to Teisha so she can lend one to me!" They both giggled some more.

After a bit they calmed down. "All right," Maddie said. "What *are* you going to do with all of this? You got some good stuff here, but how are you going to move it? I assume that's the idea. Turn it into money, right?"

"We have a guy," I said. "We don't know that he's interested in jewelry, but it looks like he wants some of the other stuff."

"If you don't mind my asking, how do you know a guy like that?"

"Long story," I said. "It starts with Byron knowing a guy who buys stolen furniture. Then that guy knows a guy who buys other things. But it turns out, I know that guy too, although I had no idea he was into anything like that."

"My guy bought all the furniture," Walker said. "The other guy, we hope, is going to buy the bikes and the jet ski and a couple other things. But we decided that we wouldn't tell either of them about the jewelry, at least until we had some idea what it might be worth."

"That was smart," Maddie said. "Course, all I can do is tell you some of it's good. I can't put dollars on it."

Teisha said. "What if I brought the best pieces into Bailey's for an appraisal? They must get that all the time."

That made sense to me. Walker nodded too. But Maddie had a problem. "Baby, you think they get *Black* girls coming in there with pearls and good gold every day?"

Everyone was quiet for a moment. I noticed that they were all looking at me.

"What if Teisha calls up Bailey's tomorrow," I said, turning toward her. "You say your name, you say that your grandmother willed you a pearl necklace and some other jewelry. You say she was a doctor or something, or maybe your grandfather was a doctor and they did pretty well and you thought the jewelry was valuable, but to be honest, you'd rather have a down payment on a house. You make an appointment to bring it in, maybe even bring your fiancée in with you. You're a good-looking couple, a teacher and an EMT. You'll seem like really good citizens. I wouldn't think that would raise too much suspicion."

"So they'd just bring in a couple of pieces?" Maddie asked. "And not really to sell, but just for an appraisal?"

I nodded.

"If they'd give us a good price, why wouldn't we just say yes?" Teisha asked.

"Two reasons," Walker said. "First, if we only get one appraisal, we won't really know if it's a good price or not."

"And second," I said, "we probably don't want to sell it too close to where we stole it. I think, if we just learn more about the value, that'll help us to figure out what to do next."

MADDIE HAD MORE QUESTIONS. She basically wanted to know the whole story. We told her most of it, leaving out some of the details, like Meghan's, Marvin's and Denis's names. Teisha had questions too. Apparently Walker hadn't told her everything. We eventually got to Maddie's big question. What was in it for her?

"Like you said," Walker said, "Realtors know who's got the good stuff. We see you as our scout. But there's more to it than just good stuff. We have certain targeting parameters." He looked over at me as he said that, a smile growing on his face. "Y'see, Andy's been teaching me the fine points of mission planning."

"My fine man," Teisha said. "Make me another drink while you talk about your par-a-matters."

Walker took her glass, and Maddie's too. "First," he said, "nobody home. No chance we're going to meet up with some homeowner with a gun. Second, out-of-sight. Someplace remote. No one driving by or walking by who can see what we're doing." He started mixing the drinks. "Third, if there's an alarm, we need to be able to see the panel from outside to make sure it's not set. Much better if there's no alarm." He paused to cut two big slices of lime and drop them in the drinks. "Fourth. Andy, what's fourth?"

"Fourth is eight-hundred-dollar sofas and three-hundred-dollar chairs."

"I don't understand," Maddie said.

"Our guy has a used furniture store. His customers are looking for good stuff, but not expensive stuff. We brought him a Bassett sofa in the first haul. He said it was worth two thousand dollars, even used, but he couldn't sell it for anywhere near that. Not fast anyway, and we want to bring him merchandise he can sell fast."

"So, you want in?" Walker asked.

"I think I do, but you still haven't answered my question."

"Your share, right? We were thinking ten percent."

Before she could respond, I spoke up. "Before you say anything, there's a few more things you should know. Byron, tell her again what we call the gang."

He looked at me a little funny before he answered. "Thousand Dolla Month."

"When we first hatched this idea," I said, "Byron said that's what he wanted to get out of it. Just an extra thousand dollars a month. So a thousand for him, a thousand for me, that's the scale we were working on. We get thirty percent of what our guy thinks he can sell it for, so we're looking at around seven thousand dollars worth of merchandise to cover a month's worth of income goal. The point is, this is a low budget operation. What you're signing on for is probably a few hundred bucks a pop. No one's going to get rich from this."

Maddie nodded. "A few hundred bucks ain't gonna get me where I want to go," she said. "On the other hand," her face lit up with a big smile, "this is totally dope!"

19

Since the Fourth had been a Wednesday, the rest of the week was a regular work schedule. I got up at 7:00 on Thursday, my normal time. My plan for the day was to make some phone calls, take a yoga class at 11:00, and chill for the rest of the day.

Walker called me from work at about 10:00. "Marvin talked to Denis. He said four thousand dollars for the bikes and the jet ski. That's twenty-seven-hundred dollars for us and we can have it on Saturday along with the other money he owes us. That sound OK?"

I told him it did. "He also said Denis wants you to call him."

I checked off with Walker and dialed Denis. "Are you free this afternoon," he asked.

"Pretty much," I said.

"Will you come by the gym at one o'clock p.m.? There is someone I would like you to meet."

"Sure," I said. "Same place, right?"

"Yes," he said. "Oh, dress to fight."

"What?" No answer. He'd hung up.

KEILA'S FRIEND JULIE was at yoga. She came in by herself just before the class started and set her mat just inside the door. She was the first person out after the class ended, but she was standing at the front counter when I came out, taking a credit card back from the Betsy, the owner of the studio. "That should do it," Betsy said. "I'm sorry about the confusion."

I held the door open for her. She didn't look at me as she walked past. "It's Julie, right?" I said. "I see you here with Keila Townes."

Now she looked up at me. "I think you mean Keila Raines."

"I probably do," I said. "I mostly know her through her grandfather. His name is Marvin Townes. I guess I just assumed."

"I think Mr. Townes is her great grandfather," she said.

"Ah," I said, "now that you mention it, I guess he is. I'm not doing too well here, am I?"

"I'm sorry. I'm a little angry. And embarrassed. They rejected my credit card."

"Over your limit?" I said. "It happens. Nothing to be embarrassed about."

"I had to use the card my mother gave me for emergencies to pay for today's class," she said. "Now I'm going to have to explain that to *her*."

"Ouch. Sounds like a mother-daughter thing. I have two sisters. I know how that works."

"Whatever you think you know," she said, "it's different with Asian mothers. And Vietnamese mothers are the most Asian of them all."

"I'll have to take your word for that," I said. This definitely wasn't going the way I expected after what Keila had told me. "Well," I said, "have a good rest of your day."

I started to walk off. I got about five steps before she called out to me. "Your name is Andy, right?"

I turned. "Yes. Andy Carver."

I walked the five steps back to her but I didn't say anything for a moment. She looked pretty uncomfortable.

"I, just, I," she finally said. "Keila said you asked her about me. She said you were interested. I was just wondering."

"That's funny," I said. "Keila told me you were interested in me."

She flushed. She might have been ready to run away. I tried for a warm smile.

"I have to meet a guy this afternoon," I said. "But next Thursday, want to have lunch with me after class? Assuming you'll be here?"

"I'll be here," she said, with a little hop and a happy smile.

"Bring a change of clothes. I'll take you someplace nice."

I HADN'T BROUGHT A CHANGE, but Denis had said fighting clothes, so I figured I was good. I did change into a dry t-shirt that I had in the car. I stopped at Chick-fil-A and got a grilled chicken sandwich with a large lemonade, then I drove on to Denis's gym.

Nothing had changed on the outside. The tattoo parlor was still there, although there was no one sitting outside today. I parked in front and walked around the corner and up the stairs. Inside the gym, it seemed brighter. The walls had been painted at some point, still gray, but a lighter shade. There were two lifting benches and racks of weights that hadn't been there before.

There was only one person in the spacious room, skipping rope in the middle of the raised cage. He was smaller than me, but not by much, and sort of a medium color so I couldn't tell if he was Hispanic or African-American. He was moving right along, with the rope slap-slap-slapping against the canvas. He kept it up as I walked over to the cage, but I could see that his eyes were on me. Then a buzzer sounded and he stopped, but he continued to hold the ends of the rope in his extended arms. "Fifteen seconds rest," he said to me. "Just one more set."

Afterward, he came over and leaned against the mesh wall of the cage. "You must be Andy. Denis told me about you. He's all pumped that you're coming over today."

Up close, I could see that he was Hispanic, but there was something about him that I couldn't quite identify. He had a wide face with small ears and big eyes. I put him at just under six feet and just under two hundred pounds. He looked to be in his early twenties.

"Andy!" Denis's voice came booming across the room. "I see you have met Andre." He jogged across the floor and climbed up into the ring. "Come up," he said to me, and when I did, he said to both of us, "*D'accord*. All right. Now shake hands and come out fighting!"

It took a moment to realize that he wasn't serious. Both Andre and I looked at him, looked at each other, and looked back at him. By that time he was laughing heartily. "No," he said, "you will not fight. But I would like you to spar. You will be good for each other. Andy, Andre will fight in the UFC. He is not ready yet, but he will be. And you, I think, will find joy in helping me train him."

Over the next half hour, Denis ran us both through our paces, doing exercises I hadn't done for more than ten years. I was rusty, but the movements I'd practiced so many times started to come back to me. Andre was very impressive. He had crazy fast hands, much faster than mine ever were. The last thing we did was side kicks at a heavy bag. He could make that dance too. I was much less impressive. Denis needled me. "Andy, we will have to get *you* into fighting shape!" I just smiled.

After the side kicks we sat and talked for a while. I learned that Andre was Brazilian. His father had come to the US to study Engineering at NC State and married a fellow foreign student from Portugal. They'd stayed in North Carolina and eventually become American citizens. Andre himself had graduated from Duke with a degree in Political Science.

"That's an odd background for a fighter," I said.

Andre laughed. "Well, there's not that many jobs for political scientists, outside of politics, which really don't interest me right now. Too much Trump, not enough governing. Maybe later on,"—a glance at Denis—"if our Republic survives."

"He is a Liberal," Denis said. "And he suffers from the liberal disease, the Trump Derangement."

They both laughed. Obviously, this was ground they'd covered before.

We talked a while longer. It turned out that Andre had a long-standing interest in Brazilian Jiu-Jitsu. His great-grandfather had trained with the Gracie brothers who pretty much started the fighting form in Brazil in the 1920s.

"It was serious for great-grandpa," Andre said. "He grew up on a reservation. He was Guarani, one of the indigenous tribes. He got drafted into the army and they made him an MP, and then he was a policeman in Rio de Janeiro. That's where the Gracie's were. The family lore is that great-grandpa carried a gun for twenty-five years, but he never took it out of its holster. If you messed with him, he took you down on the ground and didn't let you up."

"A man after my own heart," Denis said.

"My grandfather was also a policeman," Andre said. "He was a Jiu-Jitsu fighter too. But he got killed in a gunfight. Line of duty. My dad was around thirteen at the time. Great-grandpa trained grandpa, and they both trained my dad when he was young, but it was never more than kid stuff, you know, like youth-level karate classes here in the States. Great-grandpa died not too long after that and my father never trained any more. He played soccer. In fact, he played for NC State. So I grew up more soccer than Jiu-Jitsu, but I heard lots of stories."

"And I have told him some of my stories," Denis said. "But now, off with you. You work tonight, yes? Go home, shower and change, and rest yourself. Andy and I have some things to discuss."

AFTER ANDRE LEFT, Denis told me that he worked at Whole Foods, usually behind the meat counter. "It lets him train during the day. That is his priority right now. He lives frugally, but that is how a young fighter should live."

"Now, to you," he said. "How do you evaluate your first foray into crime? Do you consider it a success?"

"Well, we didn't get caught," I said.

He laughed. "Always the first measure of success in this sort of thing. But that is not what I am asking just now. When you consider the risk you took, are you satisfied with the reward?"

I thought for a moment about how much to tell him. We did far better than we expected, but he didn't need to know how much better. "Our goal," I said, "was to clear two thousand dollars. Between what we got from you and what we got from Marvin, we're close to five thousand dollars. So on that basis we're pretty happy with the result."

"But?" he said.

"I didn't really have a but in mind."

"Andy, there is always a *but*."

"OK, the but is I feel like we hit a home run in our first at-bat. I think the law of averages comes into play at some point."

He nodded. "Would you like some advice?"

"Absolutely."

"If you intend to continue with this, I would urge you to consider a very basic principle. To a burglar—*cambrioleur* is the French word—small things of large value are far better than large things with small value. To steal a sofa, you need a truck. To steal an espresso machine, you only need a car. To steal a necklace, you only need a bicycle. Do you see what I am saying?"

"We should rob a jewelry store?"

"No, no, no! That is an entirely different sort of crime. I am saying that some places have more value to a *cambrioleur* than others. But there is a contradiction. Marvin, I am sure, told you that his clientele does not buy expensive furniture. He told me that much of what you brought him was too good, under normal circumstances, for his store."

"He told us that too," I said. "He could sell it, but not for what it was really worth."

"And that is the contradiction. The house that has the right furniture for Marvin probably does not have the things I am talking about, the small things of large value."

I nodded.

"Would you be interested in knowing more about my end of this?" he asked.

"Sure," I said.

"The two motorcycles, one day next week, will go on a truck that comes through North Carolina once each month. It will take them to a place called Alice, in Texas. Anything on that truck that will continue its journey by sea goes on another truck to Corpus Christi, maybe forty miles away to the east. From there, it might go to Africa, but more likely South America. The rest goes on another truck to Laredo, about a hundred miles to the west. From there, it will most likely be driven across the border into Mexico. My buyer is the man who owns the first truck. I have known him since my fighting days in Pennsylvania. His buyer is a woman in San Antonio, but that is all I know of his business. Other than knowing that his truck picks up from many like me in its travels, and there have been several times that I had to wait for the next month's truck, because that month's was already full."

"That's pretty amazing," I said.

"Not really. As I told you, my own father was a smuggler. There have always been smuggling routes running parallel to legal trading routes."

"How about the jet ski?"

He smiled. "There is a man who travels Virginia and the Carolinas in an RV. He goes to the flea markets in the summer, the pawn shops in the winter, and the auctions all year round. We often have a meal together when he comes through Raleigh. Much of what he does is legitimate, but some of what he does is not. I called him and asked, might you know anyone who would be interested in a jet ski? I sent him photos and he came back to me with an offer the next day."

Denis's phone buzzed. He looked at the screen and shook his head. "A text from Kirsten. I am to pick up tomatoes on my way home."

I thought about commenting on his domesticity. Instead, I asked him about jewelry. "Is that something you'd be interested in?"

"Oh yes," he said. "The man I just mentioned is always in the market for watches. Another man, right here in Raleigh, is a goldsmith. He is the jewelry equivalent of a chop shop. He takes the gold from a chain and the diamond from a ring and creates a completely new piece of jewelry. All the better if he buys his materials at a *marché noir* discount!"

"Black market?" I asked.

"Very good," Denis said. "We will make a *Canadien* of you yet!"

20

spoke briefly with Walker the next day. We made plans to work out on Saturday afternoon after he and Teisha went to Baileys. They came to the gym together, all smiles and satisfaction.

"You should have seen us," Walker said. "The lovely young Negro couple down from Warren County. He's a Sheriff's Deputy. She's the Assistant Principal at the Elementary School. And oh, so excited about Grandma's jewelry!"

"Yeah, we mighta got a little carried away," Teisha said. "But we learned a lot. The lady we talked to said they'd price the two bracelets around a thousand dollars each. If we'd wanted to sell them today, she'd have paid us four hundred dollars each."

"Now tell him about the necklace," Walker said, a big smile on his face.

"White South Sea cultured pearls. The clasp is twenty-four karat gold. She said it would sell for around twelve thousand dollars. She'd have to have her boss do a final appraisal, but she thought they might pay as much as eight thousand dollars."

She nodded at Walker. "Now tell him what *you* said."

His smile was even bigger now. "I put on a sad face. I said, 'we were hopin', and just left that hanging for a few seconds. Then I said, 'I guess we were too optimistic. We were hoping this would be a down payment

on a house, like twenty-five, thirty grand. We got carried away, huh?'
She said she was sorry, it was a beautiful necklace, but not worth that
much."

"So then Byron looks at me," Teisha said, "and says, 'Maybe we
should just hang on to it until we have the rest of the money saved. You
can wear it a few times.' And he looks at the woman and says, 'It won't
go down in value, will it? Maybe it'll even be worth more in a couple of
years?' And she says, 'Oh yes, it could,' and then she says, 'You have to
promise to bring it back here when you're ready to sell.' She gives us her
card, and we're all, 'We promise,' and then we're out of there."

They bumped fists, obviously proud of their performance. Teisha
said she'd see us in a minute and headed off toward the Ladies' locker
room.

"So what do you think?" Walker asked.

"I think you did great. Now we have a better idea of the value."

"Yeah. Too bad we couldn't have just sold it all right there."

I started to say something, but he cut me off. "I know. I'm just sayin'.
Truth is, that stuff seems *more* complicated right now than it did the
other day."

"Well, I learned a few things myself," I said. "I talked to Denis on
Thursday. He wants me to help him train a fighter at his gym. But he
also wanted to give me some advice, give *us* some advice. He says the
best things for a burglar are small things with large value. He specifically
mentioned jewelry. He told me he has two people who buy it. I didn't
say anything about our stuff, but that might make things a lot simpler."

"Simpler sounds good," he said. "The playacting at Bailey's was fun,
but let's be practical. I'm all for going with Denis."

Walker being practical. It doesn't always happen. I was about to say
something wise-ass, but then I had a better idea. "One of Denis's people," I said, "is a guy who makes jewelry. Denis says he takes the gold
from one thing and the diamonds from another and makes something
completely new. Maybe we can get him to make something pretty for
Teisha, pearl earrings or something like that. Make it part of the deal?"

Walker had his big smile on again. "You know, I was very tempted to buy her something pretty at Bailey's. Spend some of that cash. But I realized it would be out of character after what we'd just told the lady. I was still thinking about going to some other jewelry store, but this is better. Thank you!"

21

I brought the necklaces and the bracelets with me on Monday when I went to Denis's gym to work out with Andre. Denis wasn't there but he'd left a workout plan. Andre was stretching on the floor mat when I arrived and he stood to shake my hand.

"Denis will be along. He wants you to drill me on my footwork. He says you know the routine."

I remembered the routine—in general. I'd never taught it but I'd been on the trainee side across from Denis many times. We started slowly but picked up the pace as I got more confident. Denis arrived after about fifteen minutes and he worked us both for another hour. We slap-sparred a few rounds in the ring, then came back to the floor mat for some wrestling exercises. Then we worked the heavy bag, first with kicks, then punches, then combinations of both. Then three more rounds of slap-sparring. I had a little trouble keeping my hands up by the third round. Andre got me a couple of good licks.

"Sorry, dude," he said afterward.

"No worries," I said. "Denis was right. I'm a ways from fighting shape."

Denis handed us both towels. "But you are in good shape otherwise," he said. "It will not take long."

Andre wanted to know how I kept myself in shape. I told him about the yoga and the running and lifting. "Besides that," I said, "I don't eat too much junk. I don't drink too much. And, really, I'm not *old*. I turn thirty-six next month."

"Ah," Denis chuckled, "when I was twenty-two, I had no idea what it might be like to be thirty-six. And when I was thirty-six, I had even less idea what it would be like to be sixty. I am, I think, in better shape than almost anyone my age. But sixty is still sixty. When I was about your age, Andy, I went to the doctor for something or other. An Algerian doctor with more of an accent than me. He did tests, he asked questions, my whole health history. And I told him everything, from the beatings I took from my father to the beatings I took in the ring. He told me that I was not going to enjoy growing old. 'I have aches and pains in the morning,' he said. He was maybe a little older than I am now. 'You will have aches and pains all day. When it starts, take two Advil, first thing every morning. Get out ahead of the pain.'"

"Vitamin I," I said. Both of them looked at me funny. "Doc Stevens, one of my guys in Iraq. He was the platoon medic. He gave out multivitamins and Advil every morning. 'Vitamins A through E, and I' he'd say. 'Let's keep your energy up and your pain down to a dull roar.'"

"I take the Aleve now," Denis said. "Most days, one in the morning is enough. And a glass or two of wine in the evening. But it is definitely worse at sixty than it was at fifty. I just hope it is not too much worse at seventy."

That got Andre to his feet. "Well, thanks, you guys, for giving me all that to look forward to. I'm gonna go home and take a nap. See you tomorrow."

AFTER HE WAS GONE, I got my backpack and showed Denis the jewelry.

"This is from the same house?" he asked. I nodded yes.

"You held it back from Marvin." Not really a question, but I answered as if it was.

"We really didn't know where it fit," I said. "We held some other things back too, a hundred or so record albums, a few cases of wine and three guitars."

"You do not fully trust Marvin?" This time it was a question.

"No, it's not really that. Like I said, we didn't know where those things fit. We still wouldn't know if you hadn't mentioned jewelry to me the other day."

"I see," he said. "Well, you did *very* well for your first effort, I think."

"I guess we did. Any idea what these will be worth to your friends?"

"I can only ask them," he said. "And I will need to show them. Let me make some calls."

He handed back the jewelry and walked off toward his little office. I loaded up a bar and cranked out a set of bench presses before he came back. "My goldsmith friend is at the Home Depot in Cary. He would like to come by here in twenty minutes. Can you stay?"

IT WAS CLOSER TO FORTY MINUTES. He turned out to be an interesting character. He was maybe five-foot-four and maybe a hundred pounds, wearing bright yellow Bermuda shorts and a black tank top. He had earbuds in his ears and his head was bopping up and down to whatever he was listening to. He came to a stop in front of Denis, bopped twice more with feeling, and then reached up, took the buds out of his ears, and put them in his pocket. "*Bonjour, Denis,*" he said. He had no trace of a French accent. If anything, he sounded midwestern. He turned to me and held out his hand. "John Knox. Nice to meet you."

I introduced myself and we shook. He turned back to Denis. "Can I see it?"

Denis pointed to the jewelry which I'd set on the corner of his desk. Knox picked up the two bracelets and looked them over. "Fourteen K," he said. "You got an ounce or so of pure between the two of these and a couple grams of silver in the white gold. Say, a thousand dollars for both."

"What is the price of gold these days?" Denis asked.

"One-thousand-two-hundred-eight dollars and ten cents this morning. Down a little from yesterday."

"That's for an ounce?" I asked.

"Yeah."

I looked at Denis. "You understand, Andy," he said. "This is not the straight market. John can buy all the gold he wants at the straight market price. He does not need us for that, and he takes no risk doing that."

"Oh, no," I said quickly. "I understand completely. I'm just wondering if it's a good deal all around."

Knox answered. "On a scale of ten, it's probably a nine for me and an eight for you. I'll go another fifty dollars if you need me to."

I held up both hands, palms out. "Not necessary. Seems to me, nine to eight's the basis of a good relationship." That brought a small smile to Denis's face. I think he approved.

"Now these," Knox said, picking up the necklaces, one in each hand, "this one is nothing special, just a string of small pearls and a ten K clasp. I'll give you five hundred dollars." That was the one in his left hand. He set it back in the box and held the other one with both hands. "This one is fucking beautiful." He counted the pearls around the string. "You got forty-one of these. They're not all uniform, but more than half of them look to be at least twelve millimeters. The rest, I don't think any are smaller than ten millimeters. I'll go one-hundred-fifty dollars each for the pearls, plus another fifty dollars for the gold clasp. Six-thousand-two-hundred dollars total."

That was at least within shouting distance of what the woman at Bailey's had said. "From what Denis told me, you're going melt the gold, separate the pearls, and make all new jewelry from this stuff. Is that right?"

"Probably, yeah."

"If you don't mind my asking, what's that likely to be?"

"Well," he said, "the small pearls, I'll probably just restring them and change the clasp. The big pearls, maybe half of them into a choker and the rest into earrings."

"How much would you charge me for a pair of those earrings?"

He looked at Denis, then back at me. "There's basically two types of pearl earrings, dangles and studs. I like to make dangles, so you got the pearl, plus the metal that hangs it from the ear. That can be gold or silver. Figure the three hundred dollars for the two pearls and another hundred dollars for the metal. No charge for the labor. Wife or girlfriend?"

I laughed. "Girlfriend, but not mine. My partner. Tell you what, how about a straight swap, the smaller necklace for a nice pair of earrings?"

"Works for me. Silver or gold?"

"Can I ask her and get back to you?"

"Sure thing. Got one other question, though. Who am I buying this stuff from, you or Denis?"

I looked at Denis. "You, right? And you'll pay me my share?"

He nodded to John and they made arrangements to meet up later in the week for the exchange. I was busy wondering if I'd stepped out of line offering the trade for the earrings. I asked Denis about that as soon as John left.

"Well, yes," he said. "But it is of no matter. We will call it a learning experience. Now, he will pay me seventy-two-hundred dollars. I will pay Marvin half of that. He will pay you two-thirds of the half. Unless..." He let the last word dangle.

"Unless we screw Marvin?"

He laughed. "That is not the word I would have chosen. But essentially, yes. He has had no knowledge of these items, is that still correct?"

"Not from me," I said. "I don't think from Walker either."

"Therefore he added no value to the exchange of these items."

I thought about that for a moment. "OK, technically he didn't introduce us to you. But he was kinda the proximate cause of getting us back together."

"If that means what I think it does, I suppose you are correct. Our reuniting was a thing that happened because another thing happened, yes?"

I think I mentioned that Denis was not well educated, but highly intelligent and very inquisitive. I told him he did a better job of explaining proximate cause than I would have.

"Still, he has benefited from the parts where he did provide value to your endeavor. Is it necessary to reward him for the parts where he did not?"

I thought about that too. "I'll have to talk to Walker," I said. "Marvin is his account."

I SPOKE TO WALKER that evening. We sat in his back yard with a couple of beers and Teisha brought out a fruit salad she'd made.

"So, something to talk about," I said. "I met the goldsmith today, one of Denis's jewelry people. He's offering seventy-two-hundred dollars for the bracelets and the pearls."

"That's great!" Teisha said. "That's almost as much as we could have got from Bailey's!"

"Not really," I said. "That was us selling to Bailey's. This is us selling to Denis. He's the one getting seventy-two-hundred dollars."

"So we'll get a little more than two thousand dollars," Walker said. "Assuming that Marvin gives us the same deal."

Teisha didn't seem happy with that. "I understand the whole fence thing. Byron explained that. But the thing I don't understand, why does Marvin get any of *this*?"

"That's what we have to talk about," I said. "Denis actually brought it up. He's willing to deal with us directly. Not on everything, not on any kind of furniture, he's not trying to cut Marvin out completely. The way he put it, if Marvin adds value to what we're doing, he should profit from that. But maybe he doesn't add any value to the jewelry. Or the other things we held back."

Walker had his eyes jammed shut. He opened them back up and looked at me. "What do you think about that?" he asked me.

"I think it's not about what I think. Marvin is your guy. It should be your decision."

"Fuck, Andy, that's not fair. You're asking me to choose between you and him."

"I don't see it that way at all," I said. "If you want Marvin in, he's in. And I'm good with it. Remember, I'm not in this just for the money."

Teisha said, "Baby, let me ask you something. You're not going to share what you got from the records, right? Not with Marvin, or the other man?" Walker had sold all the record albums earlier in the week at a local record store. He'd already given me my share.

"That's right," he said.

"So seems to me, you already decided you don't have to."

Walker nodded. "Just seems different. The records were a couple hundred dollars, total. This is more than a thousand dollars, his share, straight cash."

I stayed quiet. Teisha did too. After a moment, Walker showed a little smile. "I'm gonna give Marvin a bottle of the bourbon," he said. "I'm gonna tell him I grabbed it for myself, but got to thinking that he might appreciate it more. Then we're gonna sell him what we think he can sell, and we're gonna sell Denis what we know he can sell, and we're gonna remember that this is a business, not a charity. Everyone gotta work for their share. That sound good?"

Teisha stood up and put her arms around him. Then she stepped back and said, "It's not personal. It's just business." I think she was going for an Italian accent. Walker and I both laughed.

I STAYED FOR ANOTHER BEER. When I got home, I realized that I hadn't told Walker the other news. I sent him a text. "Forgot to mention. Seventy-two-hundred dollars plus a pair of pearl earrings. Gold or silver?"

The phone rang maybe ten seconds later. "Not sure what you mean, gold or silver," Walker said. "They'll be pearls, right?"

"Yeah. But the pin or the clip or whatever, that can be either gold or silver. Ask Teisha what she wants."

He was quiet for a few seconds, then he whispered, "I want this to be a surprise. Can't go wrong with gold, right? Especially on a Black woman's skin? Yeah, definitely gold!"

22

The next two days went by quickly. I was on a hot streak at work. I got two big orders on Tuesday and two more on Wednesday. My boss called Thursday morning while I was on another call. When I listened to the message, all I heard was "Woof, woof! Call me back Big Dog!" Which I did, and he happily told me about a conversation he'd had with *his* boss that morning.

"You're making us look good, Andy! Very much appreciated! Keep the pedal to the metal!" My boss has a very high energy level. That's probably how you get to be a sales manager. Not something I ever aspire to, but I thanked him for his encouragement.

"Y'know," I said, "the last time I got barked at by my boss it was a Colonel in Kandahar. *He* said I was making *him* look bad. We either blew something up or we didn't blow something up, I don't really remember. But he was that kind of guy. The Army had a few like that. Another thing I don't miss about the Green Machine."

"That's right," he said. "The only green machines you have to deal with now say *John Deere* on the side."

I LEFT FOR YOGA not long after that. I was dressed in my workout gear but I brought along khakis and a polo shirt because I was supposed to take Keila's friend Julie to lunch. She was already in the studio when I got there, in the middle of the back row where I usually set up, so I laid my mat down right next to her.

She'd been sitting cross-legged with her eyes closed, hands on her thighs. She opened her eyes and looked over at me with sort of a nervous smile. I asked if we were still on for lunch and she nodded her head, still looking nervous. I reached over and tapped the bridge of her nose with my index finger. Not sure why, exactly. It's not one of my regular moves. But I guess it was the right thing to do. Her smile got bigger and she didn't look so nervous anymore.

She closed her eyes again. Many people like to meditate before yoga. I like to stretch. I lay on my back and rolled one hip over in a supine twist. When I turned my head back toward Julie I saw two tanned legs standing between us. They were attached to a woman named Ellen who I'd had a thing with a couple of months before. She'd stopped coming to this class, which I assumed meant the thing was over. Now she was here, asking Julie to move so she could set her mat between us. Julie looked nervous again.

"Hey Ellen," I said. "How've you been?"

"I've been away," she said. "But now I'm back. I'm glad to see you're still here."

"I am," I said. "In fact, I'm here with Julie today." She turned and stared down at me with one of those looks that could kill. Without a word, she walked away and set her mat at the other end of the room. Julie looked a question at me. I just shrugged. Ellen always tended toward brusque. She's in her early fifties but she keeps herself in shape. Her husband is a partner in one of the big law firms downtown.

Yes, I'd had a thing with a married woman. It wasn't the first time.

THE CLASS WAS HARD. The woman who teaches it could be anywhere between forty and sixty. Her name is Ruth. She's tiny, no more than five feet tall. Silver hair cut short, no lines on her face, very little body fat except for surprisingly big breasts. She keeps the room hot, too. She put us through an hour of pretty much constant motion with one pose leading to another to another. I thought it was great.

Julie and I walked out of the hot room together. She turned right into the ladies' locker room. I continued down the hall to the much smaller men's locker room. As usual, I had it all to myself. I started the shower hot and soaped myself all over. After I rinsed it all off, I turned the hot water down in stages until it was full cold. You don't really stop sweating for a while after a hot yoga class but at least I'd cooled down some. I toweled off, got dressed and headed out the door, where I almost bumped into Ruth. She was carrying a basket of towels toward the washing machine in the back.

"It's been a while since we last saw Ellen," Ruth said.

"Yeah, she told me she'd been away."

Ruth just looked at me for a moment. "I always thought she was a little old for you."

"Excuse me?"

"And Julie? She's a little young for you too, don't you think?"

I just stared at her. I had no idea what to say.

She tapped the side of her head with an index finger. "Sees all, knows all. Knows it's none of my business too. But please don't get Ellen in some kind of cat fight with Julie. I like Julie."

Now I did know what to say. "Does that mean you don't like Ellen?"

"Andy, nobody likes Ellen. I don't think *you* especially like her." She tapped her head again. "Remember, sees all, knows all. Now go, Julie seems to be waiting for somebody up front."

JULIE LOOKED COOL in a skirt and a halter top. Cool both temperature-wise and image-wise. I didn't know exactly how old she was, but Ruth was probably right. I was pretty sure Keila was going into her second year of college, so if Julie was in the same class that would make her eighteen or nineteen. I know I didn't turn twenty until the end of my sophomore year at NC State. In any event, now I was feeling a little bit guilty about the age difference.

"So what do you like to eat?" I asked her.

"Anything," she said. "I'm not picky."

"I was thinking about Tazza, over at Cameron Village. Ever been there?"

"I have," she said. "I love their pizza!"

"OK, Tazza it is. Will you ride with me?"

She nodded yes. Her little Nissan Juke was parked right next to my car so she dropped her yoga mat and backpack in the back seat as we passed by. We made small talk about the class on the short drive over to Cameron Village. I thought about telling her about my conversation with Ruth but decided to wait on that. I was still trying to decide how guilty I was actually feeling.

Tazza was medium-busy, but we were seated right away at a four-size table near the front window. Our server came by within a few minutes to see if we wanted drinks. I nodded toward Julie, who looked up at the server and said, "I'll have a glass of Chardonnay." The server said, "I'll have to see ID," and Julie said, "In that case, I'll have iced tea." All three of us laughed. I said I'd have the same, and we went through the Southern ritual of "sweet or unsweet."

JULIE ORDERED THE SPICY SAUSAGE and black pepper honey pizza and I got a smoked brisket sandwich. I had eaten my sandwich and a couple of slices of her pizza when someone knocked on the window. I looked up to see an Asian woman about my age, in blue nursing scrubs with a big smile on her face. Then I looked at Julie to see a look of shock on hers.

"Oh God, it's my mother!"

Julie stood, and then sat after her mother made an "I'll come in there" gesture. She looked at me and said, "I'm sorry about this."

"No problem," I said. "I'm happy to meet your mother."

"We'll see if you feel the same way after," she said.

By this time, Julie's mother was at the hostess station, smiling at the hostess and pointing toward our table. Julie stood again as she walked toward us. I stood up too.

"Mom. I thought you had surgeries today."

"Yes. One this morning. Two more this afternoon. But I have time in between and I ruined my shoe this morning. I came to get new ones." She lifted her left foot so Julie could see the dark red stain along the side of her Asics trainer.

"Is that blood?" Julie asked.

"No. Fruit smoothie."

She turned to me and held out her hand. "I'm Beth Thanh, Julie's mother."

I took it as Julie said, "This is Andy, a friend from yoga class."

I said, "Andy Carver. Nice to meet you. You're a surgical nurse?"

I could see Julie wince. "I'm an orthopedic surgeon," her mother said. "Mostly knees." She waved me off when I started to apologize. "Let's sit," she said. "I could use an iced tea."

I waved our server over, and we did sweet or unsweet again. I asked for a refill. Julie didn't want one. Dr. Thanh next to me, looking across the table at Julie. "Did the pest man come?" She turned to me. "We have a squirrel inside our walls. It drove me crazy last night."

"He did come," Julie said. "He showed me a hole in the foundation where it probably got in. He put a trap there, with a big glob of peanut butter for a lure. He said it usually only takes a few hours for the squirrel to come out."

"Will he come back to take it away?"

"Yes. He said to text him."

"He'll probably kill it."

"No. He said he'd let it go in the woods somewhere."

"Do you believe that?"

"Why wouldn't I?"

"Julie, you're too trusting. I'll take the squirrel to the woods and let it go. It shouldn't have to die just for doing what squirrels do."

"Can I make a suggestion?" I asked.

"Certainly," Dr. Thanh said.

"The squirrel's only part of the problem. The hole in the foundation is the bigger part. My Dad and I fixed a hole like that on our house once. I'd be happy to come and take a look at it. And I'd be happy to take the squirrel to the woods too. I agree, a squirrel shouldn't have to die for just doing squirrel things."

"Well, thank you. That's very nice of you. Julie, will you work all that out?"

"Yes, Mom."

"Now, Andy Carver, what do you do? Obviously, something that allows you to take yoga classes during the day."

"Mom! Please don't start with the third degree!"

"It's OK," I said. "I'm a salesman. I sell tractor parts. My hours are pretty flexible. Before that I was in the Army."

"You were in the Army?" Julie asked. "I thought Keila said you were a football player."

"That's my friend Walker. He played at NC State, till he got hurt. Now he's a PE teacher. He's the one who really knows Keila's grandfather."

"Great grandfather," Julie said.

"That's right. I keep getting that wrong. But it's Keila *Raines*. That much I remember."

THE SERVER ARRIVED WITH Julie's mother's iced tea and my refill. She had our check ready too and as soon as she set it on the table, Julie picked it up and looked it over, "With Mom's iced tea on my side, it's pretty much equal. Want to just split it down the middle?" She opened her purse and pulled out a $20 bill and put it in the check folder.

I'd planned on paying for lunch, of course, but I picked up on Julie's vibe. "Sounds good to me," I said, and put my own $20 in the folder.

WE CHATTED FOR A WHILE LONGER. I mentioned that Walker had torn both his ACL and MCL the summer before our Senior year.

"Ouch," Julie's mother said. "You said he played football at NC State? One of my colleagues probably handled his case. When did this happen?"

"2003. Late July. Just before football drills started."

"I was in med school then. Just starting my second year. But Raleigh Orthopedic has been State's doctors forever. I think Hadley Callaway was already the main knee doctor back then. I'm assisting him on a TKA this afternoon." I made a mental note to ask Walker if he knew that name.

I also did some mental arithmetic. If she started college at eighteen like I did, she would have been twenty-four in 2003, which made her thirty-eight now, two years older than me. And if Julie was nineteen now, that meant she would have had Julie when *she* was nineteen.

I filed that away and changed the subject. "TKA. Does that mean total knee something?"

"Total knee arthroplasty. Surgical reconstruction or replacement of the knee joint."

We chatted on for a while about various injuries and surgeries. I mentioned my dislocated shoulder and how that's what got me into yoga in the first place. Julie was mostly quiet while her mother and I did the talking. Eventually the conversation wound down and Julie's mother looked at her watch. "Oh, I need to go next door and buy my shoes. Then back to work. Julie, what are your plans for the rest of the day?"

"I work at four. I guess I'll go home and hang out until then." She turned to me. "If the squirrel has come out, can I text you?"

"Sure," I said. "I still have some work to do today but I could get over there later."

"Well, then, Andy, it was nice to meet you," Dr. Thanh said. "Julie, I'll see you when you get home from work."

"THAT WASN'T SO BAD," I said.

"The bad part will come later. You won't believe the third degree *I'm* going to get when I get home. And I promise you, the first thing she's going to say is 'he's too old for you.'"

I smiled at that. "I probably am too old for you. How old are you anyway?"

"I'll be nineteen in two weeks. But what does that have to do with anything? I'm not looking to marry you."

Still smiling, I asked, "So what are you looking for?"

She looked quickly toward the table next to ours. Two women there were engaged in their conversation. Then she leaned forward and said, very quietly, "I want to have sex with you."

I leaned forward too. "I want to have sex with you too. See, we're both on the same page."

"I have to tell you something, though. I've never done it before. And I don't want to do it the first time with a teen-age boy. Keila told me that her first time was awful, because neither of them know what they were doing. The guy came in, like, thirty seconds, then he just pulled out and lit a cigarette. I've been waiting a long time. I want it to be better than that."

"Well," I said, "I guess I'm honored that you chose me."

"But not today, Andy. I couldn't, not after my mother. Not knowing what's coming when I get home."

My first thought was, this is probably for the best. My second thought was, yeah, but *shit!* I just smiled and said that I understood.

I MADE JULIE TAKE HER $20 back since her mother was gone. I slipped another $20 of my own into the check folder and we walked out to my car.

"I'm curious about your mother," I said.

"Everybody is," Julie said, as she got into the car. "She's even younger than you think."

"How young do I think?"

"Early forties, at least, right? To have a daughter my age?"

"Well, she said she was in her second year of medical school in 2003.

I turned twenty-four when I was in my second year in the Army. If she started college the same age as me and went right into medical school, she'd be about thirty-eight now, right?"

"She's thirty-six. She started college when she was seventeen, six months after she had me. She took a full load of AP courses *and* had a baby her senior year of high school."

"That's pretty crazy," I said.

"Tell me about it. Then you have me, expected to live up to her academically, and *not* to have sex until I get married."

"Well," I said, "since I know where you stand on the sex, how're you doing school-wise?"

She raised her eyebrows. "My mother went to Duke. She got her BS in three years and went right into med school there. I go to William Peace. I get good grades, but there's no comparison. My mother got accepted at two Ivy League schools and chose Duke. I got accepted at State and Carolina, but I wanted to go to a smaller school. I'm in Exercise and Sport Science, so she can still tell people I'm pre-med."

"Is that where you're going with it?"

"Maybe. Or I just might decide to be a gym teacher like your friend."

I laughed. "You'll have to talk to him about that. He'll try to talk you out of it. Not a lot of money."

"Money isn't everything," Julie said.

"Tell Walker that."

I PULLED UP NEXT TO Julie's car at the yoga studio and turned off the engine. "Where do we go from here?" I asked.

She said, "I'd like to see you again. It doesn't *have* to be, well, you know."

"Tell you what," I said. "There's a thing at Walker's house on Saturday. A bunch of people he teaches with and some people his girlfriend works with. She's an EMT, so you could talk about that just in case the gym teacher thing doesn't work out."

"What time would it be?" she asked. "I have to work until six o'clock, I think."

"That's fine. He told me any time after six o'clock. Would you like me to pick you up?"

"No, just tell me where it is. I'll probably tell my mother I'm going to be with Keila and the girls."

I told her Walker's address, and she typed it into her phone.

"Can I ask you one more thing?" she said.

I nodded.

"The blond lady? What was that all about?"

"Can I plead the fifth?" I asked.

"She's too old for you, you know." She said that with a teasing smile. Then she bounced out of my car and went on her way.

23

Julie called me at about quarter to four. "Andy, I'm just leaving for work, but the squirrel is in the trap. He wasn't there when I looked before."

"Give me your address," I said. "I can get over there in about an hour. He's not going anywhere between now and then. I'll pick up some Quikrete on the way so I can patch the hole."

"Thank you, Andy. I'll pay you back for whatever you need to buy."

I'D BEEN KILLING TIME until a phone call with one of my customers. He was supposed to call me at 4:00. He ended up calling ten minutes late but the call only took about ten minutes. I grabbed a putty knife from my toolbox and the canvas tarp I used to cover my bike during the winter. There's an Ace Hardware next to the gym. I stopped in there to buy a ten-pound tub of Quikrete and a trowel.

Julie lived on something called Periwinkle Blue Lane out in Northwest Raleigh, not too far from the big Crabtree Valley Mall. It was in a development of about sixty detached townhouses. I parked on the street and carried my tools and supplies toward the back of the house. The trap was about two-thirds of the way back along the left side. They pest guy had attached it to the foundation with wire and some kind of rubber adhesive and there were actually two squirrels inside. They went a little crazy as I approached. I wrapped the canvas tarp around the trap and lifted it from the foundation, first making sure that the trap door was all the way closed. Then I set the trap down on the ground and got to work with the Quikcrete.

I used the putty knife and the trowel to fill up the bottom half of the roughly oval-shaped hole. The package said Quikrete needs twenty to forty minutes to dry, but I just needed it to be firm enough to lay more into the top half of the hole. I figured ten minutes would be enough. While that was happening, I walked around the whole house to see if there were any more holes. I found one in the back corner and a developing crack on the other side of the house, so I filled the bottom half of that hole and used the putty knife to push as much Quikrete as I could get into the crack.

When I came back around to the first hole, I found Julie's mother standing there.

"Oh, hi," she said. She pointed to the tarp-covered trap on the ground. "Is the squirrel in there?"

"Two of them actually," I said. "I also found another hole in your foundation, out around the back."

She started walking that way and I followed. She was still in her baggy scrubs, but I noticed that she was slimmer and fitter looking than I'd originally thought.

"Why didn't you fill in the whole hole?" she asked.

"Got to build a base and let it dry," I said. "I'll fill about half of what's left next, and then close it off with a third level."

She nodded. "That makes sense. How about the squirrels?"

"I was thinking the wooded area across the street. I think that's far enough away they won't find their way back."

"Let me change," she said. "I'll go over there with you."

SHE WENT BACK AROUND to the front of the house. I added the second layer to both holes, then I went back to the crack and used the trowel to smooth off the face of the foundation. By the time I finished with that, she was coming out the back door in cut-off jeans and a tank top. She had her hair down and she was wearing wrap-around sunglasses. I wouldn't have recognized her from the woman I'd seen earlier.

The squirrels went crazy again when I lifted the trap. They were squealing and running from side to side. "Take it easy, guys," I said. "We'll let you out in just a minute."

We crossed the street and walked about twenty yards into the woods. "Does this look OK?" I asked. She nodded, so I set the trap down and peeled back the tarp. Then I kneeled down to take a look at the latch. It looked pretty straightforward, so I was just getting ready to unsnap it when she grabbed my arm.

"No!" she said. "Tilt it upright, with the door at the top!"

I did that, which dropped the two squirrels to the other end, which was now the bottom.

"Now, open the latch, and lower it back down, facing away from us."

I did that and the squirrels scampered away.

"You are not good at squirrels," she said, and then she burst out laughing. I could only laugh too.

WE WALKED BACK TO THE HOUSE and I filled in the last layer of Quikrete. She went inside and came back out with two bottles of Corona Light. We sat at a small table on her brick patio.

"Are you and my daughter dating?"

"I don't know if you'd call it that. We've talked a couple of times at yoga. I asked her out to lunch."

"She's too young for you."

I laughed. "You're the second person today who's told me that."

"Because it's obvious, and true. Do you have any interest in her beyond sex?"

"Mrs. Thanh…"

"Oh, please."

"Dr. Thanh?"

"Beth. For Christ's sake, you're probably older than I am. And in any event, I've never been a 'missus.'"

"Never married?" I said.

"No. You?"

"No, but I don't have a kid."

"You don't have to be married to have a kid. You don't have to be married to raise a kid. We've done just fine. Now, answer my question."

I took a deep breath. "I barely know her. I know her friend Keila better, and I hardly know *her* at all. Keila told me that Julie was interested in me. Then we ended up talking after class last week. It seemed like Keila was right, so I asked her if she wanted to have lunch after class this week. We were maybe half an hour into that lunch when you showed up."

"And where did you expect your lunch to go?"

I tried smiling. "Do I have to answer that?"

"I think you just did answer that. Now, where does that leave us?"

"I'll back off. I was feeling a little guilty anyway. But I'm not sure how I'm going to do that without hurting her feelings."

"Let me worry about that. She already knows she's going to get an earful from me when she gets home."

"Yeah, she mentioned that."

"I'm sure she told you all about Asian mothers."

"I think she said Vietnamese mothers are the most Asian of them all."

"My mother was a sweet woman. She was the exact opposite of the Asian mother stereotype. But I'll admit, I've held Julie to pretty high standards."

We both sipped on our beers. Then she asked me about the Army. "How long were you in?"

"Just over eleven years."

"When did you get out?"

"A little more than three years ago. June 2015."

"Were you in the fighting?"

"Oh yeah. Iraq and Afghanistan. Four tours in all."

"My father was a helicopter pilot in the Republic of Vietnam Air Force," she said. "He flew three groups of people out to the US Navy ships in the South China Sea during the evacuation of Saigon. The last flight, he ran out of fuel right over the deck. They just pushed his helicopter over the edge of the ship to make room for the next one. But they let him stay, and eventually brought him to the US. An American pilot he'd flown with got him a job at Ft. Bragg."

"A flying job?"

"No, at first he was a maintenance worker. Then he was a maintenance crew chief. He got married, they had me, then he died when I was eight years old. By that time, they were here in Raleigh. He started a little cleaning company and worked about eighty hours a week. My mother ran the office. And she made him buy a life insurance policy, which came in very handy when he died."

We both sipped some more beer. "Do you mind if I ask you about Julie's father?"

"No, not at all. He was my date for the Junior Prom. First time I ever had sex and I got a baby out of it. Also the last time for quite a few years, but that's a different story."

She laughed, so I did too.

"His name was Peter Fishbein. He begged me to get an abortion, then he offered to marry me, but I didn't want to do either of those things. My mother was cool, she said we'd do it together, and we did. The rest of the way through high school, all the way through undergrad and all the way through med school. She died while I was doing my residency. We had to scramble for a couple of years. I got a roommate who was basically Julie's nanny. By the time I got into private practice, Julie was in middle school, and it was a lot easier."

"Does Julie have a relationship with her father?"

"Not anymore. He was around some when she was very young. He went to Georgetown and he'd come to visit when he was home. I never blamed him, having sex was really more my idea than his. But he was never part of the family. We never let him in, so he drifted off. Last I heard, he was living in Colorado, but that was at least ten years ago."

"I served with a guy who went to Georgetown. He always said it was the world's most Catholic Catholic school."

She laughed. "Peter was Catholic. You wouldn't think so with his name, but his mother was Chinese Catholic and that's how he was raised. He looked more Asian than Jewish, anyway. Everybody called him Peter Fish Sauce."

"I'm surprised he wanted you to get an abortion," I said. "Being Catholic and all."

"Believe me,' she said, "it didn't have anything to do with his religion. It was more about his reputation. My mother was the right-to-lifer in that deal. Buddhists are mostly pro-life too. She convinced me that I didn't *have to* get an abortion, and I didn't *have to* get married, which was mostly what I was thinking anyway."

We were both quiet for a bit. I had just about finished my beer, and I was wondering if she'd offer me another one. Instead, she asked, "Do you want to have sex with *me*?"

"Ah...sure," I said.

"Not today," she said. "But let's spend some time together. Let's see what develops."

I was suspicious about her motive. Maybe it showed on my face, or else she was just plain reading my mind.

"I would," she said, "but that's not what this is."

"You would what?" I asked. I guess I wanted to hear her say it.

"I would have sex with you to keep you from having sex with my daughter. But I would also like to get to know you better. Really."

"What about Julie?"

"I'll talk to her. Let's leave it at that for now."

LATER THAT EVENING, I got a series of texts from Julie. The first one thanked me for taking care of the squirrel. The second one said she's had a long talk with her mother. The third one said that she'd probably tell me more next time she saw me at yoga.

24

The next day, in the afternoon, I drove over to Denis's gym to work out with Andre. We worked mostly on footwork for the first half hour, then we did a couple hundred sit-ups each in sets of twenty-five. Denis showed up around halfway through that and ragged on us to do "one more set" three times. Andre did them with a happy smile. Me not so much. Then he put us through five rounds of light sparring

"You are already looking better," he said to me. "The hand speed is good. The foot speed comes back a bit slower. But your foot*work* is still beautiful. Andre, that is what you can learn from this one. Footwork is balance and balance is power..."

"And power puts the other guy on his *derriere!*" we both said along with him. Then we all laughed. I'd heard those words a thousand times from Denis, and obviously Andre had too.

We finished up with some stretching and foam rolling. Then Denis left and Andre and I sat around on the mat for a while, exchanging stories. I learned a little more about his background and I told him a few Army stories. He seemed more interested in the places I'd been than the fighting I'd done, which I thought was interesting.

As it got closer to 5:00 p.m., a few woman started coming in. I had my back to the door, but Andre was facing it and greeted them all, mostly by name. "Self-defense class," he said to me. "I help out with Kirsten sometimes. Here she is now."

I turned around and there was The Big Girl. I'd never really known how old she was when I was at NC State, but I would have guessed in her middle thirties. That put her around fifty now but she still looked pretty much the same. Still big but not fat. Still reddish-blond hair. As she got closer, I could see some more age on her face, but when she opened her mouth, it was the same Baa-stin accent. "Mistah Cahvah. It's good to see ya!"

"It's good to see you too Sergeant Connolly."

She put her arms around me. "Been a while since I been called that. Kirsten is just fine. Or KC, which is what my girls call me."

"Killer Connolly!" one of the girls piped in.

Everyone had a laugh, and Kirsten squeezed me hard enough to make me say "Oooof," which made all of them laugh harder.

"OK, you two, out'a here. The ladies got the gym. Any man still here at the count'a ten gets to be a punching bag for the next hour." She pronounced it "ow-wa." All the girls laughed again and a couple started counting. Andre and I headed for the door.

ON THE WAY DOWN THE STAIRS, I asked him if he wanted to lift with Walker and me the next day. He said yes. I told him to meet us at my place at 9:00 a.m. and gave him the address. He arrived a few minutes before Walker did. I introduced them and we started walking toward the gym. We probably made for an interesting sight, three good-sized guys walking along side-by-side-by-side. Raleigh is a good town for walking, but mostly you see couples or people walking kids or dogs or both.

We made small talk on the way. Walker asked me if I was bringing one of my Namastes to his house tonight.

"What's a Namaste?" Andre asked.

"He goes to yoga, right? He takes like one class a week at five different yoga places and he's got a different woman at every one of them."

"No shit?" Andre looked at me. "That's brilliant. Do any of them have friends?"

"That's what I keep asking," Walker said. "But he doesn't share."

"Like you would if I did," I said. Then to Andre, "Walker's girl is an EMT. She'll stitch him up if he ever gets hurt, but she'll fuck him up if he ever cheats on her."

"It's true," Walker said, "but that doesn't change the fact that you're a sexual predator. How many women, all told, have you scored after you met them in yoga class?"

I didn't answer, but that didn't stop Walker, who's never happier than when he's ragging on me. "How 'bout this, have you missed any age ranges? Teens? Twenties? Thirties? Fifties? Sixties?"

"No teenagers," I said, laughing too, though I was thinking that might not have been true if Thursday had gone differently.

"Yeah, and you probably never did no senior citizens either, but I bet you got every age group in between. Now tell him your secret."

Andre said, "This I have to hear."

I didn't say anything so Walker kept right on going. "He only goes in the daytime, when every other man is at work. He's always the only dude in the class. It's just him and a bunch of hot yoga mommies, sent their hubby off to work and their kids off to school. Easy pickin's!"

Walker was having great fun and Andre and I were laughing too. Andre put his hands together like in prayer and bent at the waist. "I have much to learn from you," he said. "Apparently not just footwork!"

WE HAD A GOOD WORKOUT. Andre went at it as hard as Walker and I always did. Afterward, Walker asked him if he had any plans for the evening. "Bunch of people coming over to my house for burgers, etcetera. Six o'clockish. Andy's coming, why don't you come along?"

Andre said thank you, he'd love to come. Walker gave him the address and the ground rules. "I take care of the burgers," he said. "Everyone brings some kind of side dish, a salad or something or some kind of dessert. And bring a six pack, or whatever."

25

didn't get to Walker's house until almost 6:30. I was delayed by a phone call from Meghan. Among other things, she told me the Sanford police might be calling me.

"Want to hear something crazy?" she said. "Someone robbed Raymond and Marianne's house while they were at the beach. Allan was all freaked out when he got home. He said they stole all the furniture and Raymond's jet ski and two motorcycles. This was last Sunday when they got back. He was supposed to stay over one more night but he called me and asked me to come get him."

"Any idea who did it?" I asked.

"No," she said. "When I got there, the cops were there and they didn't even know when it happened. So I thought I could be helpful. I told them that I'd been by there the day after they left and nothing looked out of place."

Hmmm, I thought. "Did anyone think it was strange that you'd been by there?"

"Well," she said, "no one seemed to at the time, but one of the Sanford cops called me last night and asked if he could come over and talk to me today. He turned out to be a detective and he did want to know why I'd been there. So I just told him, I'd been driving by with a friend on the way back from Sunday brunch and I wanted to show you the basketball hoop in the foyer. I told him I just thought you'd get a kick out of it."

"What did he say to that?"

"He said he got a kick out of the basketball hoop too, but then he asked me for your name, and I had to tell him."

"No worries," I said. "It's not like we did anything wrong. Although looking back, aren't you glad I wouldn't let you seduce me in the pool?" We both laughed.

"The thing is, he called me again a few minutes ago and asked me for your address and phone number. So I just wanted to let you know that he's probably going to call you at some point. Detective John Stearns from the Sanford police."

"Don't worry," I said. "I'll back up your alibi."

We both laughed at that too. Then we talked for a while longer about this and that till I told her I had to get going."

"Cookout at my friend Walker's place," I told her. "I have to help him on the grill, so I better get moving."

"Do you have a date?" she asked. "Do I need to be jealous?"

"Yeah, a guy named Andre," I said. "I'm helping to train him to be a mixed martial arts fighter. So no, nothing to be jealous about."

We said goodbye after that. I promised to let her know if the detective called me. Then I gathered up the three guitars and the rest of the wine and liquor from Raymond and Marianne's house, loaded them in my car and took them to Walker's house.

THERE WERE PROBABLY twenty people in Walker's back yard but the two I noticed first were Julie and Andre. They were standing together in the back corner, talking and smiling at each other. Walker was at the grill, so I went there first.

"About time," he said. "Wanna get me some rolls? I got burgers ready to come off."

"Nice to see you too," I said.

"C'mon, don't give me attitude. Teisha went in to get the rolls ten minutes ago and I haven't seen her since."

I went into the kitchen and found Teisha at the table with another woman who was sitting hunched over with her hands covering her face. I pointed at the rolls. She nodded and I brought them out to Walker. He loaded up the burgers and carried them over to the food table. "Burgers, ladies and gents! Come and get 'em!"

He grabbed two beers from a cooler next to the table and brought them back to the grill, giving one to me. "Andre got here maybe fifteen minutes ago. Looks like he brought a date."

"I'm pretty sure she's not his date," I said. "She was supposed to be my date, but I didn't think she was coming."

He looked at me funny. "You're dating high school girls now? Jesus, I was only half serious this morning."

"She's in college. She goes to Peace. I know her from yoga class."

"Ah, a new Namaste. Well, God bless and all. Be sure to introduce her to Teisha. You know how much she loves nosing around your love life. In the meantime, Little Girl seems kind of into it with Andre."

I was thinking that too. I was wondering if this might be some kind of happy accident. I bumped fists with Walker and headed over toward the corner of the yard. Both Julie and Andre looked up as I approached.

"I didn't think you were coming," I said to her.

"I just wanted to talk to you for a minute," she said.

"I'm going to get a burger," Andre said. "See you later on."

He walked off toward the food table. Julie waited until he was a few steps away before she spoke. "I had a long talk with my mother the other night. It was really strange. She wasn't all, what the hell are you doing? She was more like just interested as a friend. We haven't been that way for a long time. Anyway, I told her that I wasn't interested in you as a boyfriend. I just decided that I was ready for sex and I wanted to do it with someone who maybe knew something about it. She told me about her first time and how she wished she'd thought of that."

She paused. "The thing is, I think I do want to wait for someone I have deeper feelings for. I apologize for leading you on."

I reached over and took her hands. "No apology necessary," I said. I was going to say something about it probably being for the best when Walker came up behind me.

"I'm Byron," he said.

I took over the introductions. "Julie Thanh, Bryon Walker. Julie studies exercise at Peace College. Byron leads children in exercise at the Barwell Road Elementary School."

Walker showed me his middle finger. "I'm a PE teacher," he said to Julie. "Are you in the ESS program at Peace?" Julie nodded. "That's a good program! I know a couple of grads teaching in the Wake County Schools."

"I might do that too," Julie said. "I'm hoping it'll lead to med school, but I'm not sure I can count on that."

"Hmm," Walker said. "Teacher, or doctor. Yeah, I'd go for doctor. Study hard would be my advice."

Andre joined us then. "Thanks again for inviting me," he said to Walker.

"You're welcome," Walker said, "but I'm confused. You two came together,"—pointing at Julie then Andre—"but you two were expecting to meet up here,"—pointing at Julie then me. "Is this one of them love triangles?"

I just smiled at Walker being Walker. Julie and Andre seemed unsure. Finally, Andre said, "We didn't really come together. She was just getting out of her car when I pulled up."

"We work at the same place," Julie said. "Whole Foods. I don't think we've ever actually talked to each other. He works in the meat department and I'm a cashier. But I've seen him around."

I could see something that looked like attraction between them. Walker seemed to see the same thing. And being Walker, he knew instinctively what to do. He took Julie by the arm and said, "Come with me. I want to introduce you to some people."

That left Andre and me by ourselves. "Listen," he said. "I'm not trying to move in on your girl. I was, like, amazed to see her get out of the car. She told me that a friend invited her. I was amazed again when it turned out to be you!"

"She's not my girl," I said, trying to keep it light. "I know her from yoga class. There might have been something. That's why I asked her here. But there isn't going to be. And it's for the better."

He looked at me like he wasn't sure about all that.

"Look, you heard Walker this morning, giving me shit. I know her from yoga. She's pretty good looking, right? She seemed interested. But she thought about it some more and I did too. Like I said, it's for the better."

"She really is good looking," Andre said. "I have to admit, I've been checking her out at work."

"She seems to like you too. Look, you've got a perfect chance to get to know her tonight. You're crazy if you don't take advantage of it."

"You're sure I'm not cutting in on you?"

"Completely sure," I said. "C'mon, I need another beer, and I could use some food."

ANDRE FOLLOWED ME to the food table where I loaded up a plate. We both grabbed fresh beers. I said hello to a couple of Teisha's work friends who I recognized and introduced Andre. I noticed that Walker had gotten Julie into a group of his fellow teachers. She seemed to be having a good time but I caught her looking at her watch every minute or so, and before too long, she excused herself and came over to our little group. Andre was more involved in the conversation than I was, so she walked around to me.

"I have to go," she said. "I'm going to a movie with a couple of girls from school."

"Isn't that what you were going to tell your mother to come here with me?"

She smiled. "Yes, but I'm really doing it. I told her I was coming here first. I told her I wanted to talk to you face to face. 'Cause there's something else I want to tell you."

I waited.

"I think you should ask her out. You're too old for me but not for her. And I think she likes you. There was something different about her when I got home the other night. She was, like, smiling for no apparent reason."

"Does she know that's what you wanted to say to me?"

"Oh, God, no. But it is why I wanted to come."

"OK," I said. "I'll make you a deal. I'll ask your mother out, but only if you ask Andre to walk you out to your car now, and say yes when he asks you to go out with him."

"He's not going to do that."

"Want to bet?"

"How do you know him anyway?"

"Let him tell you. When you go out with him."

She just looked at me, unsure of what to do, so I leaned into the other conversation. "Excuse me guys. Andre, Julie has to go. Could you walk her to her car?"

"Um, sure," he said, looking from her to me and then back again. Then a big smile. "Happy to." Off they went and I went looking for Walker.

26

When I found Walker, I told him about the call I'd gotten from Meghan.

"Are we worried about that?" he asked.

"I don't think so. I think it's all pretty routine. But just to be safe, I have the rest of the wine and the guitars in my car. OK to keep that stuff here until this blows over?"

"No sweat," he said. He paused. "Even if they have your name, there's no connection to me, right?"

"I can't see one. Meghan's heard me talk about you, but I can't imagine she mentioned you to the police."

I STACKED THE WINE and the guitars in the corner of Walker's garage. My phone range just as I finished.

"Hello?" I said.

"Andy? This is Beth Thanh. Did Julie talk to you? Is everything OK?"

"She did. I think everything's fine. She's off to the movies with her friends."

"I wasn't a hundred percent sure that was real, but I'm glad she did what she said she was going to do. Just talk to you and leave."

"And maybe you weren't a hundred percent sure I'd live up to my part of the deal?"

She didn't respond. "I'm sorry. I probably I shouldn't have said that."

"No, it was fair. You're not a hundred percent wrong. This is complicated."

"I think it's less complicated than you think. I think Julie already has someone she likes better than me. And I think she's actually hoping that you and I are going to get together."

"What makes you say that?"

"Are you doing anything right now?"

"Yes, I'm heating up leftover Chinese food. Then I'm going to watch some TV. But you didn't answer my question."

"Could I talk you into coming to a backyard barbecue? There's still plenty of food. It's maybe fifteen minutes' drive from your house. I'll personally cook you a burger and answer all your questions."

"This is the place Julie came to?"

"Yes. My friend Walker's house. There's maybe twenty people here. Very chill. Very casual. I can text you the address."

She didn't say anything for a few long beats. Thinking about it. "OK. I'll need a few minutes to clean up. Say half an hour?"

"See you then. Call me if you have any trouble finding the place."

MY PHONE RANG AGAIN about forty minutes later. It was Beth calling from out front. She didn't want to just walk into a house where she didn't know anybody. I told her to wait right there and I walked around to the front of the house to meet her. She looked good, in white jeans and a dark blue top with her hair hanging out in a ponytail from a Durham Bulls baseball cap.

"Very sporty," I said.

"If you can't wash it, hide it," she said.

Walker was back at the grill as we walked around the corner. He had a plate of raw burgers in one hand and a plate of rolls in the other.

"Perfect timing," I said to him. "This is Beth Thanh. I promised her a fresh-cooked burger."

"You gonna do the cooking?" He smiled at Beth. "Better if I do it. Andy burns meat. It's a well-known fact. I, on the other hand, am a bastion of culinary excellence."

"He's actually my alleged friend Byron Walker," I said. "But let's let him cook. Can I get you a beer? Wine? Anything?"

"Hey, Doctor Thanh!" Teisha came running over. "It's so nice to see you! Welcome to our home!"

The two women embraced while Walker and I looked on. "We never see you anymore, you not in the ER regular." Teisha said. Then to us, "My crew brought this lady lots of business. Always felt good telling 'em Doctor Thanh gonna take good care of you when we get you to the ER." Then she started pulling Beth toward the group she'd been talking to. "C'mon, Teddy and Mike are here too."

That left Walker and I standing by the grill by ourselves.

"You're up to your ears in Asian ladies tonight," he said.

"Julie's mother," I said.

"No fucking way. Older sister maybe. Youngest aunt."

"It's no lie. First time I saw her she was wearing scrubs with her hair up and granny glasses. She looked like a mother. Second time I saw her was more like this. No surprise a pretty girl has a pretty mother."

"Yeah, but she must have had her pretty young. She looks our age."

"She is our age. She had Julie when she was seventeen."

Walker said "Damn" and flipped the burgers. Then he looked straight at me. "Do you even know what's going on here?"

"Well, as near as I can tell, everyone knows everyone. Julie knows Andre. Teisha and her crew all know Beth. Marvin knows Denis, for Christ's sake. It reminds me of the Rangers. One of my old sergeants used to call us the world's smallest world."

I could tell Walker liked that line. He got a little smile around his eyes. "Well, just so you got it all under control."

"TALK TO ME," Beth said. "What did Julie say?"

"She told me that you'd talked. She said it was a great conversation, more like friends than mother and daughter. She told me she knew I was too old for her, even for a fling. And I told her I was relieved, because I knew that too."

Beth nodded along.

"And then she said I'm not too old for you, and she made me promise that I'd ask you out."

I think she blushed. It was getting a little dark by then so it was hard to tell.

"So does this count as asking you out?" I asked.

"Let's call this a social occasion," she said. "I need to talk to Julie one more time before we go out on a date."

"But that's where this is going?"

She was quiet for a moment, then she said "I hope so. I guess. But I want to make sure she's really OK with it. I felt the same way when I talked to her, it was more like friends than bitchy mother and angry daughter. We've had too much of that over the last few years."

She took a bite of her burger and chewed it thoughtfully. Then she took a sip of her beer. "Now tell me about this someone new."

"I'll do better than that. I'll introduce you to him. But first, eat your food."

SHE PROBABLY ATE FASTER than she normally would, but she didn't just wolf it down. We talked about her day and my day. She told me how much she'd always liked Teisha, and how she was one of the best EMTs she'd ever worked with. Eventually, she laid her empty beer bottle down on her empty paper plate and said, "That was good. Now, can I meet this person you think Julie is interested in?"

I pointed toward the grill, where Andre was now standing with Walker, listening intently to something Walker was saying. Then they both burst out laughing.

"That's him," I said. "His name is Andre. He works at the same Whole Foods as Julie. They've apparently been checking each other out at work and then they both show up here. I just met him a week or so ago. He's training to be an MMA fighter and I'm helping. He lifted weights with Walker and me this morning and Walker invited him to come over tonight."

"What else do you know about him?" she asked. "So far, I'm not sure I'm thrilled. He wants to be one of those cage fighters? Does Julie know that?"

"I have no idea," I said. "As far as I know, the first time they ever actually talked to each other was tonight and it wasn't any more than twenty, thirty minutes. But you could see there was some attraction. Both ways. Walker saw it too."

Teisha had joined us. "Byron told me that young man worked hard at the gym," she said. "He kept up with the two of you."

I nodded. "He's pretty strong. Apparently pretty smart too. He's got a degree in Political Science from Duke." That seemed to reassure Beth a little bit.

"Do you know where he's from?" she asked.

"From here. His father is Brazilian, came here to study Engineering at NC State. His mother was a foreign student too, I think he said from Portugal. But he was born and raised in Cary. His parents both work out at the RTP."

"He almost looks Asian," Beth said. "There's something in his features that's not quite Hispanic."

"Don't get Byron started on that." Teisha said. "I already heard him telling someone that Brazilians are Latino, but not Hispanic." Walker can be a little pedantic sometimes. Check that, he can be very pedantic. He can even tell you—at length—the difference between didactic and pedantic.

"Andre told me his great-grandfather was from a South American Indian tribe," I said, "Guarini, or something like that. His great-grandfather and his grandfather were both policemen and Jiu-Jitsu fighters."

"And he wants to be a cage fighter," Beth said. "And you were that kind of fighter too?"

"Not really. I probably did more training for less fighting than anyone in the history of the martial arts. I did that then a lot like I do yoga now, just part of an exercise regimen."

I NOTICED THAT ANDRE was texting on his phone. He said something to Walker and they shook hands. Then he started for where Beth, Teisha and I were sitting. I could see that he was a little unsure about Beth.

"I'm gonna head out," he said.

"Before you do," I said, pointing to Beth, "this is Julie's mother."

That shook him up. "Hold crap! Mrs. Thanh? Um, it's really nice to meet you?"

"Dr. Thanh," I said. Beth elbowed me on the hip. "Give it a rest, Andy. Nice to meet you too Andre."

"Are you going to meet Julie?" I asked.

"At the Krispy Kreme. She said Peace girls always go there after the movies."

"Have fun," I said, grinning at him.

"Don't keep her out too late," Beth said.

Andre sputtered out a "Yes, Ma'am" and headed for the door.

TEISHA WAS LOOKING AT US with some amusement. "That poor boy," she said. "He meets his new girlfriend's mama. And she's an Asian mama, which gotta be a close second to a large, Black, bible totin' mama. And she's a surgeon, knows her way around a scalpel. What could be worse? Oh yeah, somehow he got Andy Carver mixed up in this!" Teisha got up and walked away laughing.

"Teisha doesn't seem to hold you in very high regard," Beth said to me.

"No, Teisha loves me. She especially loves ragging on my love life, or lack thereof."

"You don't have a love life? That's not what I've heard. Julie tells me you had an affair with a married woman."

"I'm not sure I'd call it an affair," I said. "It's certainly wasn't a love affair."

"I'm not judging," she said quickly. "Full disclosure, I'm having one of those too."

"An affair with a married guy?"

"Well, that too." Just the way she said that stopped me short. "But this is not a conversation I want to have right now. I think I should be going. But listen, let's make a date for some time next week. We can talk about our sex lives then."

27

The following day was Sunday, I slept in until around 9:30, ate some yogurt and drank some juice, then I went out for a run. I did about five easy miles through downtown Raleigh. When I got home, there was a Wake County Sheriff's deputy standing by his car a few spaces down from my place, writing something on a clipboard.

I had seen this man before at the gym. He was Black, maybe fifty years old, with the big upper body of a serious lifter. His name tag said Washington.

I walked right up to him. "Hey, Deputy Washington," I said. "I've seen you at the gym." I reached out my hand to shake. "Andy Carver."

"Mr. Carver," he said, taking my hand and giving it a quick pump, "you're exactly who I'm here to see."

OK, no big surprise, even though Meghan had said a Sanford PD detective had talked to her.

"Is this about that robbery in Sanford?" I asked.

"Burglary," the deputy said. "Breaking and entering into a home. But yes. Sanford PD asked the Lee County Sheriffs to reach out to you and Lee asked us. Pretty common when an investigation crosses county lines."

"I understand," I said. "My friend called me last night and told me that I would probably be getting a call from the Sanford Police. Do you want to come in or do we do this out here?"

"Most people prefer to go inside," he said. "I wouldn't mind getting out of the sun."

I started toward my door and he followed me. I opened up and we both went inside. I went straight to the refrigerator, pulled out two bottles of water, and waved one toward him. He said thank you and took it. We both twisted off the tops and took healthy swigs. I pointed toward my front room. "Let's sit in here," I said.

After we got settled, he got right down to business. "How did you happen to be at..." he looked at his notes, "3826 Center Church Road in Sanford on July first?"

"I had gone down there Saturday and spent the night with my friend," I said. "We went out for breakfast on Sunday to a place in Pinehurst. When we were driving back, we went near enough to the house that she wanted to show it to me. She had told me before that it had a basketball hoop in the foyer."

"Your friend's name?"

"Meghan Powers."

"Girlfriend?"

"Not like a formal relationship. She works for one of my customers. We've gotten together a few times."

"Any reason you got together this particular weekend?"

"Yes, as a matter of fact. She has two kids, two boys. One was at a basketball camp and the other one was at the beach with her ex and his current wife, the people that own the house. She was going to be all by herself so she invited me down."

"You say she works for one of your customers. What do you do?"

I told him about my job. He said it sounded pretty good. Then he asked me what I did before that.

"I served in the Army for eleven years. Before that, NC State."

"What did you do in the Army," he asked.

"A few years in the infantry, then eight as a Ranger."

"You got to visit some fun places, I imagine," he said.

"Two tours each in Iraq and Afghanistan. Tons of fun. How about you? Were you in?"

"I was a Navy MP. Master at Arms they called us. Long time ago. Mostly stateside, shoreside, though I did a couple of cruises on destroyers and one on a carrier. Now, tell me more about your breakfast. Where did you go?"

"A place called the Village Inn. No, the Village Café."

"I've heard of it," he said. "Supposed to be pretty good food. Now, what did you do when you got to the house?"

"We went up the front stairs and looked into the foyer."

"And?"

"Well, it was kind of disappointing. The basketball hoop wasn't, like, a real backboard and basket. It was just one of those Nerf things. The room has a high ceiling so it might have been regulation height, but still, the way Meghan described it, I was expecting something more spectacular."

"What did you do next?"

"We walked around the house. Meghan wanted me to see the swimming pool in the back yard."

"Did you touch anything, specifically doors or windows?"

"No sir."

"Did you take anything, like from the back yard?"

"*No sir.*"

He looked up from his clipboard, where he'd been making notes on my answers. "These are just routine questions, Mr. Carver. I'm not accusing you of anything."

"I understand," I said. "Look, can I tell you something? I didn't think anything about looking in the front door. But going around the back made me uncomfortable. I was thinking a big house like that might have security cameras. And then Meghan wanted to get naked and jump in the pool and all I could think of was having to explain *that* to someone like you. I said come on, let's get out of here, and she pouted a little, but she came right along and we got in the car and left."

He looked hard at me for another moment, then he started to smile. "What's she look like, your friend Meghan? If there was video, would I have enjoyed seeing her naked?"

"*Yes* sir," I said, smiling too, then quickly added, "but there wasn't, was there?"

"To the best of my knowledge, no. If there'd been video, I think they'd of known more about the break-in itself. But that doesn't seem to be the case, so I'd say no video."

HE DID SOME MORE WRITING on his clipboard. Then he looked at his watch and wrote some more. It was all pretty benign, but I had a weird sensation that something else was coming. I was right. He looked up suddenly and said, "Do you still have the guitars?"

We used to talk about Spidey-sense in Iraq and Afghanistan. We took it pretty seriously. I remember Mike Stanton saying that Spidey must have been a Ranger. So I didn't flinch. I just put on my "not-sure-what-you're-talking-about" face and said, "Sir?"

"I'm sorry," Washington said. "I meant to ask, do you play the guitar?"

"No sir." I looked around the room. "What made you ask me that?"

He didn't say anything. I said, "Oh, I get it. There was a guitar stolen from the house."

"Three of them actually. And a jet ski. You wouldn't have one of those around here, would you?"

I laughed. "I had a snowmobile a long time ago. I damn near killed myself on it."

He laughed along with me. "Would you let me take a quick look around your apartment? Just to make sure you haven't got a jet ski hidden somewhere? You have the right to refuse, or course, and I'm not sure this would even justify asking for a warrant. We can put this thing to bed right now if you're willing to waive all that."

"Absolutely," I said. "Should I come with you or do I just wait here?"

"Please come with me. Please lead the way, in fact."

I started up the stairs with him a few steps behind. We went straight up to the third floor. He took a quick look around my office, including the closet. He opened the sliding door and took a look out at my terrace. He nodded at me and we went down to the second floor, where again, he went quickly, but seemed to be taking everything in. Back on the ground floor he looked into both closets and a few of the kitchen cabinets.

"OK," he said, "no guitars, no snowmobiles, nothing else very suspicious." He smiled, this time I think it was authentic. "And you keep your place pretty clean. OK, thanks for your cooperation. I'm sure I'll see you at the gym."

We shook hands and he left. I waited about an hour to call Walker. He was impressed by the Spidey-sense part of the story.

28

spent most of the next week on the road, my one week a month visiting customers. I called Meghan from a hotel in Richmond Monday night. She seemed relieved to hear that I'd talked to the police without incident, more relieved that I wasn't mad at her. "Nothing to be mad about," I said. "It was all just procedure. They talked to you, they talked to me, I'm sure they'll talk to a lot of people. Hopefully, they'll find the guy."

Then I laughed. "Hey, it wasn't you, was it? I can't account for your whereabouts after I left."

She laughed too. "No, but I wish I'd thought of it. Apparently they stole almost fifty thousand dollars in cash!"

"That's a lot of cash to keep around the house," I said, smiling to myself, because I knew the exact amount was $33,400.

"Raymond's a big poker player," she said. "He won a poker tournament out at the Indian casino in Cherokee." I knew about the casino, of course, from the bands on the money, but the poker part filled in a blank. Cherokee is in Western NC, out past Asheville.

We talked for a while longer. I thought about asking her about her "next" husband, but decided against it. She asked me to call her in a few weeks and I promised I would.

MY ROAD TRIP WAS pretty routine. The most interesting thing came out of
an email I got from my boss on Wednesday. He had a lead for me, from
a car repair shop in Greensboro that had somehow gotten involved with
an ancient New Holland tractor. I wrote back and told him that I was on
my northern swing and that I'd actually be in Greensboro on the next
day. I called the place and got their voice mail, so I left a message saying
that I was the salesman from Ferguson Industries and I'd be there late
morning or early afternoon on Thursday.

I ended up getting there just before noon. The owner had already
left for lunch. One of the mechanics told me he'd just gone to Chick-
Fil-A so I sat in the car, made some phone calls and answered some
emails. The owner turned out to be an Eastern European guy with a
heavy accent, maybe late fifties or early sixties. He took me out back to
show me the tractor.

"Was 1932 they made this," he said. "That much I know. Man find in
barn, he wants to restore and give to museum. I can use maybe half of
body parts. Does not need to run, man says, just status display."

I thought he probably meant *static*, but I didn't press the issue. I
told him it was unlikely that we were going to have standard parts for a
tractor that old.

"Man says, money not problem. Has a lot of money. Has big house,
private lake. My grand-daughter marries his son. He knows I am good
with the body work. Can make parts if I can't buy, but easier to buy."

"We have a guy," I told him, "who does all our fabrication. Actually,
it's two guys. One guy knows the old tractors and the other guy knows
the new technology, 3D printing and all that. I can put you in touch with
them but that's probably the best I can do."

He said that would be good and he thanked me. My Spidey-sense
tickled me again.

"I'm curious about the guy you're working for," I said. "What's his
name?"

"Grainger. William White Grainger." He pronounced it Villiam Vite.
"Always says all three names."

"He lives in Greensboro?"

"High Point. Near to Jamestown. Family is furniture. Lots of money."

"He sounds like a good guy, donating the tractor to a museum."

"Son is good boy," he said. "Is enough for me. My grand-daughter, she will marry real money. American dream, no?"

I laughed and I filed it all away. After I left, I stopped at a Hardee's and ordered a burger and a shake. While I ate, I found William White Grainger's address online then pulled it up on Google Earth. It was a big house all right and it looked to be completely secluded. Maybe it could be seen from across the small lake, but other than that, it was on a heavily wooded lot about 300-400 feet down what looked like a paved driveway off of a two-lane road. I switched over to Google Maps which told me the house was 13.4 miles from where I was sitting. It was almost 1:30 by that time, but I only had two more stops to make, one in Greensboro and one in Mebane, which was about halfway back to Raleigh. I decided to make the stop in Greensboro, then head back toward High Point to see what I could see.

THE DRIVEWAY WAS EASY to find. It was fronted by a wooden arch with a sandblasted sign that said Hidden Ivy. Lower down on both sides of the arch were signs that said Private Drive and No Trespassing. There was a low-slung building with a dirt parking lot on the far side of the driveway but there didn't seem to be anything going on there. I thought about pulling into the lot and walking back through the woods to the house but decided against it. I realized that a smarter thing would be to pass the name and the address on to Maddie to see what she could come up with. I could always come back with Walker to do a recon, just like we did in Sanford.

29

'd made a dinner date with Beth for Friday night. On the way to the restaurant, I learned that Julie was out with Andre for the second time that week. She was tentatively OK with it, she said. "I'm still a little concerned about the fighting thing, but he seems like a smart, even serious young man.

Over dinner she told me some stories about Julie. Apparently they'd had some dustups, starting around Julie's sophomore year of high school. She wanted to know if I'd been a rebellious teenager. "Not really," I said. "I got good grades, not great. I was a good athlete, not great. My Dad says I've been a good soldier as long as he's known me."

That got us talking about the Army. She was driving the conversation, asking me questions about places I'd been but steering clear of the things I'd been doing there. That was fine by me. She seemed most interested in the geography and culture of Iraq and Afghanistan. After the server cleared our dinner plates and took our dessert order, I asked her where she'd been in the world. Now it was me driving the conversation, asking questions about trips she'd taken to Scotland and the Caribbean. She was easy to talk to. I was enjoying myself. A lot.

We finished our desserts. It got quiet for a moment. I felt like she was waiting for me to make the next move. "There's a bar on the top

floor of the Residence Inn downtown," I said. "They have outside seating. It's supposed to be really nice on a summer night. Want to give it
a try?"

"That sounds good," she said, "but, could I make an alternate
suggestion?"

"Sure."

"We could have a drink at your place."

I smiled. "Believe it or not, I have outside seating on the top floor
too. And it is really nice on a summer night. Is wine OK? I have some
red and I think some white, but I don't think it's cold."

We decided to stop on the way to get a chilled bottle of white. The
Fresh Market was just around the corner so we went in there. She picked
out a Pinot Grigio and wouldn't let me pay for it. She also bought a small
melon that came in a mesh bag. When we got to my place, she asked for
a knife and quickly sliced and peeled the melon. I noted her skill with
the blade. While she did that, I opened the wine and filled a plastic bag
with ice. "Poor man's ice bucket," I said. She put the melon on the plate
I gave her and I grabbed a couple of wine glasses. Then we climbed the
stairs to the third floor.

"THIS IS NICE," she said, as we settled on my little terrace. It was full dark
and cloudy with some heat lightning in the distance. We made small
talk about my neighborhood for a while, then she changed the subject.

"I'm curious about your married woman," she said. "Julie says she's
kind of a bitch."

I laughed. "Yeah, apparently no one likes her but me. And I'm not
sure I like her all that much."

"Then why, one might ask, are you sleeping with her?"

I leaned back in my chair, stretched my arms out in front of me, then
dropped them in my lap. "She was there in my yoga class, she made it
clear that she was available. What can I say?"

"I'm not judging," Beth said. "You or her. Julie says she's an attractive, older woman. Of course, to Julie, *older* is probably younger than we think it is."

"She's in her late forties," I said, hedging a little. "Maybe older. Her husband is a downtown lawyer. They live in a big house on White Oak Road."

"She sounds very ITB," Beth said. That's a Raleigh thing, Inside The Beltline, where the old money lives.

"I was telling Julie, though, I think the thing with Ellen has pretty much run its course."

She gave me a serious look. "It needs to be, if you're going to have a thing with me."

That gave me pause. "Are you saying that you want to be exclusive? Are you saying that we even have a thing?"

She smiled. "I'm just saying that if we do have a thing, and I think we should have a thing, you can't be sport-fucking some ITB bitch who's rude to my daughter."

Now I was smiling again. "So you think we should have a thing? Is it going to start anytime soon?"

"It's going to start as soon as we finish this conversation. But there's still something I want to talk about. I think you should know what you're getting into."

I waited.

"I'm having an affair with a married woman too."

"You mentioned that last week. I wasn't sure I heard it right."

"Yes. You corrected me. You said, a married *guy*?"

"And you said, it sure sounded like, *yeah, that too.*"

"Let me start from the beginning," she said. "I told you how Julie was conceived. The first time I ever had sex. As soon as I found out I was pregnant, I swore I was never going to have sex again. And that wasn't hard at all. Until Julie was around two, I had no time or desire to have sex."

She took a sip of her wine. "By that time I was at Duke and we had a good rhythm going, my mother and I. When my father died, she used some of the insurance money to pay off the mortgage on the little house we lived in. When I got into Duke, she sold that house and bought another one in Durham. So I lived off campus, but I gradually started living something like a college life. My first year it was all classes and studying at home, usually with Julie nearby. Over time, I made some friends outside of the classroom. I started hanging out with them. I even went out on a few dates. My mother mostly worked from home so she was Julie's main babysitter, but we had two high school girls who lived next door, so we had that pretty well covered."

Another sip of wine. "I didn't really get to be seventeen, or eighteen. So here I was at nineteen. I'm a full-time student and a part-time mother and a very part-time college-age kid. But that was enough to get me wanting some of the sex that my friends all seemed to be having. I was still afraid of getting pregnant again, so I did the logical thing, right? I started having sex with girls."

She made air quotes around the word logical. I just smiled. She took a longer sip of wine.

"I was never really a lesbian. I never stopped being attracted to men. I just only had sex with girls. It's like, you know how the anti-gays talk about gay people making bad choices? It's not a choice for really gay people. It's who they are. Period. But it was a choice for me. It was a way to have sex without any risk of getting pregnant."

"I've had gay friends," I said. "I've served with gay soldiers. Male and female. In and out of the closet. It's a little weird now to think that I joined up during 'don't ask, don't tell.' I was in Iraq when the policy ended in 2011, my first tour as a company commander. Most of the company had been together for years. I remember my exec telling me that we had four gays that he knew about, all of them first-class soldiers. Then it turned out that there were two more that no one would have guessed."

"You wouldn't have guessed with me," she said. "Oh, my friends knew what I was doing, and with who. But no one else. Professors, lab partners, to all of them, I was just another highly driven Asian girl. And it wasn't like I was hanging out with the Lezzies. Most of my sex partners were more about trying it than anything else."

"Lesbians Until Graduation?"

"I'm surprised you know that term," she said. "But yes, that's mostly who we were."

"But you went past graduation, apparently."

"For a couple of reasons, starting with, I was meeting my needs. A couple times a week, I played with myself. A couple times a month, I'd play with a friend. I didn't have to worry about relationships, which I didn't have time for anyway. And I didn't have to worry about getting pregnant."

There was a rumble of thunder in the sky. Pretty far off still, but probably coming our way.

"That was my sex life, through college, through med school, and through most of my residency. As time went on, I hooked up more and more with actual Lesbians. There's lots of them in the nursing world. But I did it less frequently. Sometimes a couple of months would go by. But I was perfectly happy. Julie was becoming this little person. We could go places. We could have actual conversations. And she was, like, a natural barrier against all the pressure to get involved with men."

"You were getting that kind of pressure?"

"Oh, sure. From my mother, From my non-sex girlfriends. It seemed like everybody was trying to fix me up with somebody. But I didn't need men for sex, and I didn't need a man to complete a family. I actually liked being a single mother. Just like I like being a doctor. My mother used to say I was too self-sufficient. She might have been right, but it worked for me."

I had emptied my wineglass. I poured myself some more and topped off her glass too.

"I was twenty-four when I finished med school. I got accepted for a residency at Vanderbilt and waitlisted at Duke. My mother was all set to sell the house and move to Nashville, but then I cleared the waitlist. So we went out to celebrate that night, to this restaurant called Nana's, and our waitress was one of my sex friends, one of my first ones, a girl I hadn't seen for probably five years. She told me she was teaching high-school French and waitressing three to four nights a week to make extra money. She said she was almost engaged. We traded phone numbers and promised to get together and catch up, which I didn't really think was going to happen, but she called me the next day, and we met up that weekend, and we went to her apartment, and we've been hooking up for going on twelve years. She's been the only woman in my life for most of that."

"She's married now?"

"She is. I went to her wedding. Her husband is a teacher too. He coaches the baseball team. They have two kids, a dog, the whole sub-urban house thing. They go to church every Sunday. It's a really good marriage."

"Does he know about you?"

"He knows I'm a friend. He knows we take ballet classes together. He doesn't know that we don't always got to the classes."

"You're hiding in plain sight," I said.

"That's a good expression. Yes, that's exactly what we're doing."

"But you're still hiding."

That drew a sharp look. "What's that supposed to mean?"

"No," I said, holding my hand up, palms out, "that came out wrong. I just mean, you have to have someplace to go, right?"

"Oh, that's never really been a problem," she said. "Saturday morn-ings, there's an adult class at the Raleigh School of Ballet. Also on Sat-urday mornings, Charlie, that's her husband, runs a baseball clinic in Chapel Hill. He usually takes their two boys with him. Sometimes we do Saturday morning ballet. Sometimes we do Saturday morning sex." She smiled. "Sometimes we do both."

I could picture her as a ballet dancer. She wasn't as tall as Julie, but she was slim and athletic-looking.

"Did you grow up wanting to be a ballerina?" I asked. "Both of my sisters were into it pretty heavy."

"When I was really little, I guess. I played children's roles in The Nutcracker a few times. But I wasn't anywhere near good enough to be a professional. Marjorie might have been. She's still a beautiful dancer. For me, it's mostly exercise."

"Marjorie is your … what word should I use, lover?"

"You can say friend. She says we're playmates. We're not in love. It isn't anything like that. She's in love with her husband."

We sat quietly for a moment. "You're not buying that, huh?" she asked.

"No, I can see it," I said. "I'm actually thinking about someone else."

"Your married woman" she said.

"Yeah, she said she loved her husband too."

"Is that so hard to believe?"

"I guess not. It's just not a situation I've ever been in."

"Being in love," she said. It wasn't a question. "Me either. Aren't we a pair."

Another quiet moment passed. We both sipped more wine. There was a question I wanted to ask, so I did. "Why are you telling me all this?"

"Like I said, I want you to know what you're getting into."

"Yeah, but I have a sense this is more than just you telling me you're bisexual."

She got up and walked to the front of the terrace. There's a half-wall that goes up about thirty inches, and a foot-high railing on top of that. She looked outward for a bit then turned and leaned back against the top of the wall.

"I guess I need to tell you about my married man," she said.

"WHEN I WAS TWENTY-EIGHT, I had a hysterectomy. My mother had died. She had a very fast-moving, very aggressive cancer. My next annual checkup, my gynecologist found some fibroids in my uterus. They're not cancerous, but I'd been experiencing some symptoms. We tried a couple of things, none of them worked, finally it came down to living with it or having the hysterectomy. It's a major surgery, so it's not something you do lightly, but the main deciding factor for most people is permanent infertility, and that wasn't a factor at all for me. Julie was eleven. She was all the children I wanted."

She levered herself up and walked over and sat back down on the chair. "It took a few months to get back to my regular work schedule. It was six months before Marjorie and I got back into our thing. And during that sex drought,"—she smiled at that—"I started thinking more and more about sex with men. Like I told you, I was never a Lesbian. I was often attracted to men, I just didn't do anything about it. For only one reason, and now that risk was off the table."

She took a long sip of wine, emptying her glass. I poured her some more, and she thanked me.

"I was still in my residency. Up until then, I'd been working exclusively at the University Hospital in Durham. While I was out, they'd brought a few new people into the program there, but there was an opening at the Raleigh hospital and it would get me into the ER, on the orthopedic team, which was exactly what I wanted. So one afternoon, they bring a guy in with a heart attack and a badly broken leg. He either had the attack and fell down the stairs, or fell down the stairs and had the attack. The cardiology team got him stable and then they brought us in to work on his leg. I was the last person in the room when his own cardiologist got there, so I briefed him on what we did, and sort of helped him with his own evaluation. Then the next day, he was in the patient's room when I stopped in on my rounds."

"I think I see where this is going," I said.

She smiled. "He was right out of central casting. Tall, though not as tall as you. Middle forties, just a little gray at the temples. And cardiologists are sort of royalty among doctors. We flirted a little. He asked if I was married. I asked if he was. He didn't lie to me. He even apologized, said he was sorry if he crossed any lines. Then said he'd be back at the same time tomorrow, maybe we'd bump into each other again."

"Did you?"

"No. I was on in the ER. But he called me the day after, asked me if I'd have time to get some coffee. I was glad he did. I'd been thinking about him."

She sipped some more wine. "Anyway, we had coffee. Then we had lunch a couple of times in the cafeteria. Then we had lunch at a place near his office on my day off, and afterward we went to an apartment he has over near the NC State campus. We hooked up there for almost seven years."

"You have long relationships," I said.

"We were more active at first," she said, "like, pretty much every week. Eventually, more like once a month. I'm pretty sure he has another girlfriend."

"That doesn't bother you?"

"No. But there are a couple of other things that do. He's fifty-two now. He's about thirty pounds heavier than when we started, most of that in the last couple of years, and he doesn't carry it all that well. He started taking Viagra, and that's making him more, I don't know, aggressive might be the right word. But the biggest thing is that he found out about Marjorie, and he keeps suggesting that I bring her for a threesome."

"How'd that happen?" I asked.

"The apartment. He actually owns a couple of buildings that mostly rent to students. He's kept this apartment empty. It's on the top floor and it has a separate entrance and an elevator. He plays poker there with a bunch of other doctors and lawyers. Apparently, they play for pretty high stakes. He's got the living room set up with a real poker table and a full bar. And then, of course, there's a bedroom for his other extra-curricular activity."

She took another sip of her wine. "I've had a key ever since the beginning, and the building is just down Hillsborough Street from the ballet studio. One night last year, Marjorie and I went to an evening class. We were next to each other at the barre, doing arabesques"—she stood up and showed me the movement, sort of like Warrior 3 in yoga—"and she lost her balance and fell back into me. I caught her with my hand on her breast, and maybe kept it there longer than I needed to. For the rest of the class, we kept finding ways to touch each other. Toward the end, she said, 'Is there any place we can go?' I said, 'I know a place.' That was the first time we used Michael's apartment. Then we used it a couple more times, once on a Saturday when Charlie didn't have his baseball thing going. That was the time Michael saw us. He was just pulling up in his car as we were leaving the building. He was cool about it. It wasn't even really awkward. He texted me later on to say he'd always figured he wasn't my only lover, and man or woman, it didn't make any difference to him. But the next time we were together, he started asking for a threesome, and that's not going to happen."

There was a little extra heat on the not-going-to-happen part. Then she said, "You were right. This is more than just me telling you about my sexuality. This is me telling you that they're two separate things. The truth is, I haven't been with Michael for four or five months. All my fantasies for the last week or so have been about you. I may have sex with Marjorie tomorrow, but tonight, I want to be with you. Just know, there aren't going to be any threesomes. With Marjorie or anyone else. Please don't even ask."

She'd been leaning forward in her chair. Now, she slumped back, and closed her eyes. "Jesus, how long have I been talking? I hope I didn't bore you."

I flashed on something I'd been taught in a leadership class a long time ago. "No, not at all," I said. "Thank you for sharing."

She laughed. "That doesn't sound like something you'd say." She laughed again when I told her where it came from.

"Seriously," I said. "I'm glad you told me. I understand boundaries, and I'll respect yours."

"And I'll respect yours," she said. "Just tell me what they are. But first, point me toward the ladies room."

I WALKED HER TO THE second level and pointed down the hallway. Then I went down to the first floor to use that bathroom myself. I remembered that I had some chocolate biscotti in the cupboard, so I brought that back upstairs with me and set it down next to the melon, which we hadn't even touched.

When Beth came back, she walked to the front of the terrace again, looked out over the railing for a few seconds and then sat back down. "Should we talk about your boundaries now?" she asked.

"We don't need to," I said. "Tell me what else you were into when you were a kid."

"Besides ballet?" she laughed. "I wanted to be a pastry chef, a soccer star, and an astronaut. How about you?"

I laughed too. "I wanted to be Michael Jordan or Colin Powell. Walker says that proves I was Black in a previous life. Or else I'm going to come back as a Black man or a black dog after I die."

"He's a character, isn't he. How long have he and Teisha been together?"

We talked about Walker and Teisha for a while as we nibbled on the melon and the cookies. As I finished the last of the melon, there was a flash of lightning off toward the west. Not the heat lightning we'd been seeing but the real cloud-to-ground kind.

I said, "We probably want to get inside before too long."

"Not till we have to, OK?" she said. "I like it out here."

After few more minutes it started raining. Just a sprinkle, really, but I was pretty sure there was more to come so I stood up and said, "That's probably our cue." Beth stood up too and I picked up the now-empty wine bottle, the two glasses, and the plates from the melon and biscotti. As I stepped into the house, it started raining harder but Beth hadn't moved.

"Can anyone see us up here?" she asked.

"I don't think so," I said. "Maybe up by the edge, not back here by the door."

She kicked her sandals off, into the house. Then she unbuttoned the top front of her dress. "I have a fantasy," she said, as she lifted the dress over her head, "of being naked in the rain." She bunched it up and tossed I to me underhand. Then she undid her bra and slid it down her arms and slipped out of her panties and tossed all of that to me too. Right then, there was another flash of lightning followed immediately by a huge blast of thunder and the rain started pouring down. Beth moved out onto the terrace a little way and started turning slowly around. "This is wonderful!" she said. In just a few seconds, she was completely soaked, her hair plastered to her neck and shoulders. "Come on," she said. "Come out here. This is amazing!"

I have a healthy respect for lightning. That's a polite way of saying I'm afraid of it. But this was too good to pass up. I kicked off my own shoes and stepped out onto the balcony. Beth took two steps toward me and pulled my polo loose from my pants. As I pulled it up over my head she undid my belt buckle.

"Come on," she said. I unsnapped and unzipped my jeans and stepped out of them. They were already soaked so I just left them on the balcony floor. She reached for me and started rubbing me against her. After a few seconds of that, she hopped up, wrapped her legs around my waist, then reached down again and slipped me inside of her. She started moving, and I was holding on for dear life. She was all wet and slippery, inside and out. And all through this, the rain was falling and the lightning was flashing and the thunder was crashing. It was pretty intense. I think we both came at about the same time but it was hard to tell. She obviously felt me come, because she slowed down to a gentle motion and then she stopped moving altogether, just as the rain was slowing down.

"Oh my," she said, as she slipped off of me. "Oh my god."

There was another flash of lightning, off to the east now. The rain was still coming down but it was nothing like before. She held her head against my chest, then she leaned back and smiled up at me. "If you can come up with something to top that," she said, "I may never let you go."

I GOT HER HOME a few minutes before midnight. The garage door was just coming down as I pulled up in front of the house.

"Damn," she said. "I was hoping to beat Julie home. Now I guess I'll have to face the third degree. What do you think I should tell her?"

"Tell that we had a good time, and that I was a perfect gentleman."

She laughed. She didn't want me to walk her to her door so we kissed goodnight in the car. It was a good kiss, soft but long. "That's supposed to leave you wanting more," she said.

"I do," I answered.

30

On Sunday, I slept until almost noon. I woke up craving coffee and exercise. I took care of the coffee at Night Kitchen on my way to the gym. Once I got there, I started with some stretching in the back corner, then headed forward toward the weight machines. As I passed by the weight benches, where the heavy iron pumpers work, I noticed that one of them was Deputy Washington. He was on his back, doing bench presses with three 45-pound plates on each side of the barbell. That's 315 total with the 45-pound bar. He didn't look to be straining any, moving the bar up and down, slowly and smoothly. A sturdy look-ing, Hispanic-looking woman was spotting him. When he finished his set, they each took a plate off the bar, and she settled in to do a set with 225. She didn't seem to be straining too much either. I caught his eye as he was spotting her and we nodded at each other.

I gave myself a good workout. A lot of reps on a lot of machines. I got home feeling like I'd had a pretty good week.

A LOT HAPPENED THE NEXT WEEK. I talked to Walker on Monday and told him about the house in High Point. He promised to call Maddie later in the day. I also found out that Denis had booked a fight for Andre. They were both in his office when I showed up for our workout on Tuesday. Andre had a huge smile on his face. Denis was telling him that it was only a small step. It was a Rowan County Fight Night, at the Salisbury Fairgrounds in four weeks. Salisbury is the county seat of Rowan. It's about halfway between Greensboro and Charlotte, about a two-hour drive from Raleigh.

I saw Beth twice during the week. We had a late lunch on Wednesday. Friday night, we drove over to Durham to eat at a French restaurant she wanted to try. After we looked over the dinner menu, she handed me the wine list and told me to pick something appropriate. I told her that everything I knew about wine, I'd learned from a sergeant. That was another thing about Mike Stanton. He had a wide range of interests, but his theory on wine was that its primary purpose was to impress the woman you were eating with. Then, he said, you let the alcohol do its thing and you hopefully got laid.

The secret, he said, was to choose a wine from an obscure country— Chile and Portugal were his favorites—and something in the upper middle of the particular wine list's price range. "If they start at twenty dollars and go up to a hundred, you want something around sixty," he said. This list topped out at $75, so I ordered a Portuguese Malbec that cost $45. Stanton would have been proud of me. As it was, Beth said, "Interesting. When I think of Malbec, I usually think of Argentina. But let's give this a try."

We got back to her place around 10:00 and went right up to her bedroom, where we made love quickly and a little nervously. I don't think either of us wanted to face Julie yet. I was on my way home by 10:45.

I WORKED OUT WITH WALKER Saturday morning. I asked him if he wanted to get an early lunch at Night Kitchen afterwards but he looked at me strangely. "Late lunch at my house," he said. "Did you forget?"

I told him this was the first I'd heard of it.

"Well, shit," he said. "Maybe I forgot to tell you. Anyway, Maddie is supposed to get here at one o'clock. I'm supposed to pick up BBQ from The Pit. You can bring beer if you want."

I GOT THERE A LITTLE AFTER 1:00 with a twelve-pack of St. Pauli Girl. Maddie pulled in just as I was getting out of my car. She eyed the twelve-pack.

"How come there ain't no beer with Black girls on the labels?" she asked.

"I don't know," I said. "Must be a racist thing."

She laughed. "Andy Carver, you a funny man." She walked up and gave me a bicep hug. "So, you heard the big news, right?"

"What big news would that be?"

She stepped back and looked at me carefully. "I think you'd know if you heard it. I better not say anything more."

"Something with these two?" Meaning Walker and Teisha.

"I better not say anything more."

Teisha opened the door just as Maddie stepped up onto the front steps. She came out and they hugged each other, squealing happy and jumping up and down. Walker appeared in the doorway with a big smile on his face. After a bit, Maddie let go of Teisha and reached out to take both of his hands. "It's about time," she said. Then even louder, "It's about fucking time!"

Maddie let go of Walker's hands and hugged Teisha again. More squealing. More jumping up and down. Walker walked around them and came down the steps.

"You can probably guess," he said to me.

"You're getting married?"

"That's only half of it. The other half is why we're doing it."

"You're having a baby." Not a question. Walker nodded.

I put my arms around him. We didn't squeal or jump, but there was still a lot of emotion. He's my best friend. I'd always assumed they'd get married eventually, but I was never sure if children were in the picture. I'd ask him later if this was all part of a master plan.

WE WENT INSIDE. I handed everyone a beer, and put the rest of the twelve-pack in the refrigerator. We all twisted off caps and clinked bottles. I put it on myself to make the toast. "To a lucky man," I said, "and an about-to-be long-suffering woman."

"You'll have to make that long*er*-suffering," Teisha laughed. "But I can take it. Byron gonna be a good husband and a wonderful father."

Walker just smiled.

AFTER A WHILE, Teisha put the food on the table. We all sat down and started heaping our plates. Once everyone got some food in their bellies, Maddie asked if we were ready to talk about the house in High Point.

"I learned a lot," she said. "First of all, the Grainger family has money. Big time. They actually started out with trees. They had a couple thousand acres of timberland in Western NC and Eastern Tennessee and a couple of big sawmills. William Grainger's great-grandfather started making furniture in 1920. He was the youngest son or something and there really wasn't much of a place for him in the timber business. He'd gone off to fight in World War I, and when he came back, his father offered him the chance to start something new. They were never Thomasville or Broyhill or anything but they did pretty well. They sold a couple millions of those old school chairs with the desk part in front. William's father sold the company to some conglomerate in 1988 and started building upscale nursing homes. They have more than thirty of them now, all over the Southeast. William is the Senior Vice President in charge of Real Estate. His older sister is the President."

"Good business to be in these days," Walker said.

"The house itself," Maddie went on, "is four-thousand-four-hundred square feet. Got five bedrooms, a big kitchen, dining room, living room, family room and something the floor plan calls a solarium but it's really just a sunroom."

"What's the difference?" Walker asked.

"A real solarium is all glass. Walls, ceiling, everything but the floor. This is just a corner room with big windows."

That's exactly the kind of detail that Walker loves. I was sure he'd find a way to work it into a conversation before too long.

Maddie continued. "They're not getting any discount on their insurance policy for an alarm system. That doesn't mean they don't have one, but most people would take the discount if they could."

"You can see their insurance policy?" Walker asked.

"I can," Maddie answered, "but it's better if you don't ask how."

Walker nodded. Maddie continued.

"The most interesting thing I found is that the house is almost certainly going to be empty two Saturdays from today. William's son and your mechanic friend's grand-daughter are getting married at the Shoals Club on Bald Head Island. The ceremony is at four o'clock p.m., and if the weather cooperates, everyone gets to see a glorious Bald Head sunset at around nine o'clock."

"How did you find all that out?" Teisha asked.

"Article in the High Point Enterprise," Maddie said. "Thank you, Google."

31

We decided that Walker and I would drive out to High Point during the week to do a recon. Like the last time, we timed it for just before the sun went down, which let him work a full day and still gave us plenty of time to scope out the nearby streets. The original plan had been for him to drop me off for a solo recon, but we found a house under construction off a street that ran along the far side of the woods that surrounded Grainger's house. We pulled in behind the house. Google Maps told us that we'd have a little more than a quarter of a mile to walk through the woods.

Walker was excited that he'd get to go along. He was even more excited when I showed him a new toy I'd bought from Amazon, a pair of night-vision binoculars with recording capabilities. They weren't military spec by any means but they were pretty good.

Two steps into the woods, I used them to scan ahead of us. It wasn't full dark yet outside but it was plenty dark inside the woods. I didn't see anything that alarmed me so I started to move forward. Walker reached out and tapped my arm. "Hey, can I have a look?" he said.

I handed him the glasses. He checked a wider arc than I had and stopped, looking out toward three o'clock. "I see a deer!" he said. "Damn, there's like five of them!"

He passed the glasses back to me. "Take a look! Take a look! Isn't that cool!"

Walker, in the woods doing recon for a burglary. Jazzed like a little kid at the sight of a few deer.

THE GLASSES WERE VERY HELPFUL as it got darker and we got deeper into the woods. It was mostly cloudy so we weren't getting any moonlight. I was reminded of how dark it can get when there's no man-made light around. Afghanistan was like that up in the mountains.

We walked in the growing darkness for almost five minutes before we saw the first light from the house. In another couple minutes we were at the treeline, looking at the back and side of the house. There were lights on, both downstairs and upstairs, and the glow of a TV in one downstairs room.

"How do we do this?" Walker asked, speaking in a whisper.

"I want to circle the house," I said. "But first, could you find your way back to the car from here?"

"Oh, fuck," he said. Obviously, he hadn't thought about that.

"Look at where we are relative to the house. We're almost directly opposite the corner that joins the back and the side that doesn't have the garage on it. Remember when we looked on Google? The garage is on the left as you face the house from the front. So that means it's on the far side from where we are."

I looked at him to make sure he got that. He nodded.

"OK, from this spot, you walk as straight as you can, away from the house. If you have to go around a tree or whatever, you try to see two things on the other side of it, one near, one a little farther, straight out from the direction you're walking in. That gets you back on course."

I looked at him again. He nodded again.

"The most important thing. Any deviation to the right is good. Don't let yourself drift to the left. The road we drove in on is to the right. I don't think it's more than two hundred yards from any point on the line we walked through the woods. As long as you're bearing to the right, you'll either hit the house where we left the car, or you'll hit the road. If you hit the road, you turn left and just walk till you hit the driveway."

He nodded again.

"Last thing. It took us about eight minutes to walk here. Check your watch when you start walking back. Check it again every few minutes. If you get to twelve minutes and you haven't hit the house or the road, you might have missed on the left and gone too far. If that happens, turn to your four o'clock and start walking that way. That'll take you back to the house or the road."

"I understand," he said. "Now where are you gonna be?"

"Hopefully right there with you. But if anything happens and we get separated, you go to the car and drive at least five miles away. Hang around there for no more than ten minutes. If you haven't heard from me by then, go home."

He looked a little shaken. I patted him on the arm. "Don't worry. No reason for any of that to happen. But no reason *not* to have a plan, right?"

He nodded, then gave me a thumbs up.

"OK, let's walk just outside of the tree line. We'll still be hard to see and we're less likely to make any noise. Walk slowly and we'll stop about the middle of the back of the house."

WHEN WE STOPPED, I scanned the house for cameras and didn't see any. There were flood lights at each corner mounted just under the rain gutters. None of them were on, but I suspected they might have motion sensors. I made a second scan with the camera on before I handed the glasses to Walker. He looked for a while then handed them back to me.

The lake was more or less opposite the far side of the house. There was a forty- to fifty-foot break in the trees. We stopped at the edge. "We're just a couple of deer," I said. "We're just going to walk right across. If you want, we can stop in the middle and sniff around like maybe we found something good to eat."

Walker laughed softly. "Not all that hungry right now," he said. "But this is kind of fun."

On the other side, I stepped back into the trees. Walker followed me in. We scanned the side of the house then moved along to the front. The front lawn was considerably bigger than the back, sort of a half-oval shape with the driveway breaking out of the trees about halfway along one side. There was a light on over the front door which lit the lawn almost all the way to the driveway. Again, there were floodlights mounted on the corners of the house, and again, they were off. From this angle, I could see into the room that had the TV on. I could see the back of a man's head and the back of what looked like a recliner chair. I could also see about half of the TV, mounted on a wall, playing a baseball game.

WE GOT BACK TO OUR starting point. Walker asked, "So what do you think?"

"I haven't seen anything that scares me," I said. "But let's do one more thing. I'm going to go back to the front where I can see into the TV room. When I get there, I'll step out of the trees just a little bit and wave. When you see me do that I want you to walk about halfway from here to the house, turn ninety degrees right, and then walk straight until you hit the treeline and walk about ten feet in. I think those lights are on motion sensors, so don't be alarmed when they turn on. Just keep walking. Remember, you're just a deer. I want to see if the guy reacts in any way when the lights go on. Now they'll probably stay on for at least a minute. You sit tight until they turn off, then work your way back here. I'll probably be another two minutes getting back to you."

I reached my spot and waved. Walker started walking toward the house. He took six steps before the lights turned on. I saw him clench his shoulders, but then he turned and walked leisurely toward the treeline just like I'd told him to. He was exposed in the lights for probably twenty seconds, but I saw no reaction at all from the man watching TV. As I'd expected, the lights turned off in about a minute. There was still no reaction from the man, so I started moving back toward Walker.

WE REACHED THE POINT abeam the house at the same time. Walker had stayed in the woods, so I stepped in to meet him. He was agitated.

"I saw someone," he said. "A woman looking out one of the upstairs windows."

"Did she see you?" I asked.

"I don't think so. She looked out the window, maybe thirty seconds until the lights turned off. She stayed maybe ten more seconds, then she was gone."

We moved further into the woods. I did a 360 degree scan with the night-vision glasses then handed them to Walker and he did the same.

"I'm going to go through the woods about fifty feet that way," I said, pointing toward the driveway. "Just far enough to see the room with the TV. You keep the glasses. You can walk me back here if I have any trouble finding you. Let's give this fifteen minutes."

Walker looked at his watch. "OK ... 10:21 ... HACK!" He giggled softly. "I always wanted to do that."

I MOVED THROUGH THE WOODS, counting my steps. It took sixty-one to get to where I could see the TV room. I settled into a crouch to watch and wait. Maybe three minutes later, the light changed slightly, and then went almost completely dark. The man had turned off the TV then turned off the room light. A few seconds later it went completely dark. He had turned off a hall light. Then the light over the front door went out. With the downstairs dark, I could see some residual light coming from the front upstairs windows, but they turned dark too after about fifteen seconds. Definitely enough time to walk upstairs. Probably not enough time to arm an alarm and then walk upstairs.

I had turned about sixty degrees from my path in order to watch the house. I turned 120 degrees more, to put myself on a reverse heading. I counted out thirty steps and stopped. I still couldn't see Walker, so I counted out fifteen more.

I heard him snap his fingers twice from about my eleven o'clock. There he was with the glasses to his eyes and a big grin on his face. "You're pretty good in the woods, Tonto," he said. "You must have been able to see me, right? You came right straight at me, from the first step."

"Rangers can see in the dark," I said. "Everybody knows that."

"You know, when I was a kid," he said, "I thought he was the *Long* Ranger." I hadn't made the connection with Walker's Tonto reference. Now that I did, I saw no reason to tell him that I'd meant the Army kind of Ranger. I just laughed and said, "Not so long, Kemosabe."

"SO WHAT DO YOU THINK?" Walker asked, once were back on the road.

"I think that house is going to have the same kind of upscale furniture we took out of the other house."

"Too good for Marvin's customers?"

"Yeah."

He was quiet for a moment. "So we're going to pass?"

I was quiet too for a moment. "Tell me what you think about this. What if we come back, but not with a truck. Not looking for quantity. I keep thinking about what Denis said about small things with large value. I think we could probably park right where we did again, walk through the woods again, break into the house, and see what there is to see."

"Did you see a way in?" he asked.

"I saw a window on the second floor over the peak of the garage. It was smaller than the rest of the windows which makes me think it's a bathroom. I think it would open pretty easily with a pry bar, or if that didn't work, breaking a pane and turning the lock."

"How would we get up on the garage roof?"

"I saw four or five ladders at the construction house. I think it's pretty likely they'll be there next weekend. That house has a long way to go."

"So we'd carry the ladder though the woods. Would we carry it back?"

"Let me think on that. If we leave it, it probably leads back to the construction house, but I'm not sure how that hurts us."

"On CSI, they take images of tire tracks," Walker said, "but how about we rent a pickup truck like the construction guys probably drive. It'd be just another set of truck tire tracks and it would give us more space for whatever we find."

We fleshed out the plan a little more as we drove. By the time we were halfway home we were committed to our second mission.

32

Nothing much happened the rest of the work week, but something very interesting arose Friday evening. Beth and I went to dinner at an Italian restaurant called Gravy. She drove to my place and we walked from there. It's on Wilmington Street, maybe three-quarters of a mile away.

As we were walking home she asked if I had any plans for the next day, and if I wanted to go with her to Kinston. It's a small city of about twenty thousand, about eighty miles southeast of Raleigh. "What's out there?" I asked.

"I have to crack a safe," she said with a sly smile.

"You have to *what*?"

"I have to open a safe. It's part of an estate sale. There's an elderly woman whose husband died. She's selling the house and moving in with one of her children, so there's a whole house worth of things to sell. But the safe, she doesn't know the combination. She's not even sure what's in it. Anyway, I've worked with the auctioneer before. He wanted me for earlier this week but I couldn't get away. I promised that I'd get there well before the sale starts, so that means leaving here around seven o'clock. Want to come along?"

"Sure," I said. "But seriously, you're a safecracker?"

She laughed. "Cracker isn't really the right word. I don't use explosives or diamond drills or anything like that. I have an unusual, I guess, combination of feel and hearing. I turn the dial while I listen through a stethoscope. I can either feel or hear the tumblers click, sometimes both. It's only good on older safes, really, anything built in the last fifty years is beyond my abilities. But you'd be surprised how often someone needs to open up a hundred-year-old safe."

"How did you get started at this?" I asked.

"In high school," she said, "everything came pretty easily to me. I did the reading. I rarely needed to hear the teacher explain it to the rest of the class. One day, in a history class, I think, I was just bored out of my tree. For some reason, I reached into my backpack and pulled out my old combination lock. It was near the start of the year, and I'd gotten a new lock with a vertical combination. Do you know what I mean?"

I nodded.

"But I still had the old one, the dial kind. Anyway, I had it down underneath my desk, out of sight. I started turning the dial, slower and slower, and I felt the tumbler click! So I went back the other way, very slowly, very carefully. I didn't feel anything, so I spun it fast a few times and started again. By the end of the period, I'd opened it twice without ever looking at it."

I just looked at her in amazement.

"I tried it a few more times with other combination padlocks. Then one day, I tried the safe in the cleaning company office. The mechanism was much smoother than any padlock I'd played with, so I didn't have much luck. But then, maybe a month or so later, I was watching this old movie where the burglar used a stethoscope to listen for the clicks. I actually had one in an old doctor kit my mother had bought for me. So next time I went to the office I brought it along. And before too long I could open the safe."

"How does the word get out about something like that?"

"One of the cleaning company's customers was an auctioneer. My first year at Duke, we got hired to clean a house before a sale and we were short-staffed, so my mother and I went out on the job. It was the same sort of situation as this one. The safe was there but no one knew the combination. The auctioneer and someone from the family were talking about it while I was cleaning windows nearby. I just said, 'Let me take a shot at it.' I didn't have my stethoscope but there actually was one among the things for sale. It took me ten minutes to get it open."

"That's incredible," I said. "Anything good inside?"

"A coin collection and a stamp collection. I don't know what they sold for but the auctioneer sent my mother a check for four hundred dollars over and above the cleaning contract. And he passed the word around. I've done ten to fifteen jobs like that over the years, in the Carolinas, Virginia and Tennessee. I even flew down to Miami once in the auctioneer's private airplane."

"Well," I said, "let me know if you ever want to start a life of crime. I'll come along to help you carry the goodies home."

WE LEFT RALEIGH just after 7:00 a.m. and got to Kinston a little after 8:30. The auctioneer and his people arrived at quarter to nine. The sale was scheduled to start at 11:00.

The safe was in a room that had been used as an office or a study. Beth sat cross-legged in front of it and put the stethoscope tips in her ears. She fixed the bell to a point just above and to the right of the dial using some double-sided foam tape. Then she smiled at me, turned back to the safe, and started turning the dial.

It took her a little more than twenty minutes. I was impressed. The auctioneer didn't seem to be and Beth apologized for taking so long. She came over to stand by me while the auctioneer left the room to find the widow. They came back with two other middle-aged people I assumed to be her children. Everyone looked excited. Beth had left the door of the safe slightly ajar. The widow nodded to the auctioneer, who swung it fully open and pulled out a wooden box. He set it on a table, opened the lid and stepped back. The widow whispered something to him and he turned and walked over to Beth and I.

"They asked if we'd give them some privacy," he said.

"Of course," Beth said, and we all left the room. A couple of minutes later the widow came out with a disappointed expression on her face. She waved the auctioneer over. They spoke quietly, then he came back over to where Beth and I were standing and pulled a check from his shirt pocket.

"Not what they were hoping for," he said, "so no bonus today. Here's three-hundred-fifty dollars as agreed." He pulled three twenties from his wallet and handed those to her too. "But here's gas money and lunch money. Thank you, as always."

He shook both our hands and walked back into the study. We were back in Raleigh in time for a late lunch.

33

We burglarized William White Grainger's house the following Saturday. There were a lot of other things going on that day. Teisha came up with a list of errands for two men and a pickup truck, so I drove Walker out to the airport early to pick it up. She'd apparently told everyone she knew that we were going to have a truck for a day. That kept us busy until late in the afternoon.

WE GOT TO THE CONSTRUCTION HOUSE just before 9:00 p.m. Walker pulled quickly around to the back side of the house. There was scaffolding set up on the front side and it looked like the brick face of the house was about three-quarters complete. There were also two ladders standing up, one on each of the front corners. I shrugged into my backpack and slid my pry bar into one of the loops. I also had two sets of headlamps I'd picked up at REI. Walker grabbed his own pack, which held his two large duffels, his Skilsaw, his gloves, and a couple of pairs of booties. We took one of the ladders and headed off into the woods.

The first thing we learned is that walking in the woods is considerably harder with twelve feet of ladder. It took us fifteen minutes to get to William White's house, half again as long as the first time. The

night-vision glasses were helpful again, but harder to manage along with
the ladder. Like before, we walked around the house just inside of the
tree line. The front door light was on, but none of the motion lights
triggered. The inside of the house looked completely dark.

We set the ladder against the back side of the garage, right next to the
rear-entry door. I shook off my backpack and pulled out the headlamps.
"Let's put them on now, but we don't turn them on until we're inside,"
I said. I put the night-vision glasses back into my pack and then slipped
the pry bar out of its loop. "Leave the packs right here. After I'm in, I'll
come down and open this door for you."

I climbed up the ladder and used my hands and feet to mon-
key-scramble up to the peak. With one foot on either side of the it,
I slid the tip of the pry bar in about a quarter-inch between the window and the sill. I wiggled it a little, which let me push in another half-
inch. When I wiggled it again, the window started moving. It wasn't
even locked! I raised the window, stuck my head in, and snapped on
the headlamp. It was a bathroom. I climbed in and closed the window
behind me. The first thing I did was to put on my booties. Then I texted
Walker: "I'm in."

THE HOUSE HAD AN OPEN FOYER with a curved stairway to the second
floor. A U-shaped landing led to rooms on both sides as well as the
back. The bathroom I'd come in through was halfway down the U on
the left hand side. The door to the landing was open and I stood in the
doorway for what might have been a full minute, listening carefully for
any sounds. I didn't hear anything so I walked down the stairs, stopping on the next-to-last step to listen again. Still nothing, so I found
the back door and opened it for Walker. He put on his booties and we
started upstairs. There were two smallish bedrooms on either side of
the stairway with a bathroom in between. The whole back side of the
house was the master bedroom, with a bathroom and a huge walk-in
closet on opposite sides.

None of the smaller rooms had anything of interest in them. Only one of them seemed to have any sort of regular resident. Maybe the daughter who was getting married that night. The others all seemed like guest rooms. We scored in the master bedroom, though, with two jewelry boxes. One was a woman's, with at least thirty pieces ranging from rings to necklaces. The other was a man's, with a couple of rings and seven watches. Two Rolexes, a Breitling and three other analogs whose names I didn't recognize plus an Apple Series 3 digital.

We also found two pairs of brand new Nike tennis sneakers in the closet, still in their boxes. "Air Zoom Rafas," Walker said. "Rafael Nadal. These go like a hundred fifty dollars a pair and they're my size. These are definitely going with us!"

The main floor had just four rooms around the foyer. A big living room/family room, a dining room, the kitchen and what William probably called his study. We started there, and quickly found what the decal on the side said was a Glowforge Pro 3D laser printer. I knew our tech guys made obscure tractor parts using 3D printers but I thought those machines were, like, refrigerator sized. I had no idea you could buy one for your house.

Walker got excited when he opened the closet in the study and found a safe built into the back wall, but unlike Raymond and Marianne, William White hadn't left his open for us. "Too bad Beth isn't here," I said.

"Huh?"

"I'll tell you later."

We still did OK in the closet. We found a Microsoft Surface Pro still in its original packaging. We also found two unopened bottles of Johnny Walker Blue Label in Christmas gift boxes. "And a Happy New Year," Walker said.

THERE WAS A TOP-OF-THE-LINE Samsung curved TV in the living room. We both looked at it from the entryway.

"Sixty-five inches," Walker said. "It won't be heavy, but it will be bulky. They sell for at least a couple of grand."

"See the speakers?" I asked. "I count six so it must be surround sound. We'd need the tuner too."

"Anything else in this room?" Walker asked.

We both looked around. There was plenty of furniture but nothing in our target parameters. We went to the dining room next and found the same thing, furniture-wise. But Walker opened up the china cabinet and pulled out a wooden case that was about a foot and a half wide, a foot deep, and six inches tall. He lifted the cover and whistled.

"If this is sterling silver," he said, "it might be a jackpot."

SO FAR, WE'D FILLED one of Walker's big duffels with the jewelry boxes, the sneakers and the 3D printer. He'd had room for the scotch and the Surface Pro in his backpack. We went into the kitchen. Walker set the other big duffel on the floor and put the silverware case in it. Then he started opening up cabinets and loading up pots and pans. I took a big Vitamix blender off of the counter and loaded that in too. All they had for a coffee machine was a basic Keurig, but we took it anyway. We'd talked about filling one bag with kitchen stuff for Marvin.

There were two doors on the inside kitchen wall. One was a pantry. It had nothing of interest except a package of Mint Cream Oreos which Walker stuffed into his backpack. The other door led to a basement where Walker found four pro-style golf bags, full of clubs.

"Come look at this," he said. "This is two sets of Pings, one set of Calloway's, and one set of Taylor Made. There's a thousand dollars' worth of golf clubs in each of these bags."

We each grabbed two of them and climbed back up the stairs to the kitchen. I set one bag down and reached for my backpack. I took out the night-vision glasses and looped them over Walker's head, then picked up the golf bag again.

"Let's go out the back door and turn left around the garage," I said.

"We're going to take these to where the driveway breaks out of the woods. Then we continue around to the point where we came in, and you walk back through the woods to get the truck. While you do that, I'll get rid of the ladder and bring the other stuff out to the mouth of driveway."

"Including the TV and everything?"

"Yes. Now remember, the road we drove in on is to the right. When you get to the main road, you turn right again. Then the first right takes you into this driveway, one tenth of a mile. Use your headlights until you're twenty, thirty yards into the driveway, then turn them off. Glasses in one hand, steering wheel in the other. Go slow, try not to need your brakes."

We walked quickly to the mouth of the driveway, dropped the golf bags, and continued around to the right of the house. Walker stopped at the point we'd come in from the woods, looked back at the house, and turned 180 degrees. "I got this," he said. "See you in about fifteen."

I walked back around the house and grabbed the ladder. I carried it about twenty or thirty feet into the woods and dropped it there. Then I walked through the house to the front door and unlocked it. It took six trips for the TV, the tuner and the speakers, including the big cube sub-woofer I found under a side table. It took two more trips for the big duffels and our backpacks, including two bottles of Bud Light I grabbed from the refrigerator.

I closed and locked the front door. Just before I went out the back door, I realized that we'd missed one room, the garage. I opened up the connecting door and took a look. There was a big SUV parked right in front of me, so I walked around to the other side of it. The garage was about two and a half cars wide, with an empty space for another car and another five to six feet on the other side of that. The extra space held a golf cart that had two more golf bags on the back. Next to that was a Cannondale road bike that probably cost $3000 new.

I grabbed the golf bags and jogged them out to the driveway. If four was good, six was better. Then I ran back in to get the bike. Walker had just nosed into the clearing as I came around the corner of the garage.

We loaded the TV, the tuner and the two duffels into the rear cab. All the rest went into the bed. The top of the bicycle was the only thing visible above the bed walls. In less than three minutes we were rolling slowly back down the driveway. I had Walker stop about twenty yards from the end, still with the lights off. I got out, walked to the road and made sure I couldn't see headlights or taillights in either direction. Then I waved him forward, got in, and we pulled out onto the road.

Walked flipped the headlights on then reached over to bump fists.

"TDM!" he said. "Righteous!"

34

Marvin gave us $300 for the kitchen stuff. We'd shown him the golf clubs. He said he knew a guy in Rocky Mount who would take them and he'd broker the deal for 20%. I ran that by Denis and he gave his blessing. On Wednesday, Marvin called Walker and told him he had worked his guy up to $1425 so he had $1140 for us whenever we wanted it. He also said, "Bring me some sofas next time."

On Thursday, Denis gave us $900 for the TV and the sound system. He was waiting for his jewelry people to get back to him and also for another guy on the 3D printer. We hadn't brought him the Surface Pro. Walker was sure he could sell it on eBay for close to full price. We also hadn't brought him the bike, which I was thinking about keeping. I told Walker I'd sell my old one and put whatever I got into the kitty. He told me that wasn't necessary. After all, he said, he was keeping the two pairs of sneakers.

Denis made us an interesting offer. He'd give us 75% of whatever he could get for six of the watches in return the seventh one, the Breitling. "You like the way that'll look on your wrist," Walker said.

"No," Denis said. "It will look good on Andre's wrist. After his fight. A gift. A celebration."

Walker smiled and gave Denis a thumbs up.

ANDRE'S FIGHT WAS ON Saturday night. Beth and Julie came by at around 4:00 p.m. and we took my car to Denis's gym. He'd rented a limo bus for the trip to Salisbury. We climbed the stairs to find about a dozen people in the gym. Walker and Teisha were already there talking with a group of women I recognized from Kirsten's self-defense classes. Kirsten herself was nearby talking with two other people I recognized, Deputy Washington and the Latina woman I'd seen him with at the gym.

I could see that Deputy Washington was clocking me. I took a few steps over and held out my hand.

"Hey, Deputy Washington," I said. "Andy Carver. We see each other at the gym, and you came by my house a while back to ask me some questions about a robbery in Sanford."

"A burglary," he said, starting a smile. He shook my hand. "Call me John." He nodded to the Latina woman. "This is my partner, Arielle Estrada."

I reached out to shake her hand. "Are you Sheriff's Department too?" I asked.

Kristen answered. "Not that kind of partner. The for-all-intents-and-purposes married kind. This is Elle Estrada. Bureau of Alcohol, Tobacco and Firearms, formerly Master Sergeant, United States Army. AKA The Illustrator. AKA Wall Street."

I guess I looked a little blank, so she continued. "Elle Estrada? Illustrator?"

"OK, I get that. I'm not sure about Wall Street."

"Well, Estrada translates into street, right? And if you hadn't noticed, she's built like a frickin' wall." That came with a loud laugh and her arms around the other woman's shoulders. Obviously there was a friendship there. "We were boots together. Then we served together in Desert Storm. And again in Bosnia. And then one more time in Iraq before she got out to join the G."

"I didn't know you were in Iraq," I said to Kristen. "When was that?"

She looked at Estrada. "2006? 2007?" Estrada nodded. To me, "It was after NC State. After I went back to the real Army. Were you there then?"

"From September '06 to October '07. I had an infantry platoon. Mostly north of Baghdad. Tikrit and Samarra."

"We were mostly in the south. Basra. Working with the Brits."

"That was ugly," I said.

"All of it was ugly," Estrada said.

"But we both did our twenty," Kristen said, "and now we're both in Raleigh. I'm back with Denis, and she hooked up with George Washington here."

"John," he said, with a smile.

"Yeah, whatever," she said with her own smile. I could tell they'd done this riff before.

THE RIDE TO SALISBURY took a little more than two hours. Andre sat in the front row with Denis. Walker and I sat behind them, providing a buffer from the rest of the group. Kristen had laid in food and beverages and they were pretty boisterous, especially the self-defense women. After about an hour, Walker slid out to check in on Teisha. A few minutes later, Estrada slipped into his seat.

"Kirsten told me you were one of her cadets," she said to me. "I bet that seems like a long time ago."

"Immeasurably long," I said. "But most days, it seems just as long since I was in. I've been out for a little more than three years."

"Any issues?" she asked. "Nightmares? Cold sweats? Any of that?"

"Not really," I said." "I guess I'm lucky."

"Damn straight," she said. "If you ever do, John and I both do counseling. I'm over the worst of mine, I think. But you never take that for granted."

We talked a little about places we'd served and people we'd served with. Estrada got a big kick out of hearing what we'd called Kirsten at NC State. The Big Girl.

"We mostly called her *Bahstin*," she said, pronouncing it with a heavy Boston accent, maybe even worse than Kirsten's. "She better watch out next time she gives me any of that *Wall Street* shit."

ANDRE WAS PREDICTABLY NERVOUS in his first fight. He didn't get untracked until late in the first round when the other fighter knocked him down with a hard jab followed by a side kick. Andre got up and smiled at Denis and I, just outside the cage. "He has just learned that he can take *le dur coup*," Denis said to me. "The hard shot. He will be fine now." Over the last minute of the round, he landed a couple of hard shots of his own. In the next two rounds, he was dominant and won by a unanimous decision.

THERE WAS LOTS OF CELEBRATION on the ride back to Raleigh. About halfway home, Deputy Washington worked his way around the bus taking everybody's car keys. When we got to Denis's gym he gave some back and made others make other arrangements. Walker was on the no-drive list so he and Teisha piled into my car. Julie went with Andre. Beth huddled briefly with Julie before she joined us in the car.

"What'd you tell her?" Walker asked. "Be home by midnight?"

She smiled before she answered. "I told her I wouldn't be home tonight. I suspect she won't be either." She turned to face Teisha in the back seat. "Julie told me yesterday that fighters think having sex before a fight makes your legs weak. Do you believe that?"

"If you do it right," Teisha said, "definitely."

35

We settled up with Denis the following Tuesday. He paid us almost $7000, and that was on top of the money we'd already gotten from him. Plus there was the $1440 we'd gotten from Marvin. Walker got a little giddy when Denis gave him the earrings that John Knox had dropped off earlier that afternoon.

"My, my," he said, "Teisha is gonna love these." He held them up to his own ears and did a little twirl.

"A caution," Denis said. Walker stopped twirling. "These are not ostentatious. But they are perhaps beyond your normal budget, yes?"

Walker nodded, then smiled. "I think I know where you're going," he said. "We don't want anybody wondering how come I can all of a sudden afford fancy earrings, right?"

"Exactly right," Denis said. "But a caution, not a warning. Do you see the difference?"

"I do, and I thank you," Walker said.

I HAD A LUNCH DATE with Beth the next day. I was supposed to meet her at 12:30 at a place called Coquette. I was way early so I killed some of time at a bookstore nearby. Then I walked over to the restaurant and got us a table. I was just ordering an iced tea from the server when Beth arrived. She asked for one too.

She was still in her scrubs. "I'm having a day," she said. "We had to bump two morning surgeries to this afternoon, so I have to go back. But I'm free until two-thirty and I'm hungry!"

The server came back with our iced teas and we ordered our food. As he left, I noticed that Beth was looking at something over my shoulder. I turned and saw a tall, blond woman walking toward us, a big smile on her face. She was about our age, maybe a little older. She looked fit and strong. Beth stood up and they embraced.

"Andy," she said, "this is my friend Marjorie Maynor. Marj, this is Andy Carver."

I stood up and held out my hand. She took it, looking me up and down and being pretty obvious about it. "I'm pleased to meet you," she said to me, then to Beth, "I definitely see it."

Beth just smiled. "See what," I asked.

"Chris Pine," Marjorie said. I must have looked confused. "The actor? Young Captain Kirk?"

"Well," I said, "I used to be Captain Carver. That's about as close as you're gonna get, I'm afraid."

"Close enough for me," Marjorie said. "OK, it was very nice to meet you." To Beth, " You call me later, you hear?" She started to walk away.

"Marjorie!" Beth said sharply. Marjorie stopped. "You sit! He's going to think we set up a drive by."

"But we did set up a drive by," Marjorie laughed. "OK, I'll stay. Can I get a glass of wine?" She looked at our glasses of iced tea on the table. "Wait, no Wednesday Afternoon Wine for you?"

"I have to go back in," Beth said. "We had to bump a couple of surgeries this morning and you know how they are about operating under the influence."

I grabbed a chair from the next table and we all sat down. The server came right over and Marjorie ordered a glass of Pino Grigio. I asked for a refill on my iced tea. Beth held her hand out, palm down, over her glass. I guess she was being careful about caffeine too.

Marjorie had a not-southern accent. It took me a minute to remember where I'd heard it before. A soldier from my first infantry platoon, a private named Henslin. He was from Appleton, Wisconsin. I took a chance and asked, "Milwaukee?"

"Whitefish Bay. How did you know?"

"I knew a guy who had a very similar accent. Everyone called him Cheesehead. Where is Whitefish Bay exactly?"

"Just north of Milwaukee," she said.

"A very ritzy suburb," Beth added.

Marjorie said, "Yeah, but we were the least ritzy people there."

WE MADE PLEASANT CONVERSATION for another half-hour or so. Beth and I ate our lunch when it came. Marjorie had another glass of wine. Eventually, the server cleared our plates and Beth said it was time for her to be getting back. Marjorie hugged us both warmly and told me again that it was nice to meet me. She whispered something in Beth's ear as they hugged, and they both laughed.

"Did I pass muster," I asked, as I walked Beth to her car.

"With Marjorie? No question. I knew you would."

"Just to clarify," I said, "you don't have two friends named Marjorie, do you?"

"No, that was the Marjorie you think it was."

"So, she obviously knows about you and me. Does she know that I know about you and her?"

"No, there's no reason for her to know that."

"You were taking a chance," I said, "that I wouldn't say something stupid."

She stopped, and turned to face me. "I was," she said. It wasn't an expression of agreement. More of a statement of fact. I put two and two together.

"So, this was actually a double set-up," I said. "You were testing me too."

She looked down for a moment, then looked back up at me, a serious look on her face. "I'm starting to really like you," she said. "I guess I need to know if I can trust you. With the entirety of my life."

I wasn't sure what to say to that. "So far, so good?" was all I came up with.

"Yes," she said. Then a smile. "So far, so good."

36

The weeks leading up to Walker's wedding went by quickly. The Wake County schools started up the last week in August so he was back on his regular schedule. Beth and I were spending a lot of time together. Yoga was more about the yoga and less about Namastes.

The big wedding weekend got off to a rough start. It rained hard Saturday morning then let up for a while in the early afternoon. But by the time we got to the church at around 4:00 p.m. it was raining hard again. The wind was gusting to about thirty miles an hour. Walker's mother had to hold on to her big church hat with both hands. She arrived with Teisha's mother and step-father who'd spent the day at her house after driving in from Wilmington early in the morning. They all kept their distance from Teisha's father who'd started drinking earlier in the day. He apparently did that most days. Walker had asked Teisha's cousin William to keep his eye on him. "No problem," William had said. "He got a flask. I got a flask. We just keep a nice quiet buzz on."

The service went off without a hitch. Walker and I walked in from one side with Reverend Tate. Maddie and the two bridesmaids came in from the other side. When Teisha appeared in the doorway, the Reverend asked Walker if he was ready, then nodded to the organist and Teisha started walking down the aisle.

The rest of it went quickly. Each of the bridesmaids read a scripture, then Walker's mother and Teisha's mother read one together. Walker and Teisha were mostly staring into each other's eyes while Maddie and I made faces at each other. Then it was Reverend Tate's turn. He did a few minutes on the sanctity of marriage, then a few more on true love. Then he asked Walker and Teisha to read the vows they'd written to each other. Typically, Teisha's was sweet and Walker's was intense. The reverend did the speak-now-or-forever-hold-your-peace thing, then he asked Maddie and I to give Teisha and Walker their rings. Once the rings were on the right fingers, he pronounced them man and wife. The organist played some more as Walker and Teisha started back down the aisle.

THE FIRST HOUR OR SO of the reception was mostly eating and talking, but then the DJ ramped up the music. Walker and Teisha were the first ones up on the dance floor. Most of the rest of us stood up and clapped as they danced an energetic boogie. Before long more people were dancing. I went out on the floor with Beth, even though dancing is not my thing.

It definitely was hers, though. Probably something to do with her ballet background. She just looked completely natural and comfortable in motion. Julie had dragged Andre on to the dance floor too, and he didn't seem any more into it than I was, so Beth and Julie ended up dancing more with each other than with us. Julie seemed every bit as natural and they definitely looked more like sisters than mother and daughter.

At one point later in the evening a bunch of the women had a line-dance thing going on. Teisha was mostly the leader until Walker's mother got up and took over. She's a few years over sixty and seriously overweight, but she still had some moves.

Walker had appeared at my shoulder. "What you see there," he said, "is the result of demon alcohol on a normally sedate and godly Black woman. Ain't it something to see?" Then he went out on the floor to dance with her.

THE NEXT MORNING, Beth and I walked over to Walker's house. It was a nice fall morning,and everything had pretty much dried off after Friday's and Saturday's rain. Walker and Teisha and Maddie were sitting around the kitchen table drinking coffee and eating cinnamon rolls.

We all hung out until the middle of the afternoon. Maddie was the first to go, but before she left, she took me aside and told me that she'd left a folder with Byron, a scouting report on a house she thought had potential. "Take a look," she said. "Maybe we can all talk on the phone tomorrow or Tuesday?"

WE ENDED UP TALKING Tuesday evening. The house was in Creedmoor, about thirty miles north of Raleigh. It had been on the market for just over a month and had a contract pending. The buyers wanted to move in on January 1, which was fine with the sellers. They were waiting for their new house in Northern Virginia to be finished, hopefully by the middle of December. In the meantime, the husband was going to move to a Residence Inn in mid-October and start his new job. He would come home some weekends, on the others his wife and two kids would join him at the Residence Inn.

Maddie's notes had their tentative schedule. It looked like the house would be uninhabited at least one of the first two weekends in November. She also included the brochure that the listing agent had put together. The furniture looked like a perfect match for Marvin's store.

37

I t turned out to be the second weekend. Walker and I did our recon a few days after talking with Maddie. Everything looked good. Maddie drove by the house on Friday evening of the first weekend and lots of lights were on. She drove by again Saturday morning and there were two cars parked behind the house. The next Friday, the house was dark and there were no cars parked on Saturday morning. Walker had reserved a truck for the first weekend then rescheduled it, so were good to go for a Saturday afternoon pickup.

We left Raleigh just before 7:00 p.m. and it was full dark when we got to Creedmoor. We drove past the house a couple of times. Everything still looked good, so on our third pass, we pulled in behind it. Walker had his Skilsaw but we'd decided that would be Plan B. I had my prybar and I used that to force the back door. We made six trips together and about ten more separately and cleaned out most of the furniture. On our last trip, Walker loaded up a duffel bag with kitchen stuff and I checked out the basement. The only thing of interest down there was a freezer chest, about three feet wide and three feet high and maybe two feet deep. I lifted the cover and found it about half full, a mix of ice cream, vegetables and meat. I unplugged it and pushed it over to the base of the stairs.

"Need some help, B," I called up the stairs. Walker appeared at the door a few seconds later. We carried the freezer out to the truck where he opened the lid and smiled. He lifted up one of the packages of meat. "Bison steaks," he said. "Good and good for you!"

WE MET MARVIN at his store early the next morning. Marvin was pleased with what we brought him. "You boys are learnin' my market," he said. We unloaded and left it all in his back room, then I drove Walker to work in the U-Haul. The plan was for me to return the truck, then pick him up after school to go back to Marvin's.

When we got back there Keila had put a spreadsheet together. It came out to $5650 and showed our 30% share as $1695. Marvin counted out seventeen $100 bills, and handed them to Walker. "Don't suppose either of you boys has a five dollar bill?" he said. "No matter, we'll call it even." I smiled at Keila while she rolled her eyes at her great-grandfather.

On the way home, I asked Walker if he was satisfied with the payoff. "Not quite a thousand dollars for you this time," I said.

"No, but don't forget the freezer and all that buffalo meat." We'd taken that off the truck at Walker's house the night before, carried it down to his cellar, and plugged it in. The ice cream was a little soft, but nothing had melted. "Plus," he said, " we did way better than a thousand on the other two. No complaints here."

He suggested we split the cash $750 for me, $750 for him, and $200 for Maddie. I told him that was fine.

38

JANUARY 2019

Two interesting things happened the first week of the New Year. On January 4, I got a telegram from my boss. Actually, it was a sheet of paper designed to look like an old-time telegram, delivered in a FedEx envelope. It said, *Congratulations Andy Carver, you are the Big Dog of the Year. More to follow.* It wasn't a surprise really, I'd known I was well in the lead. Still, it was nice to be recognized. My father would be proud.

THE SECOND INTERESTING THING was running into Ellen at Fresh Market. I hadn't seen her at yoga for a few months. She told me she'd been taking different classes. She asked me if I wanted to get coffee and I had nothing better to do, so we walked over to Café Carolina. It was one of those seventy degree days that we get in Raleigh in January.

We were having a pleasant enough conversation until she asked me, with a bit of an edge, if I was still with the Asian girl. Before I even answered, she said, "She's too young for you, you know."

I just laughed. "I never had anything going with Julie," I said. "Believe it or not, I've been seeing her mother."

That seemed to offend her even more. "Really? Is she as unpleasant as her daughter?"

I laughed again. But then I put my cup down and rested my elbows on the table. "I'm curious," I said. "What's your problem? Is it an Asian thing? You have a problem with slanty-eyed people?"

She looked right back at me. "I do have concerns about Asians. And Mexicans and all the others. Even the Russians and Chechnyans and Ukrainians who are at least white. Our country is being overrun by foreigners."

I was thinking, this could go one of two ways. I could get up and leave. Or, I could soften the mood. That's what I chose to do, because of something Ellen had told me earlier. She and her husband were going to their place in Florida for the last two weeks of January. In a flash, I decided that I disliked Ellen enough to rob her. And like they say on the Law & Order shows, I had motive *and* opportunity.

"I don't disagree completely," is what I did say. "But I have to tell you, I do like this particular Asian lady. So, let's talk about something else. You said your Florida place is in Naples? My parents have been talking about moving there. What do you like about the area?"

Predictably, the two things she liked best were the weather and the demographics. I looked it up later, Naples is 94.1% white. I'm sure there are lots of Hispanics around working in the service industries, but they must actually live someplace else.

WALKER AND I BROKE INTO Ellen's house in broad daylight. It was a big house on White Oak Road, very ITB, exactly where you'd expect a big-time lawyer like Ellen's husband to live. The lots are large, heavily wooded, and you get to most of the houses via long driveways that wrap around behind.

We'd done two recons. The first time we ran along White Oak Road at dusk and slipped into the trees just short of Ellen's driveway. The second time we ran up the driveway itself just before dawn. The most promising entry point seemed to be a second-story window above a screened porch, but Walker popped the lightweight door to the porch with a multi-tool blade and found that the inside door from the porch into the kitchen was unlocked. Bad security, Ellen! We spent about half an hour walking through the house, identifying the items we wanted. We'd already decided to model this mission on William White Grainger's house. Like Denis had said, small things with large value. In Ellen's house we found all kinds of electronics, some nice kitchen appliances and a lot of what Walker called objects d'art. We also found two jewelry boxes in the master bedroom, one his and one hers. His had a Rolex that didn't seem to work but it also had $3000 in cash in it. We took all of that with us right away.

It was Walker's idea to come back later that morning. He called in sick before we left Ellen's house and then he hooked us up with a cargo van from Enterprise. We ran back to my place, grabbed my car and drove up Capital Boulevard to pick up the van. Enterprise will bring your vehicle to you, but I felt that was an unnecessary level of exposure. It turned out better anyway because we got to choose the van we wanted. They had three white ones with Enterprise graphics on the side. We took a gray one with blank sides.

We were back at Ellen's by 9:15 and on the way to Marvin's store barely twenty minutes later. We loaded up all the things we'd set aside then grabbed whatever furniture would fill the van. We ended up getting $900 from Marvin and $2200 from Denis, plus the $3000 in cash.

WE HIT SEVEN MORE HOUSES in 2019. Maddie found us six of them. She also came across a house with an outbuilding full of PlayStation 4s and LG TVs. I told Denis about it and he told us to stay away. "Whoever owns this," he said, "whoever *stole* it, you do not want them looking for you. This is a much different risk than what you have been doing." Three weeks later, he gave me $400, our share of a finder's fee he'd collected from someone who obviously had a higher risk tolerance. "A man

I know in New Jersey," he said. "He owns Game Stop stores among other things. He has a brother who owns a truck. It was a simple thing."

We gave Maddie the whole $400. "Get her to stop calling me a wuss," Walker said.

Maddie had argued pretty hard against passing. "This is a big score!" she said, and Walker had smiled at her. "Listen to you, Madeline," he said, "talking like a hardened criminal."

"Oh, fuck you, you fucking pussy wuss," she said, and stalked out of the room.

Walker looked at me and shrugged. I laughed. "You're not just a regular wuss," I said. "You're a fucking pussy wuss."

In any event, Maddie seemed to appreciate the gesture.

39

The target Maddie didn't find was the least lucrative, but maybe the most satisfying for me. It was mid-September and Beth had talked me into an evening at the ballet with Marjorie and Charlie. The headline piece was called *Rubies*. It was a Balanchine choreography, not that that meant much to me. It did to Beth and Marjorie, though, and Charlie and I agreed that it was pretty amazing. We were having drinks at 10th and Terrace afterwards, the rooftop bar at the Marriott. In between rounds I'd excused myself to go to the men's room. I'd been vaguely aware of a guy who got up from the bar as I passed by and followed me in. He was tall, somewhat overweight, but still sort of dignified looking. He spoke as we were standing side-by-side at the urinals.

"You're with Beth Thanh," he said. He had a little trouble with the "th" sounds. I realized that he'd had a few drinks, at least.

"You know her?" I asked.

"Used to know her," he said. "You know about the other one?"

I didn't say anything. Just looked at him over my left shoulder.

"The blond? Margie I think her name is."

"Yes, I know Margie," I said.

"Yeah, but, do you *know* Margie?"

I zipped up and stepped back from the urinal. "What are you saying?" I asked him.

He zipped up and stepped back too. He held up both his hands, palms toward me.

"I'm sorry," he said. "Probably shouldn't have brought it up. But I never could get Beth to bring her along. Not for lack of trying. I hope you're having better luck than me." With that he walked out. Didn't even wash his hands. And he wasn't at the bar when I walked back to our table.

Beth didn't say anything until we were walking back to my place. She had seen him at the bar and seen him get up as I walked past.

"When you went to the men's room," she said, "did you notice a man who got up from the bar as you walked past him?"

"He talked to me in the men's room," I said. "He mentioned that he knew you."

"Oh fuck. What else did he say?"

"He asked me if I knew Marjorie. As in, knew *about* Marjorie."

"What did you say?"

"I didn't say anything. He was drunk. Then he said he hoped I was having better luck than he had. Pretty sure he meant getting you both into bed at the same time. That was your cardiologist, right?"

"Yes, that was him." She sounded somewhere between angry and embarrassed.

"Beth," I said. "He's an asshole. Which you knew, right? I thought about knocking a few of his teeth out, but that would have been more trouble than he was worth."

She looked up at me and smiled. "Defending my honor?"

I smiled back. "And Margie's too. I am, after all, a knight in shining armor."

"And Michael Slattery, MD, FACC, is a very big asshole.

IT TOOK MADDIE LESS THAN ten minutes to find Slattery's addresses, both his house in Raleigh and the apartment buildings near the NC State campus. The house was in Ellen's neighborhood on White Oak Road. That gave me pause. I didn't think another mission there so soon would be a good idea. The apartments were another story, though. He owned three buildings and only one of them had a top floor apartment with a separate entrance, so that had to be the one he used as his poker parlor love nest. I did a recon on a Thursday evening a few weeks later. I found that the ground floor entrance wasn't completely separate. The outer door was unlocked and there were inner doors on each of the four floors. There weren't any knobs on the stairway side so I figured they were fire doors, and I confirmed that by going into the main building afterward. The elevator seemed to be disabled but there was a locked control box on the ground floor. I assumed that Slattery just turned it on when he was using the apartment, for poker or whatever. The stairway led to a landing on the fourth floor, with the fire door and the elevator door on one side and the apartment door on the other side. I didn't see anything that looked like a security system.

Walker rented another van from Enterprise for the following Tuesday. I rode my bike up to get it, first thing in the morning, and then drove straight to Slattery's building, where I was able to park the van right outside the back door. It was the same gray van, or else one just like it, and I figured leaving it there all day would serve as camouflage. I left my bike in the van, because a guy parking a van then riding away on a bike might have stood out to someone. I just parked the van, walked around to the front of the building, and kept on going toward home.

It was raining hard when we approached the building at nine o'clock that night. Walker had his Skilsaw in a backpack and I had my pry bar. We put our gloves on outside and our booties on as soon as we entered the building. Walker laughed as we climbed the stairs to the fourth floor. "This brings back memories," he said. On the ground floor, we could hear music playing loud on the other side of the wall. Fifty Cent, doing "I'm On It." On the second floor, it was Blake Shelton singing "Hell Right." The third floor was quiet, but we could already hear Boogie and Eminem blasting our "Rainy Days" from the fourth floor. "Perfect background sound," Walker said as he made his first cut, on a diagonal from behind the doorknob to the casing. It took maybe three seconds then he waited for a moment. We didn't hear any change in volume from the other side of the wall so he made the second cut. Now I waited a moment, then wedged the pry bar into the cut and popped the whole triangle of wood out. Walker pushed the door open and we were in.

We'd decided that we weren't worried about turning on lights, so we hit the switch just inside the door. As expected, there was a poker table with eight chairs around it and a well-stocked bar table. The chairs were nothing special but the poker table was a nice item. The only other furniture was a leather couch along the wall. There were also two fifty-five-inch TVs on opposite walls. The only thing that looked interesting in the small kitchen area was a Dyson stick vacuum on a wall charger. The bedroom had a queen-sized bed with nightstands on both sides along with a dresser, a tall cabinet and another flat-screen TV. When I looked inside the cabinet I found a high-quality set of poker chips and about fifty decks of cards, maybe half of them open and the rest still in their packaging.

We took all three TVs off the wall and took them down on our first trip. Walker carried two and I carried the poker chips under my other arm. We each took a nightstand on the second trip. I loaded the TV remotes into the top drawer of mine, and a full bottle of Chivas Regal into the bottom drawer. Walker took two bottles of bourbon, I didn't see the brands. We took the poker table on the third trip. That took both of us and the corners were pretty tight. Coming back up the stairs, Walker said, "We're not gonna make the turns with that sofa." I agreed. "They must have taken it up in the elevator." So we took the dresser on our fourth trip, then came back for the tall cabinet and the Dyson vacuum. Before we started down with the last load, Walker asked me if I wanted to do any final mischief.

"You mean, like shitting on the floor?"

"Or just breaking a bunch of shit." He was well aware of why I'd wanted to target this particular place.

"It's tempting," I said. "But it's not something I need to do. Let's just get out of here."

I drove him home and picked him up early the next morning. We'd arranged to meet Marvin at his store at 7:00 a.m. which would give Walker plenty of time to get to work. We ended getting $945 from Marvin that evening plus another $400 a week or so later when he found someone outside of the store to buy the poker table and all the chairs. We kept the whiskey and the poker chips. The whiskey was a no-brainer. Walker wanted to keep the chips "just in case."

40

I spent Friday night at Beth's house that week. We were having a late breakfast Saturday morning when her doorbell rang. It turned out to be a Raleigh PD detective, a strong-looking Black woman about our age. She apologized for coming on a Saturday as she showed her ID and asked if she could come in. Beth asked why. The detective said, "Your name has come up in an investigation."

We all sat around the kitchen table. Beth offered and poured coffee.

"You're a doctor, correct?" the detective asked.

"Yes, an orthopedic surgeon."

"And you?" she looked at me.

"I'm a salesman," I said. "Tractor parts."

"Sorry," she said. "I meant, your relationship to Dr. Thanh?"

I smiled at Beth. "Boyfriend?" I asked. "Would that be too presumptuous?" I looked at the detective. "We've never really formalized anything, but we spend a lot of time together."

The detective nodded. "I was told there was a boyfriend. I was also told there was a girlfriend." She looked straight at Beth, who looked straight back at her.

"This has something to do with Michael Slattery," Beth said, "doesn't it." It wasn't really a question.

The detective nodded again. "Mr. Slattery's home was robbed the other night. He told us you had a key to the property."

Beth looked puzzled. "His home or his apartment? I think I was only in his home once. But yes, I guess I do have a key to his apartment. I never gave it back to him. It must still be in the console in my car."

"Can we get it?" the detective asked, and they both got up from the table. I started to get up too but she told me to stay. "Just Dr. Thanh and me, please."

They were gone for a few minutes. When they came back in they both seemed pretty relaxed. The detective had a key on a plastic key-chain in her hand and Beth had a small sheet of paper.

"Like I said," the detective was saying, "this is very routine. The key isn't really even relevant because there was obvious forced entry. But he mentioned you and Mr. Carver, so you're two boxes I have to check."

"He mentioned me?" I asked.

"Not by name," the detective said. "Like I said earlier, he mentioned a boyfriend. He said he might have given the boyfriend some reason to dislike him." She looked a question at me.

"I talked to him for thirty seconds in a men's room. Actually, I mostly listened to him for thirty seconds. I didn't know who he was at first. He was drunk, he said some things, and I realized who he must be. So, yeah, I didn't like him, but it hardly rose to the level of doing something about." I put a big smile on my face. "I mean, really, I had a perfect chance to help him slip and fall in the men's room. Immediate gratification, right?"

She laughed. "I suppose so. Between you and me? Sounds like he deserved it."

AFTER THE DETECTIVE LEFT, Beth said, "That was strange. But you know what's even stranger? I kind of wish I'd done it!"

I just smiled.

41

APRIL 2019

The best day of 2019, no question, was April 14. Walker called me at about 5:45 a.m. from WakeMed Hospital.

"It's happening," he said. "She had some mild pains late last night, then it started getting serious about an hour ago. She's up on the maternity floor now. They got me doing some paperwork, then I'm headed up there too."

"Is there anything you need me to do?" I asked.

"Say a prayer, OK? Then, if you wouldn't mind, run by the house and make sure I locked up and everything. We left in kind of a hurry."

"Will do," I said. "Both things."

Neither of us is very religious, but it did seem like a good time for a prayer. *Dear God, please watch over Teisha and Byron and their baby on the way.* I threw on some sweats and rode my bike down to Walker's house. The garage door was open, the door into the kitchen was unlocked, and the television was on. Easily fixed. Then I rode my bike around Oakwood for an hour before I went home to shower and get ready for my day.

Byron George Walker, Jr. was born at 11:24 a.m. Eight pounds even, twenty-one and a quarter inches, skin as dark as Walker's, and a bunch of curly hair. When I first saw him, late in the afternoon, he was wrapped up in a blanket like a little tortilla and looked tiny in Walker's hands. "Hey Junior," Walker said. "Say hello to your Uncle Andy. Him and your Daddy been partners in crime for a while now." He looked up at me with a big smile. "Even before we started doing actual crime!"

42

Walker and I drove up to Clarksville a week after his run-in with the protesters. It was a Friday and the work on the HVAC was supposed to start the following Monday.

We took his car. It was still weird to see so little traffic on the roads. Like always, I wanted to see the house with some light and in the dark, so we left Raleigh around 6:00 p.m. We were both dressed in running gear, since exercise was one of the reasons we were technically allowed to be out of lockdown.

The target house was at the end of Lakefront Lane. We knew from Google Maps that the house was completely surrounded by trees except for a narrow open stretch leading to the water. The immediate body of water was called Owens Creek. It's part of Kerr Lake, which Walker happily told me is called Buggs Island Lake by most of the people who live on the Virginia side.

I asked him why. "Not important," he said. Which I took to mean that he didn't actually know.

WE PARKED THE CAR IN A LOT at Robbins Ballpark, which was actually a couple of baseball fields run by the city. We got out and stretched, then took off running. I had a general sense of how we could run through the downtown and end up on Lakefront Lane. It took us about twenty minutes. We ran all the way to the end which turned out to be a rounded cul-de-sac. Apparently, the original plan had been for several houses to be built around the loop. That hadn't been visible on Google maps because of all the trees.

Maddie had told us the house was built in 1977. It looked older than that. It needed paint in addition to the new HVAC that the new owners were about to put in. There was a shiny black Cadillac Escalade parked in front of a two-car garage with its rear hatch open. The back cargo area was empty, which made me think someone had brought something into the house. As Walker and I approached the rounded end of the road, two men appeared at the front door. One was older, with a big belly and a full head of white hair. The other one was our age, or maybe a little younger. Also a big belly, with longish hair and a scraggly beard. I heard Walker chuckle. "There's a certain kind of Southern boy," he said.

They watched us as we circled around the cul-de-sac. I waved. Just a couple of friendly guys out for a run. Neither of them waved back. We were maybe a quarter mile away when the Escalade passed us, a little faster and a little closer than really necessary, I thought.

"Bet we see him again," Walker said. And we did. There was something called Clarksville Health and Rehab near the intersection of the next main road. A good sized campus, I guessed it was some sort of assisted living facility. The Escalade was parked in the lot, with a good view of the road. We turned right, away from where we'd left my car. We'd gone half a mile down the road when the Escalade passed us again.

"Think he's convinced?" Walker asked.

"I'm wondering why he was so interested in the first place." I said.

"Like I said, there's a certain kind of Southern boy, don't like to see a nigger on his street. I think that's all."

"Well, let's go back, then. We'll go into the trees and take a look from behind."

WE ENTERED THE TREES about thirty yards short of the house and worked our way to a point directly behind it. There was a big oak tree there with several low branches and some higher ones that extended out over a good-sized screened-in deck. The roof over the deck was only mildly slanted, with two windows maybe three feet above the roof line where it joined up against the back wall of the house. We both smiled, knowing that we could climb the tree easily and enter through those windows.

We spent another few minutes working our way around the house, finally coming around to a spot alongside the driveway, about halfway down. By this time it was getting dark. We were surprised to see that the garage door was open and the lights in the garage were on. There were two medium-sized SUVs inside. One of them had its rear hatch open and it looked like it had two suitcases and a cardboard box inside. As we watched, a man and a woman appeared. The woman was holding what appeared to be a cat carrier and the man had a good-sized golden retriever on a leash. It was the same older man we'd seen earlier.

"Is that everything," we heard him ask.

"I think so," the woman said.

"OK, in you go," he said to the dog. He patted the floor of the cargo area and the dog jumped in. The woman set the cat carrier in the back and the man closed the hatch. They walked around toward the front of the car, the man getting into the driver's seat. I started running toward the corner of the garage. I heard Walker running behind me.

"What the fuck?" he whispered as he kneeled next to me. The car had started and the backup lights came on.

"Just stay here," I said. "Back up a little. Make sure you can't be seen from the road."

The car was halfway out of the garage. I backed up a little too. My half-baked plan depended on what happened in the next few seconds.

It worked out just the way I'd hoped it would. The man backed into the street, cut the wheels and continued to back up into the cul-de-sac, then he put the car in drive, put his foot on the gas, and reached for the button to close the garage door. He was rolling down Lakeview Lane as the door started coming down and I had plenty of time to slide around the corner and roll under it.

I GOT UP QUICKLY. The door into the house was on my left, past the other SUV which was a Jeep Liberty. There was an exterior door in the back right corner. I opened it and found Walker crouched a few feet away. I turned the lock to the open position then stepped outside.

"That was pretty slick," he said.

"It was too good to pass up," I replied. "All right, let's think about this. We don't have a truck. I don't think we're taking anything out of here tonight. But I do think we take our recon inside. I bet there's a key hidden somewhere in the garage. Let's start with that."

The key was in the third place I looked, in the far corner above the garage door. While I opened the door, Walker swept the area I'd rolled and walked on with a push broom that was hanging on the wall.

We walked through the house, room to room. All the furniture on the main floor looked like good quality, but generally older stuff. Long-used but well maintained. The electronics were a mix of old and new. There were lots of photos on the walls, but nothing in the way of art objects. There was a well-stocked bar in the family room, but not much in the way of back-up stock. Just half-full bottles of a lot of different liquors and a few bottles of wine.

THE UPSTAIRS HAD FOUR ROOMS plus two full bathrooms. The first three we looked in were bedrooms, one of them obviously being used as the master. The walk-in closet was relatively small and mostly full of women's clothes. We found more men's clothes in the two wall closets in one of the smaller bedrooms, including at least twenty suits. Again, most of what we found was older, but good quality and well maintained.

The fourth room was set up as an office with a medium-sized desk facing the door. The first thing that caught my eye when I stepped into the room was a large safe against the left-hand wall, maybe five feet tall, three feet wide and two feet deep. The second thing that caught my eye was an assault rifle leaning against it. It was an M4A1, the same weapon I'd carried throughout my time as a Ranger. Fully automatic. Military grade. Completely illegal for any civilian to own or carry. I picked it up, ejected the magazine, which was empty, and looked it over closely. There were thin smudges of Cosmoline under the barrel and alongside the magazine well. This was a brand new weapon. It had probably never been assigned to an individual soldier. What the hell was it doing here?

Walker had followed me into the room. "Is that an AR-15?" he asked.

I snapped the mag back in and handed it to him. "No, this is a top-of-the-line, current generation US military assault weapon. There is literally no circumstance in which this should be here."

"What do you mean?"

"An AR-15 is a semi-automatic weapon. That just means you have to pull the trigger every time you want to fire a round. You can buy one in any gun store, perfectly legal. You can also buy a high-capacity magazine. I think someone makes a mag that holds a hundred rounds, so great, you can pull the trigger a hundred times without having to reload and it's still all perfectly legal."

"But people modify them, right?"

"That's where it gets illegal. You can make an AR fully automatic. Then you can pull trigger once and spray your whole magazine out. A hundred rounds would take maybe ten seconds, although the gun would probably jam before it finished. We carried thirty-round mags. A gun like this, the M4A1, can empty a thirty-round mag in two seconds on full auto. Or you can set it to fire a three-round burst every time you pull the trigger. The thing is, you don't have to modify it. This is already a fully automatic weapon. And you can't buy one in *any* gun store. This has to have been stolen, and it has to have been stolen from one of two places, one of the manufacturers, or a military unit."

Walker didn't say anything. He held the rifle at what we used to call *patrol ready*, right hand on the pistol grip, left hand under the handguard. "What does this mean for us?" he finally said.

"I don't know yet," I said. "I'm going to have to think about this. This is bigger than us now. Way bigger than a TDM mission."

I pulled out my phone and took photos of the rifle, getting as close as I could to where the serial number should have been. It had obviously been filed down and I couldn't make out any of the characters. I also took a couple of photos of the safe, which had sort of a steering wheel thing on the front with a combination wheel above it. While I did that, Walker looked in all the desk drawers and in the closet. When he was finished, I laid the rifle back the way I found it and we worked our way back through the house, turning off all the lights. When we were back in the garage, I put the key in my pocket. "I'll make a copy of this tomorrow," I said. "We'll put the original back when we come back."

"You think we're coming back?" he asked.

"Oh yeah," I said. "One way or another, I think we're definitely coming back."

HALFWAY BACK TO RALEIGH, Walker held up his right hand, index finger pointing upward. "I know," he said. "I know where I've seen that guy."

"What guy?" I asked.

"The Bubba in the Escalade. It's been bothering me since we first saw him. He looked very familiar and I think I finally remembered where I saw him. At the cemetery. I'm pretty sure he was one of the assholes at the cemetery, all dressed up in their camo gear, carrying their guns."

"Was he the one who called you the N-word?"

"No, just one of the ones standing around. But the more I think about, the more I think it was him."

"Coincidence?" I asked.

"Maybe. Probably. Nothing too remarkable about two gun nuts knowing each other. Interesting, though."

I thought about that. "Now you've got me wondering if he was there to make a delivery," I said. "One of the things I've been thinking, why wasn't the M4 in the safe? Or at least somewhere out of sight? Maybe it just got there and somehow got lost in the shuffle of them packing?"

"Hard to know," Walker said. "But we should get ourselves home. Teisha has a long shift tomorrow, and I've got the baby all day. I need my rest."

43

slept until about 8:30 on Saturday, ate some breakfast, then did a yoga class on YouTube. With all the studios closed down it had been more than a month since I'd taken a live class. After I showered, I sent a text to Mike Stanton: "Got something to talk to you about. Got any time?" My phone buzzed almost immediately: "Always got time for u amigo. I call u in 20."

My phone rang almost exactly twenty minutes later. "Andy, how the hell are you?"

"I'm good, Mike. How about you?"

He caught me up on his life. I caught him up on mine. We agreed that things were weird.

"And speaking of weird," I said. "The thing I wanted to talk to you about? I was in this guy's house yesterday. I happened to see an M4. An A1 model. It looked factory new. It still had some Cosmoline on it."

"One of our guys?" he asked.

"No."

"A civilian?"

"Yes."

"That's not possible."

"I know. But it was there."

Stanton was silent for a couple of beats. "Who's the guy?"

"Can we not go there just yet?"

"Andy, for Christ's sake!"

"I know," I said. "The thing is, I was somewhere I wasn't supposed to be."

"Oh really? Why doesn't that surprise me? OK, you're fucking some guy's wife, in his house, and you come upon a fully automatic assault rifle that has to have been stolen. From us. Probably by one of ours. You know all that, right?"

"I do."

"Are you trying to protect the wife?"

I almost said no, but I held back. Better to let him think that for now.

Instead I said, "I know how important this is. And I won't hold out on you when push comes to shove. But tell me, for now, what will you do with this information. What's the next step. And keep in mind, I'm right here on the ground. I can probably help when push comes to shove."

He was silent for another couple of beats. "Well, now that you mention it. I'm not sure I *know* what to do. Which means I should talk to my boss. Will I be able to reach you later today?"

"Any time you need me. Just call."

THE NEXT TIME MY PHONE RANG, it was Walker. I'd apparently dozed off. It was almost 1:00 p.m.

"The gun guys are back," he said. "They've been parading around downtown. The news just showed them walking into the Subway down on Fayetteville Street. One of them's carrying an anti-tank gun."

I flipped on the TV and turned it to WRAL. Sure enough, there was a flabby-looking guy in a red, white and blue wifebeater with what looked like an AT-4 tube slung over his shoulder. But I seriously doubted it was a live weapon. The AT-4 is a disposable. It comes as a tube packed with a cartridge round. Once you fire it, the tube, which is mostly made of fiberglass, is functionally useless. You can find expended tubes at most Army-Navy stores.

I told Walker that. I asked him if he recognized anyone. He said no, but the news had only shown a couple of faces.

"I'm just getting ready to take Junior out for a ride," he said. "He's been cranky and the car usually puts him to sleep. Want to come along?"

I said no, and filled him in on my conversation with Mike Stanton.

"Wheels in motion," he said. "OK, let me know what happens next."

WALKER CALLED AGAIN ABOUT fifteen minutes later. "So we're driving down Blount Street," he said, "me and Junior. And I see Bubba from yesterday getting into his Escalade parked by the Marbles Museum. Him and the guy who called me nigger the other day at the cemetery. They both put long guns into the back seat before they got in. I drove past them, but I watched in the rear view. They turned left on Martin Street so I turned left on Davie and we all turned left on Person Street. Right now we're heading north on Capital Boulevard, so maybe they're going to Clarksville. I'm going to follow them and see."

"Are you sure that's a good idea?" I asked.

"Why not?" he said. "Junior's sleeping. We have to be somewhere. I'll stay back. If I lose them, I lose them. But it might be interesting to see what they're up to, right?"

Yes, I thought, it might be.

MY PHONE RANG AGAIN an hour or so later. I didn't recognize the number but it was a 571 area code which meant a cell phone in Northern Virginia. Stanton had the same area code. I said hello and a slightly Southern voice asked me if I used to be Captain Andrew Carver. I said yes.

"My name is John Collins. Your old sergeant, Mike Stanton, works for me. We had a talk this morning, and I think you and I need to have one now."

I didn't know the name but I knew who Stanton worked for. "Sergeant Major, it's an honor to speak with you."

He chuckled. I think. Maybe just a grunt. "Yeah, but it may not turn out to be a pleasure. Now tell me, what the *fuck* is going on down there?"

I told him what I'd told Stanton. Then I told him I had new information, a possible connection between the gun and armed protesters in Raleigh.

"Jesus. I just heard from the Chief about that nonsense. He wants me to find out if the retard with the AT tube slung over his shoulder was ever one of ours. Do you have any information on that?"

I assumed the Chief he was talking about was the Chief of Staff for the Army. Hard to believe I was talking with people at this level, the people who actually run the Green Machine.

"If you want a guess," I said, "it would be no. They look like wannabees to me. But that's only my guess."

"What's your guess about the M4?"

"Well, it has to be stolen, right? So that means a military unit, or from one of the manufacturers. Did you see the photos I sent. The serial number had been filed away pretty well, but from what I've read there are ways to bring it back."

"Yes," he said. "At some point we'll seize the weapon and I'm sure whoever gets it will try that. It might not be us, though, as in, *the Army*. As you might imagine, there are jurisdiction issues."

"For what it's worth, I know an ATF agent down here," I said.

"Do you really? That might be helpful. OK, I'm looking at the photos you sent to Sergeant Stanton. I'm interested in the safe. Specifically, why was that gun not in that safe?"

"I have the same question," I said. "What seems most likely to us is that it got lost in the shuffle. We're speculating that the guy in the Escalade had just delivered it to the guy who owns the house, who's in the process of moving out of the house, temporarily, for some work that starts on Monday."

"When you say *we*," he said, "you're not talking about Sergeant Stanton."

"No, Sergeant Major. A friend of mine named Byron Walker. He was in the house with me."

Collins was quiet for a moment. "Stanton told me you were someplace you weren't supposed to be. He implied that there was extra-marital sex involved. That's not what this is, is it."

It wasn't a question. I didn't answer. He was quiet for another moment.

"OK, for the moment, let's say that's none of my business. You were unwilling to give Stanton the names of these, shall we say, persons of interest. That won't fly with me."

"I understand. I don't know anything about the guy with the Escalade, the delivery man. The guy who owns the house is named Wayne Pelham. I was told that he was some sort of political guy in DC. Retired now."

"Wayne Pelham? Are you sure you don't mean Pelham Wayne?"

I'd dug up a sheet of paper that Walker had brought to my place after he first talked to Maddie. It said Wayne, Pelham, and Jessica. Eighty-eight Lakefront Lane, Clarksville, VA. I hadn't noticed the comma between Wayne and Pelham before.

"Apparently I do," I said. I told him about the comma.

"Well, son of a bitch," he said. "Pel Wayne. That makes this even more interesting."

"Who is he?"

"Ever hear of OCS?" Collins asked.

"Officer Candidate School?"

"No, no," he said. "Onward Christian Soldiers. A non-profit. Dedicated to upholding Christian values in the military. Not a bad bunch, generally, but we kept our eyes on a couple of them, including Wayne. He cornered the Chief and the Commandant of the Marines once at a ceremony out at Fort McNair. Went on what the Chief described as a mild homophobic rant with a little racism thrown in on the side. OCS eventually got rid of him, apparently over some financial irregularities. That was late last year as I recall."

"So he might be the kind of guy hooked up with a bunch of pro-gun, anti-lockdown, probably racist protesters?"

"I would think so. But let's remember, our interest, and by that, I mean my interest *and* the Army's interest, is very specific to one gun, and I don't want that gun in anyone's hands but ours. That includes ATF, at least until I have a better handle on the situation."

My call waiting beeped. I looked quickly. It was Walker. I let it go.

Collins said, "Would you be willing to visit that house again?"

"I can be there in an hour. Just over, maybe," I said. "This is, ah, informal, right?"

"And likely illegal," he said. "But justified in my view. Are you a gun guy, Mr. Carver?"

"No. I don't think I ever held a gun outside of my time in service."

"I grew up in a gun culture. Hell, I was president of the Rod and Gun Club in my high school. I hunted from the time I was eight years old. I shot trap and skeet and precision rifle. I can certainly get behind someone wanting to have a gun in the house to protect themselves and their family. But I can't have *our* warfighting weapons out on the street. So, if you'd be so kind, go take the weapon back and let me know when you have it. I'll make arrangements to transport it from there."

I CALLED WALKER BACK as soon as I was in my car, heading north. "What's up?" I asked.

"I'm headed back," he said. "The Escalade pulled into a driveway about eight or ten minutes ago and I saw the passenger get out as I drove by. I swung back around a couple of minutes later. The Escalade was gone but I wrote down the address."

"We can give that to Maddie," I said. "See what she can do with it."

"Yeah, plus I got the license plate on the Escalade."

I told him to give that to Maddie too. Then I filled him in on my conversation with Collins.

"So you're on your way back to the house?" he said. "Want me to meet you there?"

"No, not with Junior with you. You guys go home. I'll be OK."

44

parked in the Rehab lot and worked my way through the woods to the house. I looked into each of the ground floor windows. No lights were on and I didn't see any sign of life. There were no windows into the garage, so I unlocked the side door and opened it a crack. The Jeep was there, the other SUV was not. I already had gloves on so I slipped into booties and moved quickly to the inside door. I unlocked it and waited for maybe ten seconds. Then I opened it and entered the house. I went immediately upstairs to the office room. The rifle wasn't there. It wasn't in plain sight, at least, so I looked in the closet, then I checked the closets in each of the bedrooms and looked under the beds. I went back downstairs and looked in every closet and under the big pieces of furniture.

OK, Wayne must have come back to the house and secured the gun. He may have placed it in the safe. He may have taken it someplace else. Either way, this mission hadn't achieved its objective.

AS SOON AS I WAS BACK on the road, I dialed Sergeant Major Collins. The call went to his voice mail, but my call waiting beeped before his "leave a message" message started. It was his cell number calling so I clicked on "answer" and said hello.

"Mr. Carver, you're on a conference call. Let's just say for now that it's an interested party. What do you have for us?"

"I don't have the weapon," I said. "I entered the house. It wasn't in plain sight and it wasn't in anything I could look into or under."

"It's in the safe," he said.

"Probably," I said. "Hopefully. Unless it's been taken somewhere else."

The other voice spoke. "The safe is free-standing, correct?"

"Yes, sir," I said. In the Army, standard practice dictates that if you're not sure who you're talking to on a telephone, you always assume that it's a superior officer. I suspected that I was now talking to the *most* senior officer.

"John," the voice said. "Four men and a truck?"

"That should be enough," Collins said. "Mr. Carver, what do you think?"

"Well," I said, "they obviously got it up there. No way to know how much additional weight might be in it now, but it's a straight shot up the stairs and no other obstacles I could see."

"John, where could we get those assets?"

"Ft. Bragg, obviously. There'd be a wide range of assets there, including Special Forces. But I think we should use MPs for this. And the more I think of it, I'd recommend that we use the 110th." That didn't mean anything to me but I assumed it was some sort of special-clearance MP unit.

"That's what, five hours travel time from Rock Creek, plus however long it takes to put a team and equipment together?"

"Call it six hours total, best case," Collins said. "That takes us to O-dark-thirty, which is fine. Do we have any reason to expect further movement between now and then?"

They seemed to be waiting for me to answer that. Instead, I said, "I may have another option."

A full beat of silence. Then Collins said, "Go ahead."

"I know someone who can open safes. She does it mostly for lawyers and auctioneers, situations where someone died and the family doesn't have the combination to the safe."

"Hard entry?" the other voice asked. Drills and explosives I thought he meant.

"No, sir, touch and hearing. She's actually a doctor. A surgeon. This is just something else she knows how to do."

Another full beat of silence. "How long?" Collins asked.

"I'll have to call her, see if she's even available. But I can do that immediately."

"Do it," the other voice said. "Then call the Sergeant Major. John, get the other wheels moving too."

We both said, "Yes, sir." I was a little quicker than Collins.

I TURNED INTO A SIDE ROAD and pulled up the best of the photos I'd taken of the safe. I texted it to Beth and then dialed her number. It rang six times before she answered.

"Hey Sweetie, what's this?" she asked. "A gun safe?"

"Yes," I said. "Do you think you could open it?"

"Probably. It looks like a pretty standard combination set."

"What are you doing right now?" I asked.

"Right now?" she said. "I'm toasting a bagel. I've got some chicken salad and I have another bagel. Want to join me?"

"I would," I said. "But I'm sort of on a mission. And it involves getting into that safe."

"Andy? What are you talking about?"

"There's a gun in that safe that was stolen from the Army. I've been tasked with getting it back."

"I don't understand. Are you in the Army again?"

"Not in the Army. But working with the Army."

A pause. "Andy, what's going on here? Is this a joke?"

I took a deep breath. I probably should have prepared for this call a little better.

"Let me start again," I said. "I stumbled into something and I reported it to military authorities. I reported it to a soldier I served with who's in a pretty high position right now. It's a tricky situation for the Army, and the next step depends on knowing whether this stolen weapon is actually in that safe. They're looking at sending a team to confiscate the whole safe, which would be a big step, and it would take time. I thought of you, and I raised it as a possibility, and they asked me to see if you'd be willing."

"This is crazy," she said.

"No argument here," I said. "But it's real."

"Where are you?" she asked. "Where would I be going?"

"I'm in Virginia, just across the state line. I'm on my way back to Raleigh, though, hopefully to pick you up. The safe is in a house in Clarksville, Virginia. It's temporarily vacant and I have a key."

A pause, then she asked, "Is this legal?"

I thought about how to answer. "*Legal* is sort of a gray area. There's national security involved. All I know is that I've been tasked by very senior people."

Another pause. "OK. I'm in. When will you be here?"

"About an hour. Maybe a few minutes more."

"I'll be ready," she said.

I CALLED COLLINS AND TOLD HIM that I expected to be back in the house with my asset in approximately two and a half hours. He told me that he was waiting on confirmation from Army assets but it looked like I'd be well ahead of anything he could put together. He asked me to call as soon as I had something to report.

Beth came running out as soon as I pulled into her driveway. She had the same teardrop shoulder bag she'd brought to Wilson. She also had a lot of questions, which I answered, though not 100% honestly. She seemed satisfied that we were on the side of right.

I PARKED IN THE REHAB LOT AGAIN, but this time we walked along the road. Just a couple out for a stroll. The house was still dark. So far, so good. Beth had her stethoscope in the shoulder bag. I'd put gloves and booties in there too. We stopped at the garage back door and put them on. I asked if she was ready, she said yes, and I opened the door.

We went quickly into the garage, then into the house, then up the stairs. I had a small flashlight that I keep in the car, but when we got to the office room, I turned on the desk lamp and pointed it toward the safe.

"Will that give you enough light?" I asked.

"More than enough," she said. "I usually close my eyes anyway."

She kneeled on the floor, set the stethoscope, and started turning the dial.

"Just getting a feel for it," she said. "It feels like it's supposed to. OK, let's go to work."

She turned the dial slowly now, maybe ten degrees at a time. After maybe a minute, she said, "Got one." She started turning in the other direction. Another minute or so later she said, "Got number two." The third one took a little longer but she finally found it. Then she turned the wheel and opened the door.

The M4 was in a rack along with two other rifles and three shotguns. I removed it and laid it carefully on the floor. There were also nine hand-guns in vinyl pockets on the inside of the door and maybe two dozen boxes of ammunition. I took out my phone and started taking photos of the interior of the safe. I noticed a zippered canvas bag on a shelf above the long guns. I pulled it out and opened it. Four banded bundles of bills, one of which looked like Euros, and six passports. Two of them were standard US passports, for Wayne and his wife. The others were one set of US and one set of Canadian with Wayne's and his wife's photos but different names. I dropped the bag by the M4 and closed the safe.

"We did good?" Beth asked.

"We did very good," I answered. She put her stethoscope back in the bag and I dropped the canvas bag in there too. I slung the rifle over my shoulder and we headed down the stairs.

45

We walked back to my car. Again, just a couple out for a stroll although this time it was more of a power walk. I held the gun against my side in case anyone was watching. When we got to the car, I put it in the trunk and spread a yoga towel over it.

As we pulled out of the parking lot, I dialed Collins' number. As I pressed send, I told Beth that he would probably want to talk to her. "Just answer any questions he asks you," I said.

"Who is this you're calling?" she asked.

I realized that I hadn't told her that, but the phone was already ringing. "I'll tell you after."

Collins picked up on the fifth ring. "Sorry," he said. "I was talking to the MP's. They're assembled now, ETA a little under five hours. What's your status?"

"We have the weapon," I said. "There was nothing else of particular interest in the safe except for a zippered bag that contained three sets of passports for two people and four banded stacks of currency. US and Euros. On quick inspection, all hundreds."

"You have that bag?" he asked.

"Yes. I left the rest of the contents of the safe as it was. Two more rifles, hunting types. Three shotguns, nine handguns, and a lot of ammunition. I took photos of all of it."

"Good work," he said. "You know, I don't think I asked you before, how is it that you know someone who can open safes?"

I didn't answer. I looked over at Beth and smiled. "I'm his girlfriend," she said. "I'm also pretty good at knee surgery."

Collins laughed. "Well, thank you Doctor. You did the Army a solid tonight. OK, Mr. Carver, let's talk about taking that weapon off your hands. I'm thinking I'll send the MP's to Raleigh. That's where you live, correct?"

"Yes," I said.

"I'm also thinking that we don't have to do this tonight. Give me a time and a place, let's say noon or around there tomorrow."

I gave him my address and we arranged that the MP's, probably two of them, would call me when they got close to Raleigh to fine tune a pickup time.

"Just one more thing," Collins said. "The current thinking is that this thing has two parts. Ours is where the weapon came from. These MPs are from the 110th Special Unit and this is one of the things they do. By that, I mean sensitive situations. Everything else, including Pelham Wayne, is civilian. I'll be making some calls tomorrow about how to route that and it probably comes down to FBI, ATF or local law enforcement. You mentioned that you know an ATF agent. How well?"

"We have mutual friends. Her husband is a Sheriff's Deputy. I see them at the gym and we've seen them socially. She's ex-Army, by the way. Retired Master Sergeant. Her name is Estrada, Arielle Estrada."

"Elle Estrada? No kidding? When you see her in the gym, she looks like she could bench press the whole damn thing?"

Beth laughed. I don't think she knew about Estrada's background, but she said, "She's definitely a big girl. The two of them together are really something."

"Estrada and her husband?"

"Well, them too," Beth said, "but I was thinking of the woman who's the mutual friend."

"Another old Master Sergeant," I said, "named Kirsten Connolly. She was one of my ROTC instructors at NC State."

"Kirsten Connelly from *Bahstin*?" he asked. "My God. I had those two working for me in Bosnia. Good soldiers, and yes, they were quite a pair. Please be sure to give them both my regards next time you see them."

Wow, I thought. It's a very small world.

46

called Walker just after 9:00 the next morning. He ended up being my fourth call of the day. Collins had called me just after 8:00 a.m.

"What we'd like to do," he said, "is arrange a meeting between the MP's that are heading your way and Agent Estrada. Can you make that happen? I can, through channels, from here, but the Chief thinks it's better if this initiates at the field level."

I didn't have her phone number but I knew where I could get it. "I can certainly make a call," I said. "I can't guarantee that she's available, or even around."

"I understand," he said. "Make the call. I'll be out of pocket for the next hour or so. Virtual church with my family. But I'll call you after that to see where we stand. In any event, the MP's won't be there before eleven o'clock a.m."

I dialed Denis's cell. He grumbled when he answered. "Andy? You are interrupting an old man's sleep!"

I laughed. "I thought you still got up with the dawn."

"Every day but Sunday," he said. "What do you need?"

"Elle Estrada's phone number," I said.

I heard him speaking to Kirsten, slightly muffled, like he had his hand over the microphone. "It is Andy. He is asking for Elle's phone number." Then to me, "Kirsten will text it to you. I must admit, we are curious. Why are you calling Elle on a Sunday morning?"

"Believe it or not, I stumbled across something that ATF needs to know."

A pause. "You will tell me if there is anything I need to know, yes?"

"Definitely."

Another pause. "Andy, I will tell you something you may need to know. I do business with John Washington."

My turn to pause. "Business, like...?"

"Yes. He sometimes encounters contraband. He sometimes has questions about others who deal in contraband. We have helped each other several times over the years."

"Jesus. Have I told you how I first met him? He came to question me about our first burglary!"

"You did not tell me but he did. On the ride back from Andre's first fight. We laughed at the coincidence. And that is what he believes, that it was only a coincidence. An example of *petit monde*, the small world."

"Well, hell," I said, "I've got another small world story to tell you, but it'll have to wait."

I was ready to hang up, but he wasn't.

"One more thing, Andy. I assume you know about Marvin Townes?"

A little chill passed through me. "What about him?"

"Then you must not know. He is in the hospital. He has the Covid. I spoke with his granddaughter yesterday, his great-granddaughter I mean. The prognosis is not good. He is an old man, and he has other health issues."

"I'll make sure Walker knows," I said. "We'll reach out to Keila."

"That will be good," he said. "Please keep me in the loop on the other matter."

I WAS TEMPTED TO CALL WALKER right away but decided it would wait. Estrada answered on the first ring.

"This is Special Agent Arielle Estrada," she said. "This is an unsecure line."

"Elle," I said. "Agent Estrada. This is Andy Carver. I called Denis this morning to get your number. I've been asked by the Army to contact you and set up a meeting."

"But you're not in the Army anymore," she said. "Neither am I. OK, what's up?"

"First of all, John Collins sends his regards."

"*Sergeant Major* John Collins? As in, the senior enlisted soldier in the United States Army?"

"Yeah. He told me you served with him."

"And you're somehow involved with *Sergeant Major John Collins*?"

"I guess you're about to be too," I said. "Quickly, I stumbled across something and I reported it up the line to an old sergeant of mine who works in the Sergeant Major's office. Next thing I know I'm talking to the man himself and assisting in recovering a stolen weapon. There are a couple of MP's from something called the 110th Special Unit on their way to Raleigh right now to pick up the gun. I was asked to call you to see if you could meet with them."

"What kind of weapon?" she asked.

"An M4A1," I answered.

"And it found its way into civilian hands." she said. It wasn't a question. "OK, I get it. And somewhere in all of this, you told John Collins that you knew an ATF agent, which turned out to be me."

"Yes," I said.

"OK," she said, "when and where?"

"They're supposed to get here before noon. Probably not much before. I was just going to have them come to my place. That's where the gun is."

"Give me your address," she said. "I'll be there at noon."

WHEN I CALLED WALKER, he answered the phone by saying, "I just heard some shitty news."

"I think I may have heard the same news," I said. "Marvin?"

"Yeah. I was talking to my mom. Where did you hear it?"

"I was talking to Denis," I said. "We should reach out to Keila."

"I already did. She's pretty scared. He can't have visitors and the doctors can't really tell her anything. It's in God's hands, my mother says."

Neither of us said anything for a moment. Then he asked about the day before.

"Holy shit!" he said after I told him the highlights. "So what happens next?"

My call waiting beeped. I looked at the screen and saw Collins' number. "Well, I've got the Army calling right now. I'll call you back when I know more."

"WERE YOU ABLE TO connect with Estrada?" Collins asked.

"Yes. She's coming to my place at noon. Are the MP's still on schedule?"

"I haven't heard otherwise," he said. "You should still expect a call from them. It's a Captain named Reece and a Staff Sergeant named Lombardi. They're primarily investigators. I spoke to their CO and she says they're very good, especially the sergeant."

"Are they going to want anything from me?" I asked. "Other than the weapon?"

"That's a good question," Collins said. "My advice to you would be to answer any questions they may have. Same goes for Estrada. I think my office gives you cover on everything that happened after you called this in." He paused for a moment. "I am personally somewhat curious about the events leading up to that call. You admitted to Sergeant Stanton that you were someplace you weren't supposed to be. I'm not going to ask you about specifics. I'm especially not going to ask if any crimes were committed. But I do have some more advice for you. If you made mistakes, don't compound them. Understand?"

"I understand," I said. "Listen, Sergeant Major, I think you're reading too much into what I told Mike. But I do understand, and I appreciate your advice."

47

called Walker back. It turned out he'd been on the phone himself. Maddie had called and her news was very interesting. The passenger in the Escalade was named Truman Wayne and his father had cosigned the mortgage on the house in Oxford. Pelham Wayne. The Escalade was registered to someone named Paul Tribble.

"I been thinking about our probable cause situation too," Walker said. "As you know, that has to be our reason for going in the house. We had probable cause to believe that a crime had been committed."

My first impulse was to laugh and tell him he watched too many cop shows. But this wasn't a laughing matter so I didn't say anything.

"The other thing," he said. "The story has to start with something true. We may have to make some shit up, but let's start with a solid foundation. Which is, I spoke with the protesters at the cemetery and one of them called me nigger. That's where the story starts."

"OK, where does it go next?"

"To your house," he said. "With me telling you what happened and telling you I'd like to find a way to fuck those guys up."

"All true so far."

"Yeah, here's where that ends," he said. "I asked you to give me a ride home. As we passed the cemetery, the crowd was breaking up. I saw that guy get into the Escalade with the other guy. I said, let's follow these motherfuckers."

"And we followed them all the way to Virginia?"

"Why not?"

I didn't say anything. Walker took that, correctly, as me being skeptical.

"Andy, we're making lemonade here. It doesn't have to be perfectly rational, it just needs to be somehow, somewhat believable."

"What happens next?" I asked.

"We follow those boys to Clarksville. We're looking at Google Earth before we turn the corner onto Lakefront Lane. We see there's only one house down there. I suggest we park the car and jog by the house. You remind me they've seen me before. We decide you'll jog down by yourself while I drive your car around the block a couple of times. When you come up on the house, you see the two boys and the old boy standing around the Escalade, and somebody's holding what sure looks to you like a military gun. You decide you need to know for sure. We decide to stake out the house from the trees. Later on, we see an opportunity so we go in."

This time I did laugh, but it was from pure admiration. "That's a hell of a story," I said.

"You just gotta tell it with confidence," he said.

"I'll practice on that," I said. "In the meantime, I got Elle Estrada and a couple of MP's coming by this morning. I'll let you know how that goes."

48

The MP sergeant called me at quarter to twelve. She introduced herself and told me they were ten minutes out. "By the way," she said. "The GPS shows a Krispy Kreme across the street from you. Are they open? With Covid?"

"The drive-through is for sure," I said. "Why, do you guys want some donuts?"

"Captain Reece says they're not to be missed. I'm a Dunkin' girl myself, but he's a Captain and I'm just a Sergeant. So, you know how that goes."

"I guess I do," I said. "Listen, I'll walk over there and get a dozen. I already have fresh coffee working. Anything else I can get you?"

She said no. I walked quickly across the street. There was one car in the drive-through lane and it was Elle Estrada. She saw me coming and lowered the passenger side window. "Great minds thinking alike, huh?"

"I wouldn't have even thought of it," I said. "But the MP Captain has a thing for Krispy Kreme. They called me on the way in. They're just a few minutes out."

"I'm getting a dozen," she said. "Here, jump in and you can show where to park."

ALL BUT ONE OF THE VISITOR'S SPOTS were taken. I suggested that we leave that for the MP's and showed Estrada where to park on Blount Street. As we walked back to my place a plain black sedan pulled into the spot we'd left open. Perfect timing. Estrada and I reached the sidewalk in front of the car as the two MP's got out. They were both in fatigues, both holding masks in their hands, and Lombardi carried a briefcase. They both clocked us immediately.

"I'm Andy Carver," I said. "This is Agent Estrada from ATF."

"Arielle Estrada," she said. "Special Agent, based here in Raleigh, which falls under the Charlotte Field Office."

"Mark Reece," The captain said. "Captain, investigator, assigned to the 110th MP Unit. This is Staff Sergeant April Lombardi, same job, same unit."

We were all standing, a little awkwardly, about six feet apart. Reece and Lombardi were still holding their masks in their hands. No one spoke for a moment until Reece smiled and said, "Normally we'd offer to shake hands but we don't want anyone to be uncomfortable. And Sergeant Lombardi thinks fist-bumping when in uniform in undignified. So how about we go inside and get our business done?"

"Sounds good to me," I said.

I opened the door and stepped aside to let everyone enter. Reece and Lombardi had their masks on and I noticed that Estrada now did too. "Just head into the living room," I said. I left the back door open, and then I walked into the living room and opened the front door. "I have the AC on," I said, "and with the doors open we have pretty good ventilation. I'm OK without the masks if you guys are. And for what it's worth, I've already had it."

"I have too," Lombardi said. We compared our symptoms. Hers had been similar to mine. A week of not feeling well but nothing worse than that. They all took their masks off.

I took coffee orders and Estrada opened up the donuts.

"I'm not a hundred percent sure who's leading this meeting," I said, "except I'm pretty sure it's not me."

Reece looked at Estrada and said, "I think it's me. Is that OK with you?"

She nodded. He looked at me. "You have the weapon?"

I got up and went to the closet by my front door. I came back with the M4 and the zippered bag. I released the magazine from the rifle and handed both to Reece. I dropped the bag on the coffee table. Reece looked the M4 over quickly and handed the magazine, which was still empty, to Lombardi. He handed the rifle to Estrada.

"It's the real thing," Estrada said. "Any thoughts on how it got out of the barn?"

"No," Reece said, "but that's our tasking. I understand you'll be working the receiver side, Mr. Wayne."

"First time I've heard that name," Estrada said.

Lombardi opened the briefcase and took out a file folder. "Pelham Wayne," she said. "Formerly an executive with a non-profit organization called Onward Christian Soldiers. The Army's apparently had its eyes on him for a while. Not our unit, and not related to this matter, but there's a file on him. Here it is." She handed the file folder to Estrada, who opened it and started reading the first page.

Lombardi turned to me. "We understand that you have some information linking Wayne to a militia group here in Raleigh?"

Estrada stopped reading. Obviously that was of interest to her.

"I don't know about a militia group," I said, "although that seems likely. What I do know is that he's connected to at least two people who were here in Raleigh on two separate occasions, protesting against the shutdown, wearing military-style clothing, and carrying guns while they were doing it."

"Yesterday?" Estrada asked.

"And last week. At the cemetery."

"Keep going," she said.

"I actually know more right now than I did the last time I spoke with Sergeant Major Collins. The guy I saw with Wayne was named Paul Tribble. And Tribble was at the protests with Truman Wayne, who appears to be Pelham Wayne's son."

"What's your source on this?" Reece asked.

"Wait!" Estrada said, looking straight at me. "I need to know how you're involved in this in the first place."

"With all due respect," Reece said to her, "you don't. Mr. Carver is assisting in an official US Army investigation. Not to say we won't share that with ATF down the line, but not right now. My instructions are clear on that."

Estrada looked like she had more to say but I held my hand up to her and turned to Reece.

"Captain," I said. "I appreciate that. The Sergeant Major told me I'd have cover from his office, but he also gave me some advice. He said don't compound any mistakes I've already made. I don't think I've done anything indefensible, and I think it would be helpful to everyone if I answer Agent Estrada's question."

He looked over at Lombardi, who had taken a laptop out of her briefcase and was typing on it. Then he looked back at me and nodded to go ahead.

"I mentioned the protest at the cemetery. A friend of mine had an exchange with the protesters. You know him," I said to Estrada. "Byron Walker. It wasn't anything heated or violent, but under his breath, one of the protesters, who turned out to be Truman Wayne, called Walker the N-word. He was on his way here when that happened. He told me about it when he got here. We talked a little bit about teaching them a lesson. But it was purely hypothetical at that point. Just, you know, it would be great if we could fuck these guys up. The next Friday we happened to be in Clarksville VA, outside of Pelham Wayne's house. We saw him talking to Tribble."

"You just happened to be in Clarksville VA?" Estrada said.

"Let me come back to that." I said. "Later on, we watched Wayne and his wife drive off. So we went inside. The M4 was in an upstairs room, just basically leaning against the wall."

"Andy…" Estrada said. I held up my hand again.

"The next morning, I spoke with Master Sergeant Mike Stanton.

He works in the Sergeant Major's office. He was my platoon sergeant in Iraq. We haven't kept up all that well, but I knew where he worked and he seemed like the right guy to call. He spoke with Collins. Collins called me. He asked me to go back to the house and secure the rifle. I went back to the house. I entered the house. The M4 was no longer leaning against the wall. I should mention, there was a gun safe in the room. We speculated, Collins and I, that the gun had been put in the safe. He spoke of mounting a mission to remove the whole safe. That involved your unit, I believe," I said to Reece. He nodded. "But I told Collins that I knew someone who could probably open the safe."

Lombardi spoke up. "A question," she said. "Who the hell *are* you?"

Reece laughed. I did too. "I know," I said. "It probably strains belief. I was a Ranger Captain. Now I'm a salesman. And I just happen to know a safecracker. You know her too," I said to Estrada, who was not smiling. "Beth Thanh."

"Jesus," Lombardi said. "Everybody knows everybody around here."

"Not just around here," I said. "Agent Estrada knows the Sergeant Major."

Reece and Lombardi looked at each other. Lombardi shrugged. "I know Mike Stanton. I play bridge with his wife."

We all looked at Reece. "Ah, I played poker with Doyle Brunson once," he said. "He took all my money."

Lombardi and I laughed. Estrada seemed to lighten up a little. Reece reached for another donut. I took a sip of coffee and continued my narrative.

"I contacted Beth and made arrangements to pick her up. She's a doctor, by the way, an orthopedic surgeon. Somewhere along the line she taught herself how to open combination locks and it's something she does for lawyers and auctioneers. Apparently, it's not that uncommon for someone to die and no one knows the combination to a safe. She took me along on one of those gigs once, which is how I knew about her talent. Anyway, we entered the house yesterday at about nine o'clock p.m., she opened the safe, and we recovered the weapon and brought it back here."

Estrada turned to Reece. "Are you going to have problems with probable cause?"

"I don't think so," he said. "We're not expecting to prosecute any civilians. We think we're going to find that one of ours committed the theft."

Lombardi added, "One, get this gun off the streets. Two, close down the source. I suppose there could be a three if we find that other weapons are missing, but I think it's more likely we'd refer that to your agency. As you may remember, in military justice it's less important *how* we know than *that* we know. We know, we act."

Her computer beeped. She looked down and moved her fingers on the touch pad, then hit a few keys and looked up at Reece. "The VA has a Paul Tribble living in Stovall, North Carolina. He got out on an ELS in 2006. The active duty database has an E-4 Peter Tribble stationed at Bragg. He's an 89A." She moved her fingers some more. I knew that ELS stood for Entry Level Separation, which basically meant getting kicked out of the Army within the first 180 days. I'd had a couple of soldiers separated for medical reasons, but ELSs were also issued for behavior or attitude problems. I didn't recognize 89A, but I knew it was a MOS, or Military Occupation Specialty code.

Lombardi looked up and smiled. "Anyone want to take a guess?" she asked.

"Transportation is the 80s," Estrada said, "but I don't recognize 89."

"Ammunition Stock Control and Accounting Specialist," Lombardi said. "Ammo and guns tend to go together. It can't possibly be that easy, can it?"

REECE STOOD UP AND REACHED for the M4 which Estrada had leaned up against my coffee table. Then he reached into his pocket and came out with a business card which he handed to Estrada. "We'll keep you in our loop if you'll keep us in yours," he said. Estrada nodded.

Lombardi had put her laptop back in the briefcase and she stood up too. "How do you happen to know the Sergeant Major?" she asked Estrada.

"I served with him in Bosnia," Estrada answered. "Best boss I ever had."

"For sure," Lombardi said. "I've heard him speak a couple of times. He's who I want to be when I grow up."

"I though you wanted to be just like me." Reece said.

"In your dreams," she said. "Sir."

Reece smiled at me. "Never ends, does it." He stuck out his hand. "Nice to meet you, Andy. OK if I take a couple more of those donuts?"

Estrada handed him the box. I picked up the zippered bag. "How about this?" I asked.

They all looked at me. "What's in it?" Reece asked. I opened the bag and shook the contents out onto the coffee table. No one said anything for a moment. Estrada reached down, picked up the passports, and thumbed through them, one by one. "I'll take these," she said. "I'm not sure they'll ever be admissible in a prosecution, but I think they belong in my investigation."

"How about the money?" I asked. Reece had picked up the packet of Euros and was turning them over in his hand.

"Spoils of war?" Lombardi said with a smile. "The Captain gets the funny money?" We all laughed.

"As much as the Captain would like a little cash bonus," Reece said, "I don't think the money does anything for our investigation. You guys do seizure all the time, right?"

Estrada nodded.

"All yours then," he said. "You put it into the government till, maybe some small fraction of it comes back to me and April in our paychecks someday."

49

We shook hands all around and the MP's left. Estrada walked to my kitchen sink and started washing her hands. After she finished, she turned to me. Before she said anything, I said, "I know. We have to talk." I poured myself more coffee and we went back into the living room.

"Everything you've heard so far is true," I said, "but not complete."

"No shit," she said.

"Before I continue," I said, "can we leave Walker out of it?"

"For the moment," she said.

I took a deep breath. "*I* was casing the house. *I* was thinking about robbing it. I had intelligence that the house would be empty for a period of time while repairs were being made. I had no knowledge of the assault rifle, or the protesters, or any of what it turned into. But I saw the gun on my recon, exactly the way I described it, and that changed everything. I had to let somebody know. If I hadn't had a relationship with someone in the Pentagon, I would have called you. But it's obviously a military weapon, so I went to the military."

"You've done this sort of thing before," she said. It wasn't a question, but I still nodded yes.

"And this is all connected to Denis Chaisson." That wasn't a question either, but this time I didn't respond.

"Oh, come on Andy. I know all about Denis. It's too much of a coincidence that you're into stealing and he's into stolen property and you're not into it together."

"How much trouble am I in?" I asked.

She sighed. "I don't know. It all depends on how much I might need you to make a case down the line. Your official status as of right now is *informant*. If push comes to shove, I can probably waive prosecution in return for the information you're providing. But you may already have fucked up my case by going into that house. Like Lombardi said, the Army doesn't have the same constraints we have. I'm going to have to think about how to make this work."

"How about Walker, and Denis?"

"If nothing else puts Walker in the house, I can probably keep him out of that. I'm going to need him on the other thing, though, his involvement with the protesters."

"But that makes him a witness, right?" I said. "Not an informant?"

"Probably."

"How about Denis?" I asked.

"Is he directly involved in this specific episode?"

"No."

"Then he's OK. As far as this goes. Now, how about Beth? Is she also part of your little crime syndicate?"

"No!" I said. "Oh, God, no. She has no idea about that part of my life."

"And she hasn't questioned your involvement in this whole mess?"

"I just told her I stumbled onto something," I said. "That's been good enough so far."

"Yeah, good luck with that," she said. "I think I can promise you it's going to come up again. But that's your problem, not mine. Who's the other person?"

"I'm sorry?"

"There's at least one more person involved in this. Your intelligence source. Who told you the house was going to be empty."

I didn't answer. She didn't press it. After a long moment, she stood up and gathered up the money and the passports. She stared at me for another long moment.

"I'm ATF," she finally said. "I care about alcohol, tobacco, and especially firearms. I really don't give a shit about petty theft. So I won't break your balls and I'll try to keep you out of trouble because the end justifies the means. Are you going to be talking to the Sergeant Major again?"

"I don't know," I said.

"You probably are," she said. "Give him my number. Ask him to call me. And tell Denis to expect my call."

I LEFT A MESSAGE FOR DENIS. He called me back an hour later. He'd already spoken with Estrada.

"She is not going to make things difficult for you," he told me. "It has been decided that the information she got from the Army gives her probable cause to begin an investigation. They will deal with the origin of that information if and when it becomes necessary. Apparently, much can be shielded by the simple words 'National Security.'"

"I'm sorry if I brought any heat down on you," I said.

"The real heat is on our friend John Washington," he said. "She is angry with him, because his dealings with me compromise her. But I think it will all end well. She told me that her agency is very interested in these protest groups. This opens a door for her to investigate them."

I asked him if he'd heard anything more about Marvin. He hadn't. He asked me if we had any further plans for *le vol*. I told him we did not.

"That is good," he said. "Best to lay low for now."

50

did just that. My life was quiet and small for the next couple of weeks. I made my phone calls and processed orders. Even though much of the economy was shut down, the people who used tractors and other heavy equipment continued to use them and they continued to wear down and break down.

I only saw Beth a few times, though we talked every day. None of the hospitals were doing elective surgery, but Raleigh Orthopedic had their own surgery center. The volume was down, but she was still doing a few knees every week and doing follow-up visits with previous surgery patients. Beyond that, she was working ER shifts at WakeMed Hospital. With Covid plus the normal flow of emergency cases, the ER teams needed all the help they could get.

On May 26, a Tuesday, we got the word that Marvin had died. He'd been on a respirator for more than three weeks. That was also the day I heard George Floyd's name for the first time.

WALKER CALLED ME in the middle of the morning. "My mother just called," he said. "Marvin's gone. Happened last night."

It wasn't really a surprise. We'd known that the prognosis wasn't good. We also knew that Keila was already talking with a business broker about selling the store.

"There won't be much of funeral," Walker said. "I'll send some flowers from both of us and I'll tell Keila to call if she needs anything."

We were both quiet for a moment, then he asked if I'd watched any TV news that morning.

"No," I said. "Did they mention Marvin?"

"Something else," he said. "Three white cops killed a Black man in Minneapolis, Minnesota. There's a video of one of the cops with his knee on the dude's neck. You can hear him saying he can't breathe and crying for his mother."

"It keeps happening, doesn't it," I said.

"This is gonna be different," Walker said. "You can't watch this and not want to pull the fucking cop off the dude and beat *him* to death."

"Jesus, B," I said.

"I'm telling you, Andy. Watch the news and you'll see what I mean."

I TURNED ON CNN. I didn't have to wait very long before they showed the video again. It was horrible. I agreed with Walker. I was sure plenty of other people felt the same way.

I read something once about murder being a blood crime, either hot blood or cold. I'd watched snipers work in Afghanistan and I'd always thought that kind of killing was the coldest of cold. But the expression on that cop's face, the one with his knee on George Floyd's neck, that was even colder.

I SPENT A LOT MORE TIME watching TV over the next couple of days. I had mixed emotions about the protests. There's something pure to me about people showing up and standing together. I was proud to see so many white people standing with their Black brothers and sisters. But it bothered me that many of them seemed to want to take over the cause. I mentioned that to Denis when we spoke on the phone Thursday morning.

"Do not walk in front of me," he said. "Do not walk behind me. Just walk beside me and be my friend."

"That's a quote, right?"

"Albert Camus," he said. "Though perhaps I do not have it exactly right."

I WAS WATCHING TV Saturday night when Beth called. Not the news, but an episode of *The Expanse*. Andre had turned me onto the show and I was binge-watching a couple of episodes a night.

She was clearly agitated. "Are you watching the news?" she asked.

"No, *The Expanse*," I said.

"Put on the news. I'm watching WRAL."

I switched to Channel 5. And saw Walker, standing in front of the CVS Store downtown with his hands stretched out in front of him. He turned his head to the right and said something to someone off-camera. Then he backed up a couple of steps. It looked like he was trying to block the door, which I could now see had been broken. The camera switched to a shot of a burning trash can, then back to the front door. There were a few other people in the shot now, circling around Walker. It looked to me like they were getting their courage up to rush him.

"I'm going down there," I said. "I'll call you when I know what's going on."

I was out the door in less than ten seconds, my phone still in one hand, my keys in the other. The CVS is on the corner of Fayetteville Street and Hargett Street, maybe three-quarters of a mile from my place. I ran down Blount Street past the Governor's Mansion. There were maybe fifty people milling around in the street, and maybe twenty-five police officers. I cut through the big parking lot between Blount and Wilmington. There were probably twice as many people around the State Capitol—twice as many protesters and twice as many cops. I cut across the southwest corner of the Capitol grounds. From there it was a 100-yard sprint down Fayetteville Street to the CVS.

Walker was nowhere to be seen. People were running in and out of the CVS. The people running out were carrying whatever they'd grabbed in there, everything from six-packs of soda and twelve-packs of toilet paper to cases of bottled water. One asshole was pulling one bottle at a time from a case and hurling it toward a firetruck that was parked across the street. The trash can I'd seen on the TV was still burning. Half a dozen firemen stood around the truck, but they hadn't approached the fire. They seemed mostly concerned with not getting hit by water bottles.

As I stood in the street in front of the CVS, I realized that everyone around me now was Black. And not middle-class Black or college-student Black. Ghetto Black. Angry Black. Taking advantage of an opportunity to get some. To get some of anything they could take. To get some payback for real or perceived prejudice. This sure as hell wasn't about George Floyd. This was *get some for me!*

The next thing I realized was that everyone was either looking at me, or pointedly *not* looking at me. I didn't really feel threatened. It was more like curiosity. *What's this white boy doing here?* I found myself in eye contact with the guy throwing water bottles. He was about eight feet away. He tossed me a bottle, underhand.

"Hey," I said. "Did you see the guy who was standing out here a little while ago? It looked like he was trying to keep people out?"

"He wen' thataway," the guy said, pointing east down Hargett Street. "Wasn't no way he was keepin' alla these niggas outa here. This all ours now, right?"

"I guess so," I said.

"Maybe you best get gone too," he said. "Not threatnin'. Just sayin'."

I took a step toward him. He turned and ran. I set the water bottle down in the street and walked around the fire truck. There was some empty space behind it in front of the Christian Science Reading Room, which had all of its windows broken. I lifted my phone and dialed

Walker. When he answered, I asked him where he was, and if he was OK.

"I'm walking past Gravy," he said. He was only about a block away. "I'm fine. Where are you?"

"Across the street from the CVS. I saw you on TV."

"And you came running like a madman, huh? That shit was only a couple of minutes ago!"

"Well, you were gone when I got here. Seems to be pretty much out of control."

"I could see it was getting there. I did what I could, then I left."

"I'm headed your way," I said. "See you in a minute."

He waited for me in front of the restaurant.

"Bad night for Raleigh," he said.

"How long have you been down here?"

"I came down a couple hours ago," he said. "Right after we put Junior to bed. I was with the people around the Capitol. I felt like I should be there, you know?"

I didn't know, really, but I didn't say anything.

"I fucking hate this," Walker said. "I'm gonna go home and turn on Fox News and this is all they're gonna show. Not thousands of people doing legitimate, peaceful protest. A whole different bunch of people, burning shit, breaking shit, stealing whatever they can get their hands on. And they're all going to be Black. What a waste."

I agreed, but I didn't say anything. Just put my arm around his shoulder as we walked toward home.

51

My father called me on Tuesday the following week. I saw "Dad" on the caller ID and had a flash of concern. He rarely calls me. When someone calls from home, it's usually my mother. Most of the time it's me calling them.

"Hey Dad," I said.

"Andy," he said. "How's everything?"

"All good here. Staying busy. Staying out of trouble." I had a tiny guilty flash as I said that last part. "How's everything with you?"

"Oh, your mother and I are fine. We talked to your sisters over the weekend and they're fine too. No, the reason I called is that I'm going to be in your area tomorrow. I'm hoping we can get together."

I'd known that my father's company had a big deal in the works with a company in Rocky Mount, about an hour east of Raleigh. He told me how it had gotten to the point where I's were being dotted and T's were being crossed. One of those details was a machine in the Rocky Mount plant that either could or couldn't do something that was critical to my father's company. Apparently he was the guy who could make that determination and it had to be done with a physical inspection.

"And guess what," he said, "because of the coronavirus they're sending me on a private jet!"

"Well, that's pretty cool," I said. "I assume you'll be flying into the Raleigh-Durham Airport?"

"No. They can fly right into the regional airport in Rocky Mount. But then the plane goes somewhere else before it picks me up again the next day so I asked if the pickup could be at RDU. I can rent a car in Rocky Mount and drop it off there."

"I've got a better idea," I said. "I'll come pick you up in Rocky Mount and take you to the airport in the morning. You'll stay with me, right?"

We made plans for me to pick him up at the plant around 5:00 p.m. He'd call me if he was going to be earlier or later.

I WAS GETTING READY TO LEAVE for Rocky Mount the next afternoon when I got a couple of emails from the president of my company. The first one was addressed to all of the salespeople.

I am saddened to tell you that Pete Dayle passed away this morning. My sales manager. *You may have known that Pete came down with Covid-19.* I didn't. *You may also have known that he had some other health problems.* He was fat and wheezed when he walked. *We're all going to miss him. In the meantime, I'm sure your thoughts and prayers, like mine, will be with his family.*

I liked Pete. He was an easygoing boss. Maybe a little heavy on the rah-rah, but I always figured that was just part of being a sales manager.

The second email was addressed just to me.

Please call me. I should be available the rest of the day. Otherwise, please call first thing tomorrow morning.

The president's name was Alan Radatz. He'd been a soldier in the late '70s, after Vietnam. Like me, he'd gone to college on an ROTC scholarship. He told me once that he'd hated every minute of it.

I called him from the car on my way out of town. I got his voice mail, so I left a message. He called me back within a few minutes.

"Andy, you got the news about Pete?" he said. "He thought a lot of you. He was very proud when you made Big Dog last year."

"Sad news," I said. "He was a good boss."

"He had a good shot at being the next president," Radatz said. "You know, we do an exercise at our annual Management Retreat about who should succeed us, if something like this should happen. He was my choice to succeed me."

"I could see that," I said.

"You were his choice to succeed *him*."

Really? I thought. "That's, ah, very flattering. And very surprising."

"He certainly felt you were capable of more than just a salesman's role. He never talked to you about it?"

"No, sir. He'd ask me where I wanted to be in two years or five years, but it never went any further than that. I mean, I think all I ever said was I'd like to be doing this and not getting shot at."

Radatz laughed. "Well," he said, "the fact is he did recommend you for the job, and you would have been high on my list anyway because of your performance and your background. So congratulations. It's probably bittersweet, I know, because of the circumstances, but I'd like you to be our next VP of Sales."

I had questions. I started to ask one but he cut me off. "Andy, I have a call on the other line. Can you hold for a second?" I held. It was more like forty-five seconds. "Sorry about that. Listen, I know you have questions, but I have a situation. I'll ask Charlie Wyman to call you. If you have any questions he can't answer, call me in the morning, OK?"

He hung up before I answered. Charlie Wyman is the Human Resources guy. I zoned out for a moment while I considered what had just happened. Did I want to be a sales manager? Not something I'd even remotely considered. But, something worth thinking about.

MY FATHER WAS WAITING OUTSIDE the plant when I drove up. I popped the trunk, got out of the car, and accepted his hug.

"You look good," he said. 'That's usually the first thing he says to me. "You always look good. It's good to see you."

"You look good too," I said. "How'd everything go today?"

"Better than I'd hoped," he said. As we headed off, he told me about the testing he'd done with the machine in question. Apparently, it would do what they needed and more.

We spent most of the ride talking about family things. That's an established pattern. We talk about everyone else before we talk about ourselves. He knew a lot more about what was going on with my sisters than I did, but like always, he acknowledged that it was mostly things he heard second-hand from my mother. She talked to them numerous times each week. He might talk to them once or twice a month, about the same frequency he talked to me.

When it got to be time to talk about me, I told him about my conversation with Alan Radatz. He was pretty excited. "That's great news, Andy! What are you, three or four years into the job? And already a big promotion. I'm proud of you, son!"

He stuck his left fist out and I bumped it with my right.

A moment later, he asked, "Does this feel anything like when you got promoted in the Army?"

I hadn't even thought about that. "Not really," I said. "I only got two promotions, you know, and they were both pretty much automatic. If you don't screw up as a Second Lieutenant, they make you a First Lieutenant in eighteen months. Another two, two-and-a-half years and they make you a Captain. I guess it does feel kind of like when I made Rangers. That was based on merit. But it was also something I wanted. I'm not sure I want this."

"Why not?" he asked. "More responsibility. I assume more money. That never hurts."

"Yeah," I said. "I'm not saying I won't take the job. But if you'd asked me yesterday if I ever wanted it, I would have said *no*. And one thing I can tell you, I don't want to move."

He smiled at me. "Does that have anything to do with the doctor you're dating?"

I smiled back at him. "Is this where you ask me all the questions Mom told you to ask me?"

We both laughed. "She's coming over tonight," I said. "She'll be coming from an ER shift so she's probably not going to stay very long. I told her about your Bojangles addiction, by the way, so she says she's coming hungry."

We both laughed again. My father and I both discovered Bojangles when I came to school at NC State. It was always at the top of his list whenever he visited me.

MY PHONE RANG JUST AS WE pulled up to the drive thru. It was Walker. "I'm here," he said. His normal routine when he rang the doorbell and I didn't answer. I hadn't been expecting him. I realized I hadn't told him about my father coming.

"I'm not," I said. "But I'll be there soon. Just stopping at Bo's to get some chicken. Want anything?"

"Chicken sandwich combo," he said. "You got beer?"

"Could probably use some more," I said. "Hey, I have my father with me. We'll be there in about ten minutes."

"Excellent," he said. "I've got Junior. We'll walk over to the mini-mart and get some more beer. Tell your Dad he's gonna meet his great-godson."

WALKER WAS SITTING IN THE GRASS in front of my place when we got there. He had Junior sitting up, more or less facing him. Walker was playing at patty cake except Junior wasn't having any of it. He seemed more interested in the front wheel of his stroller, which was parked just out of reach. Walker had bought one of those big-wheel jogging strollers on Craigslist.

I parked the car and my father and I got out. I popped the trunk and went around to the back to get his bag. My father walked right over to Walker and Junior.

"Hello Byron," he said. "And hello Byron Junior! What a handsome little boy!"

"Yeah, well," Walker said. "A little bit of me, a lot of his mother. So I'd have to say he's more cute than handsome." He smiled proudly. "But he is really cute, isn't he?"

BETH ARRIVED A FEW minutes later. She was wearing a yellow sundress which surprised me a little, knowing she was coming right from work. Typically she showed up in scrubs so I supposed she was dressed up for company. That actually made me feel good.

Everyone was hungry so we all made up plates and settled in the living room. We made small talk while we ate, everything from Junior's development to the protests and riots. After a while I collected up all the plates and brought them into the kitchen. When I got back into the living room everyone was standing. Walker had Junior in his arms and Beth and my father were facing each other, holding hands.

"It was so nice to meet you," Beth was saying.

"Same goes for me," my father said. "I hope we'll see you again."

"Is that the royal 'we,'" I asked, "or are you including the missing Mrs. Carver in that thought?"

"I'm sure your mother will be very happy to hear all about Beth," he said.

"Yeah, as compared to all the skanks he used to hang with," Walker said.

Beth turned toward Walker and raised her middle finger. Then she kissed the tip of her index finger and held it out to touch the tip of Junior's nose. He grabbed at her finger, but she was too quick for him. Then she kissed the tip again and reached out and touched Walker's nose. "Say hi to Teisha," she said to him. "Walk me to my car?" she said to me.

WHEN I GOT BACK INSIDE, Walker was sitting in my recliner. Junior was in his stroller and he seemed to be asleep. I sat down beside my father on the couch.

"You were asking if we were anywhere near the riots," I said. "Black Panther here managed to get right in the middle of it, trying to keep a mini-mob from looting a drug store."

"Unsuccessfully as it turned out," Walker said. "But The White Shadow here saw me on TV and ran right down to back me up," Walker said. "Literally."

"I did," I said. "I ran right out the door and down the street. All of this was happening less than a mile away. Course, he was already gone when I got there."

"Discretion being the better part of valor," Walker said. "Those people were going in. There were a lot more of them than me."

"It sounds like you made the right choice," my father said.

52

Everyone got quiet for a moment. My father was the first to break the silence. "I grew up in a town that had one Black family. One of their boys was my age. Robbie Johnson. I have very strong memories of everyone referring to him as the colored boy."

"When they weren't calling him *nigger*, I bet," Walker said.

"There was some of that," my father said. "Probably more than I ever knew about. There was plenty of *mick* and *wop* and *spic* too."

My father turned to me. "How much do you know about the Carver family. You remember my father, of course, your grandfather. His father was still alive when you were born but I'd be amazed if you remembered him. He was born in 1900 and he died in 1984, so you were what, two?"

I nodded.

"He came to America when he was about ten, and he still had a little bit of an English accent. *His* father had been in the British Navy and moved the family over here when he was promised a job piloting a ferry between Rochester and Toronto. I actually remember him pretty well, my great-grandfather. He lived to be ninety-two, so he was around until I was nine or ten years old. Anyway, he hated the Irish, and his son, my grandfather, did too. I couldn't tell you if either of them even knew any Irish people, but the hatred was there. It was visceral. In fact, I'm not sure I ever heard either of them say the word 'Irish' without 'bloody' or 'fucking' or "bastard" or 'scum' attached to it."

"Don't imagine they liked Black people too much either," Walker said.

"Well, I'm pretty sure the first time I ever heard the N-word was out of one of their mouths," my father said, "but again, I'd be surprised if either of them knew many Black people."

"Hate doesn't require knowledge," Walker said.

"In fact," my father said, "it seems to thrive on ignorance."

WALKER GOT UP to hit the head. He promised to bring back fresh beers.

After a bit, my father said, "I've always been proud that you seem to be completely color-blind."

"I learned some of it from you," I said. "You and Mom."

"That's nice of you to say. I think I'm *mostly* color-blind. But I have to admit that I have a gut reaction sometimes that I'm not proud of. I saw two middle-aged Black men today. They were *slovenly*, that's the only word I can think of to describe them. This was at the factory. They were supposed to be painting the enclosure around one of the machines. They were moving at about the speed of dirt. I just couldn't help flash on the stereotype of lazy, shiftless Black men."

Walker had just come back into the room. "That's cause that's what you were looking at. Two lazy, shiftless niggers. They exist. I know a bunch of them."

My father looked down at the floor. "That's such an ugly word, but I have to admit that sometimes I hear it in my own head."

"Cut yourself a break, Mr. C. The word's in the world. It turns up in your head. The question is, do you let it back out of your head? Do you treat Black men like they're less than you? We all have impulses. We all have *bad* impulses. What matters is if you can control them. As for Andy..."

"Yes?" I said.

"Andy came to State pretty innocent. Maybe open-minded is a better way to say it. He ended up in a dorm with a bunch of Black guys, but we were mostly athletes. Most of us had discipline. Most of us had purpose. We studied, we practiced, we took it seriously. Sure, we partied too, but Andy got in with a bunch of guys who were mostly *not* lazy, shiftless niggers. His experience with Black guys was regular guys with black skin."

"But better dancers," I said.

"Oh yeah. Natural rhythm. That goes unsaid."

"He's right," I said, to my father. "But it's even more than that. The Army has its share of racists, that's just a fact. It's mostly at the lower levels. You might find a squad that's full of white-power assholes, or even a platoon, which means there has to be a racist squad leader or platoon leader, because most of the people who get to those levels won't tolerate that bullshit. I had a couple hundred sergeants under me over eleven years. I can think of a few that were white power guys, but only a few. In my Ranger company, I had a Lieutenant who went that way. I found a way to get rid of him and make that he'd never make Captain, so I think mostly that process works. Once you get beyond all that, especially in Special Ops, the Army is the most non-prejudiced organization you could ask for. Only one thing matters, can you soldier or not? Can you do your job? In my own experience, most of my best soldiers were Black or brown. Now that doesn't mean everybody *likes* everybody. But everybody understands what it means to go to war together."

Everybody was quiet again for a moment. I'd never really talked like this with my father before. Or Walker.

"We talked about being brothers and going to war together on every football team I ever played on," Walker said quietly. "I maybe never thought about how shallow that was. That whole part about people trying to kill you, I guess that makes a difference."

WALKER AND JUNIOR LEFT AT around 9:00 p.m. I offered to drive them home but that would have involved waking Junior up. Walker took the last of the Bojangles with them. "Little treat for Teisha when she gets home."

My father and I sat in the living room for another hour or so. I had another beer. He asked if I had any decaf, which I didn't, but he settled for some herbal tea. We talked about work a little more, his job and mine. We talked about my sisters a little more. Eventually we got to talking about Beth.

"So what can I tell your mother," he asked, "besides that she's very attractive and she seems to like you?"

"What you're asking is, is this serious?"

"Well, yes," he said.

"It's pretty serious, I guess. I don't think either of us feels any need to run off to the altar, but I think we both want it to last."

"She mentioned her daughter," he said. "How old?"

"Julie's twenty-one. She'll be twenty-two in a couple of months."

"So Beth is a few years older than you." It wasn't a question. "She certainly doesn't look it."

"You'd think so," I said. "She's actually one month younger."

"Wait, how old are you?"

"I'm thirty-eight, Dad. I was born in 1982." I smiled. "You were there, right?"

"It's just that, OK, she had a baby when she was sixteen or seventeen. I assumed a first marriage, but it wasn't that, was it." Again, not a question.

"No," I said. "She's never been married. She and her mother raised Julie. Beth went to college and med school as a single mom. "

"Do you know anything about the father?"

"A little. He's not part of their lives. Hasn't been for a long time."

I told him some more about Beth's family. He told me something I hadn't known, that one of his best friends from high school had been on the USS Blue Ridge, one of the Navy ships in the South China Sea during in the evacuation of Saigon. "He was a deck hand. He told me about pushing Vietnamese helicopters into the water. Wouldn't it be something if one of them was Beth's father's?"

"It wouldn't surprise me," I said. "It already seems to me like everyone I know knows everybody else."

"Well," he said, "I can already tell you what your mother's going to say when I tell her all of this. She's going to say Beth stayed single because she was waiting for you, and you've stayed single because you were waiting for her."

I laughed. "Maybe that's true," I said, "but don't let Mom start hearing wedding bells. We're not there yet."

53

The airplane was sitting on the ramp in front on the General Aviation terminal at RDU when we arrived the next morning. The pilot was at the counter paying for fuel, and he walked my father quickly out to the plane after we said our goodbyes. I called Beth as I was driving out of the airport.

"I just dropped my father off at the airport," I said. "I was thinking about swinging by your place."

"Will you bring me a scone," she said.

"Is that the price of admission?" I asked.

She laughed. "Yes, and one for Julie too."

I stopped at a Panera Bread. They had blueberry, orange and cinnamon crunch. I bought one of each.

My phone rang just as I was turning onto Periwinkle Blue Lane. It was Charlie Wyman.

"Andy," he said, "Charlie Wyman from the home office. Got a few minutes to talk?"

"Sure," I said, as I pulled into Beth's driveway. I left the car running so my Bluetooth wouldn't disconnect.

"First of all," he said, "congratulations. I know it's not the way you wanted to get the job, but we all feel you're the right man for it."

"Thanks," I said. "Pete was a good guy, a good boss. But I have some questions…"

"I'm sure you do. And I have a couple of stipulations, but let's start with you. What are your questions?"

"The first," I said, "the biggest I guess, is whether I'd have to move there." *There* being Trenton, NJ, where the home office was located.

"Ha," he said. "That's actually our first stipulation. No, we don't want you to move here. Obviously, very few of us are in the office because of Covid. But that got us thinking about how many people can, and even should, work remotely once it's over. Alan has a vision of a much smaller headquarters staff."

"How about travel. How much time would I be expected to spend with the other salespeople?"

"Your decision," he said. "However much time you need to do your job, which means helping them reach their quotas, so you reach yours. You'll have to do that remotely for now anyway. If you can figure out a way to do it after Covid, more power to you. Now, we'll want you up here every once in a while, and part of your job will be planning and staffing the trade shows. But how much have you been on the road since you joined us? One week a month? Probably not more than that under any circumstances."

I was nodding to myself. It sounded good so far. "You mentioned my quota," I said. "Does it work the same for a sales manager as it does for a salesman?"

"We use different terminology," he said. "The sum total of the individual sales quotas is your volume objective. And you get bonuses based on achieving your volume objective and several other factors. I have a document that describes Pete's compensation plan for this year and I'll send that out to you. It's probably the easiest way to explain it."

Beth had appeared at her front door while he was talking. I waved and she started walking toward me. I lowered my window and held up the phone so she could see I was on it. She held out her hand and whispered, "Give me the scones."

Wyman and I talked for another few minutes. He'd answered my most important questions and the two other stipulations weren't anything that bothered me. I'd have to sign a non-compete and I'd have to complete a program on maintaining a fair and harassment-free workplace. No problem at all.

WHEN I GOT INSIDE, Beth and Julie were sitting at their kitchen table. Julie was typing on her laptop. There was a mug of coffee and a scone on a plate in front of one of the empty chairs.

"What's going on at the home office?" Beth asked.

"They're offering me a promotion," I said.

"Andy, that's terrific!" she said. Then her smile faltered "Oh, wait…"

"I won't have to move," I said. The smile came back. "That would have been a problem for me too."

Julie looked up from her typing. She smiled at her mother, then at me. "Oooh, is this where you get all lovey-dovey? Start talking about making a life together?"

Beth stuck out her tongue at Julie, and nodded to me. "Tell her where your home office is."

"Trenton, New Jersey," I said.

"Oh, yuck. OK, I get it. Nothing to do with your relationship. Nothing at all. Yeah, right." She stuck her own tongue out at both of us, picked up her laptop and left the room.

I waited until I heard Julie climbing the stairs before I said, "It actually has a lot to do with our relationship."

She nodded. "I was wondering when we were going to talk about this."

I started to say something, but she held up her hand. "Let me go first," she said. "I've sort of been rehearsing this."

I waited. She lowered her voice almost to a whisper and said, "I haven't been with Margie for a while now. And it's not just because of Covid. I was starting to feel like that was cheating on you."

I said, "I haven't been with anyone else for a while either."

She stood up. "Let's go for a walk. This isn't a conversation we should have at a whisper." She called to Julie that we were going out and led me to the door.

We walked toward the woods across the street, the same place we'd freed the squirrels almost two years ago. I mentioned that. Beth said, "Yes. It's a little hard to believe, isn't it. And to think that, back then, my first instinct was to rescue Julie from you."

She took my hand and we walked along.

"I haven't been *with* Margie but we still talk all the time. Sometimes we talk about you. She has a theory, that the reason you never got married was that you were waiting for me. And the reason I've never been serious with a man is that I was waiting for you. She's a pretty hopeless romantic."

"So is my mother, I guess. My father says she'll say the same thing.

"Your father is very nice," she said. ""I was expecting more questions about *us*. But you probably got them all after I left."

"Yeah. He used the 'your mother's going to want to know' approach. I promised to call her, by the way. I need to remember that."

"What are you going to tell her?"

"Well, that's it, isn't it?" I said. "What should I tell her?"

She was quiet for a moment. "If I could tell my mother," she said, "I would tell her that I've fallen in love with Andy Carver. I would tell her that I'd like to spend the rest of my life with him. I would tell her that doesn't have to mean marriage, but it might be nice, when Julie moves in with Andre—which, by the way, they just told me about last night—if we started talking about living together too."

"Wait a minute," I said. "The two of them?"

"Oh yes," she said. "But I've been expecting it. Truthfully, I've been encouraging it. I've told Julie many times that it wouldn't bother me at all if they moved in together. They're too young to get married, but they're not too young to take the next step. If they live together for a couple of years and still want to get married, I'll be all for it."

"Well, damn," I said. "OK, I agree with you all the way. It's a good intermediate step for them. But, are you thinking the same thing about us?"

"I suppose so," she said. "It seems like a logical next step. If you feel the same way, of course."

It was my turn to be quiet for a moment. I wanted to get this right. I stopped walking and turned toward her and said, "When I talk with my Mom, I think I'll tell her that I've fallen in love with Beth Thanh. That we're talking about spending the rest of our lives together, but she, being practical, has proposed that we move in together and see how that works for a while. I think that will make my mother happy. Will it make you happy?"

She pulled me into a tight embrace. "I think it will," she said.

WE TALKED ABOUT DETAILS as we continued walking. I thought my place would be easy to rent and a good investment as a rental property. She thought her place would be fine for a while, but eventually we'd want something that was more *ours* together. We decided that we'd pool our income but separate our savings and the equity in our houses for now. About ten minutes into it, I had a moment when I wondered if all of this was really happening. We'd gone way past where I thought this would go when I drove up to Beth's house less than an hour ago. But then I thought, *yes, it's happening, and I'm good with it.*

I LEFT A LITTLE AFTER 11:00 A.M. When I got home, I went up to my office and turned on the computer. Then I went back downstairs to get some iced tea and found Walker at the door. He had Junior on a carrier on his back today. I let them in and helped him shed the carrier. I poured us both some tea while he reached into his fanny pack for a juice box for Junior.

"Maddie called this morning," he said.

"She still mad at us?" I asked.

"No, she's still not happy we bailed on Clarksville, but she's moved on from it."

We hadn't told Maddie the whole story about Clarksville. We—mostly me, but Walker was OK with it—had decided she didn't need to know. We told her we'd done a recon, but we'd been seen and followed. Which was true, of course. In any event, we told her we'd decided it was too risky after that.

"Maddie has something new," Walker said.

There was something in the way he said it. "But there's a *but*…," I said.

"We're not invisible anymore," he said. "That scares me a little. It scares Teisha a lot."

I nodded.

"This has been good," he said. "The extra money's made a big difference. We've even built up some savings. But Teisha thinks, and I agree, that it's time to stop."

"That makes three of us," I said.

Now he nodded. "I thought you'd feel that way," he said, "I was hoping. Anyway, we came to another decision, Teisha and me. I'm gonna get out of teaching. I'm going to find a job that pays more." He chuckled. "Teisha says I should find a job like yours, be a stay-at-home Daddy."

A JOB LIKE MINE. Why not *my job*? He'd be good at it. Did I have the authority to hire him? I'd have to find out how that worked.

"Andy?" Walker said. I realized I'd zoned out on him for a minute.

"Sorry," I said. "Just thinking it's a big change. And speaking of change, I have something to tell you. Beth and I, we're going to move in together."

He half-opened his mouth, then closed it. Then he did it again. Walker, speechless, for maybe the first time since I've known him.

"Well. God. Damn," he finally said. "I can't wait to tell Teisha. She's been saying, if anyone could tie you down, it'd be Dr. Beth. I don't think she really believed it, and I'm not sure I believe it." He put his arms around me and squeezed. "But I'm happy as hell for you, brother."

WALKER AND JUNIOR STAYED for a few more minutes. My phone rang just after they left. Estrada.

"What are you going to be doing at around four o'clock?" she asked.

"Nothing in particular," I said. "I'm working, but I don't have a lot left to do today."

"I'm meeting those two MP's out at the airport, at the National Guard facility. They're stopping on their way to Bragg. You're invited."

"I can be there," I said, "Want me to bring Krispy Kremes?"

She laughed. "No, this time Reece wants BBQ. Someone told him about Clyde Cooper's. Would you be able to stop in there and pick up a couple of meals to go? Pork for Reece and chicken for Lombardi, plus whatever you want. Nothing for me. Get a receipt and I'll reimburse you."

"Sure," I said. "But I'll get the check. You got the last one."

"Whatever," she said. "OK. See you there. Four o'clock p.m."

54

got to the Guard base before Estrada. The sentry had my name, though, so I parked in the lot, put on my mask, and carried my Clyde Coopers bag into the main building where a PFC in an olive drab mask led me upstairs to a small conference room looking out over the ramp. The same private led Estrada in about ten minutes later just as a UH-60 Black Hawk taxied up to the building. I watched Reece and Lombardi jump out and head inside.

I made a little small talk with Estrada while we waited for the MPs. A different private led them in, all three of them wearing the olive green masks. Reece went immediately to the Coopers bag. He opened it and looked inside.

"That smells good," he said. "OK, we're a little pressed for time. What we came to tell you is that we're making an arrest tonight. April, you want to run it down for them?"

Lombardi handed each of us a folder. I opened mine to see a photograph stapled to a document I recognized as the summary page of a service record.

"Michael James Merriman, E-5 sergeant," she said. "This is the man who removed the M4 you recovered, and two others, from an inbound shipment at Ft. Bragg. Records were falsified in an attempt to cover the theft. Merriman transported all three weapons to a still unidentified third party who attempted to remove the serial numbers using a combination of chemicals and a grinding tool. As you saw, that action was successful at the visual level, but we were able to raise the serials and match them to the shipment."

"Help from FBI," Reece said. "They're the best at that sort of thing. No offense, Agent Estrada."

"None taken," Estrada said. "Good to know the Feebs are good for something."

Lombardi continued. "Merriman got the weapons back from the unidentified third party about three weeks ago. He has two of them stored in an attic space at his girlfriend's apartment. We don't think she's involved. The other one, the one you recovered, was given to Peter Michael Tribble, Specialist E-4, who we believe assisted with the falsification of records. We don't have proof of that, nor do we have proof that Specialist Tribble passed the weapon along to his brother, Paul Harbin Tribble." She paused and looked at Estrada, then me. "You remember those names, right?" We both nodded.

"But we know that both of those things happened," she continued. "And that Paul Tribble passed the weapon in turn to Pelham Wayne. Again, though, I want to stress that we don't have actual proof beyond Merriman."

"But we know for sure that Wayne ended up with the gun," I said.

"Let's come back to that," Reece said. "Our Sergeant Merriman has a reputation as a tough guy. He's very popular among a certain element at Ft. Bragg. Sergeant Lombardi's investigation paints him more as a bully. And an abuser." He nodded to her to continue.

"The girlfriend has been treated for injuries very suggestive of domestic abuse. The neighbors have confirmed at least verbal abuse. Lots of it. She's been given the opportunity to press charges by local law enforcement, but she's always declined. It's immaterial anyway, he's going down for the gun, but it's part of a profile we see too much of. And we take particular delight in addressing."

Reese chuckled. "It's entirely possible that, during the arrest, Sergeant Lombardi is going to kick Merriman's testicles into his upper esophagus."

Lombardi rolled her eyes above her mask. "He's exaggerating," she said. "He does that. No, we're just going to explain to him how domestic abusers tend to get treated at Fort Leavenworth, which he's likely going to be calling home for a while. We'll give him a chance to roll on Tribble in return for keeping the domestic issue out of his jacket."

"Timing," Reece said. "Merriman and Tribble are both on four to midnights tonight. They work in different buildings. Merriman, in fact, is all the way out by Pope Field. We're coordinating with the MPs at Bragg. Sergeant Lombardi and a couple of the locals will take Merriman. He'll be charged immediately under Article 121, larceny of military property. At the same time, I and some more of the locals will pick up Tribble. He'll be held on suspicion. Depending on how quickly we can convince Merriman to roll, we may be ready to charge Tribble as early as tomorrow morning."

"What does that mean for me?" Estrada asked.

"We're officially notifying you of our suspicion that a civilian within your jurisdiction, Paul Tribble, is involved in this conspiracy," Reece said. "We plan to keep a lid on this until at least this time tomorrow. I assume you'll make arrangements to pick him up during that window?"

Estrada nodded. "I'll coordinate with the US Attorney here in Raleigh tonight, then probably the Granville County Sherriff. Best case, we'll be outside his house when he wakes up tomorrow morning."

"What about Wayne?" I asked.

"That's where it gets tricky," Estrada said. Reece and Lombardi both nodded for her to continue.

"If we can get to Wayne through Tribble," she said, "we don't have the complication of *you*."

They were all looking at me now, straight-on cop eyes visible above their masks. I felt a flash of, not guilt, but embarrassment.

"Will that work?" I asked.

"Probably," Estrada said. "Especially if the Army shares its leverage on the brother."

"Which we will," Reece said. "I've been given guidance that the big fish here is Wayne. We'll make deals with Merriman and Tribble to clear you a path to Wayne."

Estrada nodded. "OK, if there's nothing else, I need to get to work." She shook hands with Lombardi and Reece and then turned to me. "Why don't you plan to meet me at Denis's gym, tomorrow at about four." It wasn't a question. I nodded that I'd be there.

55

When I got home, I found emails from Radatz and Wyman. Radatz said he knew I'd talked to Wyman, but if I had any questions for him personally I should feel free call at any time. Wyman sent the document describing Pete's compensation plan. I scanned it quickly. Base salary, $132,000. Incentives up to $45,000, based on individual performance and overall profitability. Upgraded company car. I could be looking at more than twice what I made last year, not to mention the possible opportunity for Walker.

Radatz said to call at any time, so I did. He seemed happy to hear from me.

"Have you made your decision?" he asked.

"I think so," I said. "I wouldn't have wanted to move to Trenton, but Charlie put my mind at ease about that. The main thing I wanted to ask you about was covering this territory. How much latitude do I have in hiring my replacement?"

"That's a good question," he said. "Pete had pretty wide latitude, but he had a lot more experience hiring salespeople than you do, didn't he?"

"That's part of the reason I'm asking," I said. "The other part is that I know a guy I think would be a perfect fit. He's never been in sales. He's a middle school gym teacher. And he's a good friend of mine.

I guess what I'm asking is, does any of that prevent him from being considered?"

He laughed. "He's not a relative, is he?"

"No."

"OK, so we don't have a nepotism problem. Why do you think he's a good fit for the job?"

"He's good at the same things I'm good at. Better at some of them. He's probably better suited to the job than I was when I started."

Radatz laughed again. "Talk to Charlie," he said. "Set up a time for them to talk on the phone. We'll see where that takes us. Now back to you. Are you the new VP of Sales?"

"I guess I am," I said.

WE TALKED FOR A FEW more minutes, then I went downstairs and made myself some dinner. I ate it in front of the TV, watching Lester Holt do the news. Between Covid and the continuing backlash over George Floyd's death, there wasn't much to be happy about.

After the news, I called my mother. She answered on the first ring. "So, tell me all about Beth," she said. I told her the basics, then answered all her questions. Half an hour later, she let me go. After that, I called Beth and told her about all of the conversations I'd had today.

Towards the end, I asked her if she was having any second thoughts.

"Do *you* have any second thoughts?" she asked.

"None at all," I said. "I love you."

"I love you too. Good night."

JUST A FEW SECONDS after we hung up, my phone beeped another text message. Two hearts. I texted two back at her.

56

Walker and I had made plans to work out at Denis's gym the next morning. Andre was there when we got there, finishing up his own workout. We all shot the shit for a while and made plans to run together the next morning, which was a Saturday. Andre said Julie would probably be there too. After they left, Walker and I got down to it. We worked hard for almost an hour and a half, finishing up with four sets of fifty sit-ups. Walker sounded like a freight train grunting through the last set.

James and a few of his boys were sitting outside the tattoo shop when we came down the stairs. He greeted us happily. "Yo, Cassius and Rocky!"

"How's business?" I asked him.

"Oh, you know," he said. "Ain't never that good, ain't never that bad. Payin' the bills, mostly. Denice been good about the rent since the Covid started."

I noticed that one of the others was looking sort of sideways at Walker. Then I noticed that Walker was looking straight at him.

"Yeah, I'm him," Walker said. I assumed he was talking about Byron Walker, ex-football player.

"Thought it was you," the guy said. "Why you do that?"

"Because it wasn't helping," Walker said. "A Black man got murdered and people came out to protest. That was righteous. Other people came out to break shit and steal. How was that helping George Floyd? How was that helping you for Christ's sake?"

"Got me some shit," the guy said. "Got my voice heard."

"By stealing from a drug store? By breaking their windows?" Walker was speaking quietly, but it still felt loud. No one else was talking now. The guy finally lowered his eyes. "Guess I a different kinda nigga than you," he said.

"Damn straight," Walker said. Then to me, "C'mon."

WE'D DRIVEN OVER in Walker's car. He didn't say anything as we got in and drove away. I waited until he was ready to talk.

"You didn't see that asshole at the CVS, I guess," he finally said.

I said no.

"He was one of the first ones to go in. Not *the* first, he didn't want to fuck with me. But a couple of other guys went behind me and threw a trash barrel through the window. That's when I decided to give it up. As soon as I walked past him, he ran right into the store. He must have been in and out before you got there."

"Disappointing to see that he's one of James's boys," I said. "I kind of like James."

Walker said. "Can't fault him for keeping bad company I suppose."

He was quiet for a few blocks. Then he said, "I am a different kind of nigger. I do a different kind of stealing. Not sure I have the moral high ground here."

I thought about that. "Not sure it matters," I finally said. "I think there's bad and worse in this situation. What we've been doing is definitely bad, you can't escape that. But turning a peaceful demonstration into looting and rioting is worse."

"A matter of degree, huh? OK, I can live with that. But it's another thing that makes me glad to put that shit behind us." He smiled. "Don Cheadle. Made that movie. Moving on."

"Speaking of which," I said, "I want to talk to you about a job."

"A job for me?

"Yes," I said. "My job."

We were just pulling up at a red light on Person Street. He turned to me and said, "Say what?"

"I'm getting promoted. Vice President of Sales. Gotta hire someone to replace me, so I'm thinking why not you?"

"Wait a minute," he said. "First of all, that's amazing. Congratulations!" A car honked its horn behind us. The light had turned green. Walker drove forward across the intersection and pulled over to the side. "That's fucking amazing!" he said again. "What happened to, what's his name, Pete?"

"Died of Covid," I said. Walker's face fell, like he was sorry he asked.

"I know," I said. "Dead men's shoes. Bloody wars and dread diseases."

I could see him processing that. I was actually surprised he didn't know the reference, but he put it together pretty quickly. "British Army?" he asked.

I nodded.

"Well, still," he said, "congratulations. But, shit, does this mean you're moving to New Jersey?"

"Nope," I said. "I can stay right here. And hopefully show you the ropes and keep you out of trouble."

WALKER HAD LOTS OF QUESTIONS. I had some of the answers and told him he'd get the rest when he talked to Charlie Wyman. Finally, he said, "One last thing…"

I waited.

"I won't have any problem working for you," he said. "You know I love you, and I respect you." He was getting a little choked up. "Don't ever worry about giving me orders or hurting my feelings or any of that shit. I can be coached. I always could. You know what I'm saying, right?"

"Sure," I said. "You're Cheadle. But I'm Clooney."

He flipped me the finger. I just smiled.

57

was back at Denis's gym at four o'clock. I found Denis himself sitting
with James outside the tattoo parlor. I told him I was meeting Estrada.
He told me she wasn't there yet and waved me to a chair.

James said, "Thought we was gonna have some fireworks before."

I nodded.

"Saw them both on the TV that night. Your boy standing guard, like.
My boy just itchin' to do some damage. Thought I saw you come by a
minute later, but I wasn't sure about that."

"Yeah, I was there," I said. "I saw Walker on the TV too. I live nearby."

"So you came a runnin'?" he laughed. "Pretty sure most of the white
people goin' in the other direction about then."

"What can I tell you," I said. "Seemed like a good idea at the time."

Denis asked what we were talking about. Estrada drove up as I was
starting to explain.

She got out of the car and walked over to us. "Denis," she said.
"James."

They both said hello.

"Andy. Let's take a walk."

I got up and followed her. She waited until we were fifty feet down
the sidewalk before she started talking.

"Everything went as planned at Ft. Bragg," she said. "Better than planned, actually. Merriman rolled on Tribble right away. Tribble asked what kind of a deal he could get. Reece asked him what he had to trade, and he told them his brother never touched the weapon, it went directly from Merriman to Truman Wayne to Pelham Wayne. We're not sure we believe that, but I still grabbed the brother first thing this morning and then we went back and picked up both the Wayne's. Papa Wayne's lawyer showed up after lunch, and they'll all be out on bond before suppertime. The three civilians, I mean. Merriman and Army Tribble aren't going anywhere."

"So you'll be able to make your case?" I asked.

"Without you, you mean? We can probably get at least one of them on receiving stolen property based on testimony. Peter Tribble can give us Truman Wayne, or else Merriman can give us Paul Tribble. Either of them could give us Pelham Wayne, but only on the receiving charge. It's unlikely we can get anyone on possession of an illegal firearm without producing the actual weapon, and doing that brings you into play, which at best is an illegal search and seizure."

I started to speak, but she waved me off.

"It's been decided that the United States Government is satisfied that one stolen military weapon is off the streets, the other two have been recovered, and the military side of the theft ring has been closed down. It has further been decided that we'll take what we can get on the civilians, even if one or more of them walks on these charges. Because," now she smiled, "we found several very strong connection points between Paul Tribble, Truman Wayne, Pelham Wayne especially and a Southern Virginia-based white power group that has been designated as a domestic terrorist organization. They were prominent in Charlottesville back in '17. FBI has been trying to break them since well before then. They think it's going to be easy from here."

"That all sounds good," I said. "I have to ask, though…"

"You are not on anyone's hook. Byron Walker is not on anyone's hook. Your mystery member is clean too, and so is Dr. Thanh, who I'm

willing to believe was never part of your little game. But Andy, I'm warning you…"

"I understand." I said. "I give you my word. I already gave Sergeant
Major Collins my word. No more extracurricular activity."

"OK," she said. "But let me finish. I'm warning you that if my
John ever finds himself in trouble that can be traced back to you—or
Denis!—I will come after you. Understood?"

I tried to look like I didn't know what she was talking about.

"John knows what I know about you, Andy. And I'm sure you know
what Denis knows about John. So let's all continue to be friends, yes?"

"Works for me," I said.

DENIS ASKED ME TO COME upstairs after Estrada had gone.

"You are *d'accord* with Arielle?" he asked. "Everything is OK?"

"She says so," I said. "She did sort of threaten me. You too actually."

"She has made her position clear to me in the past," he said. "Several
times. But I can think of no situation in which John would be at risk
from me. No situation in which I would incriminate him, at least."

"Honor among thieves?" I asked. With a smile.

"Honor among *men*," he said. "I have given him my word."

He opened his little refrigerator and pulled out two beers. We each
drank some.

"There is something we must talk about," he said. "It is time for you
to retire from stealing."

I started to speak. He held up his hand.

"It is also time for me to retire from my own activities beyond the
law. Do you believe in *trois*, that certain things happen in threes?

I smiled. "I've never known you to be superstitious," I said.

"I have my beliefs," he said. "I admit, not all of them are rational, but
they are what I believe."

He took a sip of beer.

"The first thing, Marvin's passing. I knew him a long time." He crossed himself. "The second thing. This whole situation with the Army gun." I nodded. "The third thing. I have cancer."

"Jesus, Denis!"

He held up his hand again. "It is cancer of the prostate. It was diagnosed early. It is treatable. My doctor has very high confidence that this will not kill me. But it has made me think. I do not need the money. I do not need the risk. I do not want another shoe to drop. So, with Marvin gone, and me no longer an option, it only makes sense for you to retire too, no?"

I set my beer down and put my arms around him. He was stiff at first, but then he relaxed and put his arms around me too. We held that for a moment, then we both let go.

"The fourth thing," I said. "Walker and I already made that decision. We're not invisible anymore. That scares him and it scares his wife even more. What scares me is Beth. She seems willing to believe that we just stumbled into the gun thing. But I don't want to press it. I want her to see me as a guy still serving my country, not a crook."

58

spent the night at Beth's place. Her alarm went off at 6:30 a.m. the next morning. She was working an eight-to-four shift in the ER at WakeMed.

I stayed in bed while she showered and dressed, then we both went downstairs for breakfast. We walked out to our cars together. She kissed me and told me she loved me. I said it back.

The plan for the day was to meet up at my place for our run. Walker was just pulling in when I got home. He had Junior with him. I held Junior while Walker set up his jogging stroller. All the while, Junior was pointing at him, saying, "Dada, dada, dada."

"When did that start?" I asked. Junior hadn't done any talking yet as far as I'd known.

"Just the other day," Walker said. He smiled. "Boy only got one word, but it's a good one."

JULIE AND ANDRE SHOWED UP a few minutes later. Julie was wearing yoga tights and a running bra crop top. I couldn't help thinking how her appearance had changed over the last two years. She'd been very pretty in a nineteen-year-old girl sort of way. Now she was a beautiful young woman.

We all stretched, then started off running down Blount Street. The plan was to take turns pushing the stroller with Walker taking the first turn. Andre and Julie led the way, then Walker, then me.

We had to stop for traffic at Martin Luther King Boulevard. I stepped up and took over the stroller. Andre took over from me when we turned onto the Walnut Creek Greenway which took us out behind the NC State Campus. We switched about every mile on the Greenway. I had the stretch from the end of the Greenway to Hillsborough Street, which left us with about two and a half miles to go. Julie was dragging a little by that point.

"Why don't you guys race yourselves down Hillsborough Street," she said. "Junior and I will take our time."

The three of us pushed ahead and ran the two miles to the State House in a little over twelve minutes, quite a bit faster than the eight-minute mile pace we'd been running with Junior. Andre just nosed me out as we sprinted the last fifty, sixty yards.

THERE WERE A HUNDRED OR SO people gathered on the east side of the Capitol grounds where a seventy-five-foot tall monument stands. It has a statue of a Confederate soldier at the top. There were two people perched about fifteen feet up where, up until last weekend, there'd been two other soldier figures. They'd been pulled down on the first night of the protests by a crowd of mostly white protesters. The two on the monument now were white. I watched Walker shaking his head at them.

"In from the suburbs to spearhead the revolution," he said. "How many of them thought Black lives really mattered two weeks ago?"

I SPENT MOST OF OUR waiting-for-Julie time stretching, trying to work a kink out of my left shoulder. I'd been noticing more aches and pains like that over the last few years. Thirty-eight isn't really old, except it is.

When Julie and Junior did arrive, we all walked north on Salisbury Street then east on Edenton. There was another group of people gathered at the top of the Bicentennial Plaza, a pedestrian mall between the Department of Agriculture and the Museum of History. This group was also mostly white. In fact, it was all white except for a small group of Blacks who seemed to be counter-protesters. The main body wore MAGA hats and carried Trump flags. I noticed quite a few holsters and some long guns slung over shoulders. I also noticed John Washington, in uniform, standing with two Capitol Police officers on the opposite side of Edenton Street. I waved to him. He waved back.

There was a tall man with long, greasy gray hair on the steps of the History Museum. He wore black jeans, heavy boots, a black leather vest and a TRUMP 2020 hat. He was speaking into a bullhorn.

"Yes, we had a civil war," he was saying. "We may have to have another one. That may be the only way to return this to a white, Christian nation, the way God intended. If we let the Democrats have power, it will only get worse. They don't love or respect this country. They don't love or respect Jesus. They want to cancel us out. They want to cancel *you* out! I say, we can't let that happen. Whatever it takes, we must do."

That brought applause. When it died down, Walker called out. "I have a question!" The speaker ignored him, but most of the people surrounding the Museum steps turned to look at us. "I have a question," Walker said again, louder this time.

"What is it?" the speaker said.

"My mother," Walker said, "is a Black Christian woman. She most definitely loves and respects Jesus Christ. I'm wondering, is there a place in your white Christian nation for her?"

"Can she cook and clean?" the speaker said.

"Probably better than your mother," Walker said.

The speaker smirked. "Well, then, she can cook and clean for me. She can serve my wife and my children. We'll call her Mammy." That brought laughter from his group. I noticed several of the armed men moving in our direction. They weren't laughing. Neither was Walker. He took a couple of steps forward but before he could say anything else, I had my hand on his chest.

"You can't be doing this," I said. "You've got Junior here and this kind of shit could get you in real trouble."

There were five or six men at the front edge of the crowd now, maybe fifteen feet separating us. Andre had moved up alongside Walker. I was still in front of them, my back to the crowd.

"Not you either," I said, quietly. "You're a professional fighter. You have too much to lose."

Julie was right behind Andre. "Julie," I said, "take Junior please." I pointed toward Washington and the two Capitol Police. "You know Deputy Washington. Go over there with them."

I turned to see that two of the MAGA hats had walked out into the street. One of them, a skinny twenty-something with acne scars was pointing at Walker.

"We know you," he said. "You were at the cemetery."

The other one was older, probably early forties, and big. Maybe six-feet-five and fat, but some of it hard-looking fat. He didn't say anything, just bounced a little on the balls of his feet.

Another guy stepped out into the street. "We know both of them," he said. "I saw them in Clarksville, looking at Mr. Wayne's house."

Walker spoke softly, just to me. "The guy in the Escalade. One of the Tribbles, right?"

I turned and pushed both of them back.

"I'm serious," I said. "We're not doing this. We're walking away."

I turned back to the three in the street. "Fellas, we're just going to continue on our way. Best if you just let us. No one needs to get hurt."

"You're the ones likely to get hurt," the skinny one said.

I didn't say anything. Two more of the MAGA hats walked out into the street. The big guy took a step forward.

"You're the one I hate the most," he said to me. "Your nigger friend, your spic friend there, they can't help what they are. The yellow bitch too. Although I gotta say, I wouldn't mind fucking her."

The skinny one laughed and stepped forward too.

"You're a race traitor," the big one said. "You're a nigger lover. You're a disgrace."

The skinny guy turned to the rest of the crowd and started chanting. "Race traitor. Nigger lover." He raised both of his arms, wanting people to join in. Most of them didn't, but more than a few did. They kept it up for five to six rounds but when it didn't catch on to the whole crowd, they gave it up. The skinny one turned back to us.

"Why don't you turn around and walk away the other way," he said.

Walker was pushing forward. I turned and pushed him back again. "You guys," I said. "Back up about three, four steps."

"We're not backing down," Walker hissed.

"You're right," I said. "But I got this. Please, three, four steps."

They did it grudgingly. But they did it. I turned back to the MAGA boys. The big one and the skinny one had come forward another step.

"So, is this going to be the first battle of your civil war?" I asked.

The big one smiled and made a come on gesture. I took a big step forward and side kicked the skinny one in the middle of his stomach, doubling him over. I followed up with a clubbing left, the bottom of my fist hitting the side of his head. He went down on his side, out of the fight for the moment at least.

I stepped back to my original position. Not it was my turn to make a come on gesture to the big guy. He wasn't smiling anymore. He made a roaring noise and charged at me, trying for a tackle. I stepped aside and put an elbow into his shoulder as he went by. He turned quickly, and shuffled a few steps to his left so he wasn't right in front of Walker and Andre. He started forward and I did too. I let his wild punch go over my shoulder and hit him hard a couple of times in the gut. It didn't seem to bother him too much, but I pushed him back and landed a right cross between his nose and his ear. Then I put a left under his chin, catching some jaw and some throat. He backed up and shook his head, trying to clear it. I noticed that the kink in the shoulder seemed to be gone.

I also flashed on an image of Max Karpenko, a Ukrainian Special

Forces sergeant I'd met on a training rotation in Germany. He was the hand-to-hand instructor for his unit. Someone in my platoon, Doc Stevens, I think, had told him that I'd done some MMA-type fighting. He invited me to spar. We had a good workout. I more than held my own, which definitely impressed my guys. But he sat me down afterward and critiqued me as hard as Denis ever had. The last thing he said was, "In real fight, for your life fight, always attacking. Only retreating if you need to. Clear you head. Clear vision. That sort of thing. Otherwise, attack, attack, attack. Not points, yes? Life or maybe death!"

So when the big guy backed up, I moved forward. His hands were down so I hit him in the face. He raised them for protection, so I kicked him in the balls. That doubled him over, so I round-house kicked him in the side of the head. He went down hard.

THERE WAS A MOMENT OF complete silence. I guess everyone was stunned. Then I heard a series of sharp cracks. Something slammed into the back of my leg and I went down on the street. I got my hands down just before my face hit. I tried to push back up, but I couldn't.

In a moment, Walker's face was right next to mine. His lips were moving. I could see that he was saying "Andy! Andy!" but I couldn't hear him. Then I could. And I could talk.

"B," I said. "I'm OK. I got shot, huh? Can you believe that? Four combat tours and I get shot in downtown Raleigh." I realized I was laughing. I realized I was probably in shock.

I half rolled myself. I could see Julie. She was taking off her yoga tights. She was standing there in her panties and her crop top. That seemed funny too. Then she was wrapping her yoga tights around my leg.

"We need to elevate his leg" she was saying. Then Walker was there with Junior in one arm and his other hand on the stroller. He flipped the stroller sideways on the ground and slid it up close to me while Julie rolled me onto my back. She lifted my leg up and laid it over the stroller.

"Perfect," she said. Walker pulled the padding from the stroller and laid it under my head.

I heard sirens. I saw Andre pulling off his running shorts and handing them to Julie. I saw the two Capitol cops moving everyone out of the area. I saw John Washington leading the skinny guy away, his hands cuffed behind him. I guess that's who shot me.

Walker crouched down next to me with a bottle of water. Julie took it out of his hand before I could drink any. "He's probably going to need surgery," she said. "Better not to put anything else into his stomach."

The sirens got very loud. Then they stopped. Then Teisha was crouched next to me, feeling around the back of my leg. She was asking Julie if she'd seen an exit wound. I didn't hear the answer. Then Teisha swung around and talked to me.

"You're gonna be fine," she said. "It looks like you caught one small caliber bullet."

Another EMT was sliding a blood pressure sleeve up my arm. "Cops said a Seecamp twenty-five. Shooter had it in an ankle holster," he said.

"OK, Andy," Teisha said. "We're gonna sit you up, get you on a gurney, start an IV, and take you to the hospital. First thing, though, let's take some deep breaths. Six count in, six count out. Nice. Good. How's that feel?"

I held a thumb up.

Once I was up on the gurney I could see that the crowd had been dispersed, but there were still twenty to thirty people milling about. Walker, Andre and Julie had stepped to the side while the EMT's worked on me. Now they came over. Walker handed Junior to Teisha and he squealed happily. No one else spoke. Finally, I said, "So, what's new?"

That broke the tension. Walker said, "How do you feel?"

"My head's pretty clear," I said, "but my leg's staring to hurt like a son of a bitch. What happened after I went down. Was anyone else hit?"

"No one else," Walker said. He pointed at Andre. "This one dove right onto that asshole before he could empty his clip. Washington told me it held seven shots. He only got off three."

I looked at Andre. "You ran towards a guy with a gun? That's not too bright, you know."

"He wasn't looking at me," Andre said. "I knew I could get there." Julie had both her hands around Andre's left arm.

"What about the other guy, the big one?" I asked.

Teisha answered. "The other EMT crew carted him off a minute or so ago. You might see him at the hospital."

"ANDY," WALKER SAID. "I never saw anything like that."

"Like what?" I asked.

"Like the way you kicked ass on those two guys. It was, I don't know, *violent* isn't a big enough word for it. It was like a whole action movie in ten seconds."

Andre and Julie were both nodding. "I'm glad all I've ever had to do was spar with you," Andre said. "You were on a whole other level from anything I've ever done."

"Well, remember, I've had some training that you haven't. The Army doesn't teach you sportsmanship."

59

Walker wanted to ride in the ambulance but Teisha told him to take Junior home. "He needs to be fed. He needs his nap. He needs normal," she said. "You take care of him, I'll take care of Andy."

She promised to keep him updated and he promised to text everyone else. After she closed the door, Teisha asked me if I had any preference on which hospital they would take me to.

"You know what?" I said. "Beth is working the ER at WakeMed today."

Teisha laughed. "Oh, well, then. Let's definitely go there!"

BETH, AS IT TURNED OUT, was attending the prior arrival. "I'll tell her," Teisha said, "but I'm gonna wait until she's done with your friend. We don't want to strain her Hippocratic Oath."

The doc who attended me was named Case. He asked Teisha how much blood loss she'd observed.

"Minimal," Teisha said. "A bystander wrapped him tight with a pair of yoga pants."

"God, another reason to love spandex!" Case laughed. "That was good thinking."

"She's in that Sport Science program at Peace College," Teisha said. "Plus, her mother's Beth Thanh."

"The bystander? No shit?" Case said. "I just met Thanh this morning. Seems like a fine doctor." He paused for a moment while he poked at my leg. Then he turned back to Teisha. "Do you know her, by the way? Do you know if she's married or anything?"

"Anything," she said, smiling, then pointing at me. "With this guy."

"Oh God," Case said. "I'm terribly sorry."

"No worries, Doc," I said. "But what do you think about my leg?"

"I think," I said, "that the bullet hit the femur. There's no exit wound, so the bullet itself is still in there. Let's get some imaging, then we'll know more. How much pain?"

"Enough that I'm gritting my teeth most of the time," I said.

"OK," he spoke to the two nurses who were hovering nearby. "Patty, let's get him some morphine in the IV. Maria, call down to Radiology."

THE MORPHINE TOOK THE EDGE off the pain pretty quickly and someone from Radiology came to get me after about ten minutes. We passed Big MAGA in the hallway, apparently on the way back from X-rays of his own. He was flat on his back and didn't see me. About a minute after I got back to my exam room, Beth walked in. She kissed me hard, lifted up for a moment, shook her head quickly, then kissed me hard again.

"Oh, Andy," she said. "Is this connected to that stolen gun?"

"Indirectly," I said. "Some of the same players, but it's not a straight line."

"I'm still mad as hell that they shot you!"

"Yeah, well, me too. Have you seen the X-rays?"

She was just starting to say *no* when Dr. Case walked in. He walked over to the computer on a side table and clicked a few keys. The X-ray image popped up on a wall screen. Beth got up and stood beside Case.

"Obviously, there's the bullet," Case said, pointing at the screen. I couldn't really see it with them both in the way. "That won't be any problem. The rest of it is kind of a mess."

"That doesn't sound good," I said.

They both turned around to face me. "You've got what's called a comminuted fracture," Beth said. "There's a break through the bone and a number of fragments around the point of impact. Do you know what you got shot with?"

"I think I heard it was a twenty-five caliber," I said.

"From how far away?" Case asked.

"Maybe fifteen feet?" I said. "Twenty at the most, I'd say."

"That's all good," Case said. "Anything bigger, or closer, would have done a lot more damage." He turned to Beth. "Do you want my recommendation?" he asked.

"Of course, doctor," she said.

"Take out the bullet, secure the femur with a rod, put the fragments back in place as best we can, secure all that with a plate, close it up and give it time to heal."

"Andy," she said to me, "when's the last time you ate or drank anything."

"Before I left your house. Eight-thirty or nine o'clock."

"It's noon now. We want at least another hour before anesthesia. Five or six hours would be better." She turned to Case. "Who's on this afternoon and evening?"

He clicked some more on the computer. "Paul Cox comes on at five o'clock p.m. I'd call him our second best trauma surgeon."

"Who's the best?" Beth asked.

"Dr. Raynor. But he's got Covid. I heard they put him on a respirator yesterday."

"OK," Beth said. "Let's start the ball rolling for this evening with Dr. Cox. I'd like to assist. How do we make that happen?"

She patted my hand. "Don't worry, Baby. I'll take good care of you."

BETH WAS IN AND OUT of my room over the next couple of hours. She left her phone with me for a while, so I was able to call Walker. He'd already spoken with my parents. I decided to wait until after the surgery to call them myself. He told me Andre had talked to Denis, and John Washington had apparently called him too.

Eventually, an orderly came to take me down to pre-op. There was no one there when we arrived.

"Ghostville," the orderly said.

His pager went off, and he clicked a couple of keys.

"Gotta go," he said. "I'm sure somebody be here soon."

He left me on my gurney, just inside the door. Soon turned out to be a few minutes, and it was Beth who came through the door next. She looked at me, looked around at the empty room, and shrugged her shoulders.

"One of my professors had a theory," she said, "that when doctors die, before they can get in to heaven, they have to wait in hell for exactly the amount of time they kept patients waiting."

"Remind me to tell Walker about that," I said. "He'll love it."

EPILOGUE 1

was in surgery for just over three hours. First, they put a titanium rod down the middle of my femur. Then they fit the bone fragments back into the main bone as well as they could and wrapped a stainless steel plate around it. They fastened the plate to the bone with four screws. Beth showed me the before and after x-rays. She told me she'd get copies so we could take them home and frame them.

I had three visitors Sunday morning. The first one was a Raleigh Police detective named Monroe. The second one was a Capitol Police detective named Grimaldi. The third one was Elle Estrada. Each of them stayed about half an hour. Each of them asked me basically the same questions. Each of them tried to explain the jurisdictional issues. They all agreed that it was a complicated mess.

In the end, the powers that be decided not to charge me with anything. Someone had apparently taken video which made it pretty clear that my action was "provoked and invited," at least by the big guy, whose name was Frederick Bauer. He ended up with a suspended jail sentence and a $1200 fine for carrying a weapon at a public demonstration. He turned out to have a KA-BAR knife sheathed against his leg. Probably a good thing I didn't give him an opportunity to use it.

The skinny guy, the one who shot me, was named Robert E. Lee. Really! The locals wanted to charge him with attempted murder, but he was eventually allowed to plead to lesser charges in return for testimony on other cases. Specifically, his testimony helped ATF and FBI to put some serious hurt on the whole Southern Virginia White Power scene. Lee served four months in Raleigh Central Prison, after which he apparently left the area for Gainesville, Florida.

Truman Wayne did fourteen months in federal prison for possession of an illegal weapon and receiving property stolen from the US Government. Paul Tribble only got six months. His lawyer argued, successfully, that he had never "possessed" the weapon. Army Tribble and Michael James Merriman both spent time in Leavenworth after which they were dishonorably discharged.

Pelham Wayne wasn't charged in the gun case, but he still ended up spending time behind bars. With some encouragement from the Department of the Army, Onward Christian Soldiers decided to press charges regarding those "financial irregularities." They turned out to be irregular enough to get him twelve to twenty months in the low security federal prison in Butner North Carolina.

WALKER GOT MY OLD JOB. We did a lot of Zoom calls together to introduce him to his customers. I backed him up as he learned the products and the business, and I wasn't surprised that he picked it all up quickly. I did a lot of Zoom calls with the rest of my sales team, too. By the end of July, I was starting to feel pretty comfortable as a sales manager. Being the Big Dog of the Year bought me a lot of credibility, and it turned out I hadn't forgotten all of the leadership skills the Army taught me.

I WAS ALSO RIDING MY BIKE for at least an hour a day by the end of July. Every other day, I rode to Denis's gym. Forty-five minutes there, an hour or so working out, then another forty-five minutes riding home. Some days I'd lift weights, some days I'd do online yoga classes. Andre joined me a few times. Walker only worked out with me on the Saturdays or Sundays. He wouldn't take time off during the work week. Something about not slacking off on his new job.

THE LAST WEEK IN JULY we moved all of my stuff out of my condo. Maddie had listed it on a couple of rental sites and I had a tenant moving in the first weekend in August. Walker and Andre did most of the heavy lifting. Most of my furniture and kitchen stuff went to Keila, who was still running the store until she could sell it. The only big thing I kept was my Fuego grill.

EPILOGUE 2

M y phone rang just before noon on August 12. I was at my desk in what had once been Julie's mother's room. We'd set it up to be my office. It was a 703 area code. Northern Virginia. When I answered, a crisp female voice asked me to "Please hold for the Sergeant Major of the Army."

I had been proofreading a proposal that Walker had written. I tapped the speaker icon on my phone so I could keep working while I waited. It was almost a minute before Collins came on. "Mr. Carver. I was thinking about you this morning. I signed a pair of commendations for those two MP's, Reece and Lombardi. We've pretty much locked up our end of that little adventure you all had down there. I wanted to ask you, how are you doing?"

"I'm fine, Sergeant Major. Not a hundred percent yet, but getting there."

"That's good to hear," he said, then paused for a moment. "There was some talk about a commendation for you as well, but I quashed it. I thought I should tell you why."

"That's not necessary," I said. "I understand why. And I want you to know, I followed your advice."

"Hang on a minute," he said. I heard him talking to someone else, muffled like he had his hand over the receiver. At that moment, Beth walked in. I motioned her to the other chair in the room.

Collins came back on. "I apologize, Mr. Carver. Something I have to deal with. Immediately. But it sounds like you're telling me that you're back on the straight and narrow, and that's what I wanted to hear. So stay there. Do you copy?"

"Yes, Sergeant Major. Message received and understood."

AFTER I HUNG UP, I turned to face Beth. She had a question on her face.

"What did he mean by that?" she asked. "Were you ever *not* on the straight and narrow?"

I smiled at her, took a deep breath, and let it out. "Dennis uses a different phrase. He says straight and bent. It sounds better when he says it in French. *Droit* and *courbe*."

She didn't say anything, but she was still looking the question at me. I took another breath and continued. "Walker and I were casing that house," I said. "We were planning to break in and rob it."

Her mouth opened slightly. Other than that, she didn't move or speak.

"Not that it really matters," I said, "but it was mostly his idea. You know he was always trying to make ends meet, always feeling underpaid. One night, purely by accident, he found out that a guy he'd known all his life was buying stolen furniture to sell in his used furniture store. So he talked to the guy, then he talked to me, and we decided to go into the house-robbing business."

She smiled a little, so I did too. "This is the thousand dollar a month thing," she said.

Now I was the one surprised. "How do you know about that?" I asked.

"I heard Teisha say something about it, to her friend Maddie. They were giggling and flicking at their earrings. It's just something I remembered for some reason."

"Yeah, that's what we called it," I said. "The whole goal was to find

Walker another thousand dollars a month, so he could quit his part time jobs."

"And you?" she asked.

"I was never in it for the money. I guess I was in it for the adrenaline rush."

"I understand," she said. "I won't ever forget the way I felt when we went in that house. How long did this go on?"

"Almost two years? I think we hit about a dozen places."

Her eyes opened wide. "And one of them was Michael Slattery's apartment!"

I nodded.

"Son of a bitch," she said, but not angrily. "Now Byron has your old job, and he'll be making more money, so you stopped?"

I nodded. She was nodding too. Agreeing with me, I thought.

"But we have to do it one more time," she said. Maybe not completely agreeing.

"What do you mean?"

"We talked about taking my little talent to the dark side once. Do you remember?"

I did remember. It was the day after we'd gone into Pelham Wayne's house. I hadn't taken her very seriously.

"You said something about needing intelligence. About knowing where there was a safe worth opening."

I shrugged.

"Well I do," she said. "It's in Michael's house, and I have been fantasizing about doing it ever since *someone* robbed his apartment and brought the police to my door."

She stood up, grinning now. "I'm serious, you know. Well, maybe not *completely* serious, but I wouldn't mind feeling that rush again."

I DIDN'T SAY ANYTHING. And Beth didn't mention it again, though she did take to calling me Raffles. Walker had to explain that to me. David

Niven played a gentleman burglar by that name in an old movie. Niven was the Clooney of his time, Walker said.

About six weeks later, though, I found myself looking at the notes we'd gotten from Maddie before we hit Slattery's apartment. His house was on White Oak Road, not far from Ellen's. I pulled it up on Google Earth. Big house, big lot, surrounded by trees.

The next day, I rode my bike out that way. I told myself it was a bad idea. But I did it anyway.

Dave Fellman is the author of four business books.
He lives in Raleigh, North Carolina.
A Thousand Dollars A Month is his first novel.

www.davefellman.com